Praise for Lexxie Couper's *Death, The Vamp and His Brother*

"Lexxie Couper has crafted a clever, fast-paced story that will capture your attention and never let it go. Everything in this story exceeded my expectations from start to finish. This is one story I gladly recommend to anyone, especially those who like stories where sexy heroes are forced to look at themselves and decide whether or not to accept who they really are."

~ *Karin, The Romance Studio*

"Lexxie Couper has created a marvelous adventure into the world of the supernatural, with a number of surprises in store for the reader. The title is what originally caught my interest, but I sincerely enjoyed every minute I spent with these characters, and I hope Ms. Couper will revisit this world to give us a view of the future with these three."

~ *Holly, Whipped Cream Reviews*

"I loved Death, the Vamp and His Brother. It is great fun. There is humor and pain in this tale. Things are not what I expected them be...I liked how everything fit together and worked well to give me a book I couldn't put down. I hope there will be additional stories about the other Horsemen of the Apocalypse. Very creative and different, Ms. Couper!"

~ *Sheila, TwoLips Reviews*

Look for these titles by

Lexxie Couper

Now Available:

Savage Retribution

The Sun Sword

Death, The Vamp and His Brother

Lexxie Couper

A Samhain Publishing, Ltd. publication.

Samhain Publishing, Ltd.
577 Mulberry Street, Suite 1520
Macon, GA 31201
www.samhainpublishing.com

Death, The Vamp and His Brother

Print ISBN: 978-1-60504-734-8
Digital ISBN: 978-1-60504-643-3

Editing by Heidi Moore
Cover by Natalie Winters

First Samhain Publishing, Ltd. electronic publication: August 2009
First Samhain Publishing, Ltd. print publication: June 2010

Dedication

For my brothers—I wouldn't say you were the inspiration behind Patrick and Ven, but you were pretty damn close. Well, except for the fangs, that is.

Dawn—You are just that to me.

Sexy Man…of course.

And my friend, Paula. You know why. Love you.

"And power was given unto them, the Four Horsemen, over a fourth of the earth to kill with sword, and with hunger, and with death, and with the beasts of the earth."

Revelation 6:8

Prologue

The Realm

It's not easy getting a date when you're the Grim Reaper.

Looking at herself in the bathroom mirror, Death sighed. It was way too long since she'd last had sex and she was horny.

She flicked a critical eye over her naked body. High, round breasts, a narrow waist and smoothly curved hips. Long legs and firmly toned arms. Not a dot of cellulite in sight, not even on her inner thighs, the one place an immortal female Entity was likely to experience such a mortal affliction.

She looked good. Damn good. Not that anyone noticed. Millennia of traipsing around the world of man, severing life threads in a long, body-concealing, head-covering cloak did little for her reputation as a hot babe. About the only entities that had any idea what she *really* looked like were her fellow Horsemen and, despite her escalating sexual frustration, the idea of a physical relationship with any of them made her shudder. It'd be like sleeping with her brother, or in Famine's case, her sister. Eww.

Death, or as she preferred to call herself in this millennium, Fred—she'd been a fan of The Flintstones since 1960—sighed again and turned from the mirror. She couldn't stand around moping about her lack of a sex life for the rest of eternity. She had work to do.

In an instant, the iconic black cloak so immortalized by popular culture covered her body from head to foot.

She scowled and wrinkled her nose. The robe vanished, a pair of faded Levis, a snug Ramones t-shirt, six-inch stiletto boots and a New York Yankees cap replacing it in a shimmering instant of light and color. Fred nodded her head with a grin. She didn't feel like conforming to the dress code today. If the Powers had a problem with that They could stick it in Their metaphysical ears. Her first claim was in Sydney, Australia, and she'd be damned if she was going to stalk around in the Aussie summer sun in a stifling cloak, whether the living could see her or not.

Killing the light, she left the bathroom, throwing her scythe a quick look where it sat propped against the head of her bed.

After a brief consideration, she shook her head. *Nope. Not today.*

A pair of sunglasses materialized in her hand—large, black and bug-like with two small diamond scythes embedded in each temple.

Fred grinned again and slipped them onto her face. She maybe sexually deprived and as horny as hell but she looked good. And really, when a girl was going to work in a demanding job, looking good was vital.

Even for the Grim Reaper.

Chapter One

"I. Don't. Care." Turning from the sea-spray-crusted window, Patrick "Wato" Watkins ground his teeth. He clenched his cell phone in his right hand, frustration making his blood boil. If his brother wasn't already dead, he'd kill him. "I'm not coming home, Ven. I have a job to do and I'm not leaving the beach just because you've got a bee in your bonnet."

Ven, aka Steven, aka annoying-as-hell older brother, ground his teeth in return. Patrick could hear his sibling's molars connect and press together through the phone.

"When are you going to listen to me, brother?" Ven asked, his normally deep voice unnaturally deeper. Whether from anger, worry or the high position of the sun, Patrick didn't know. Ven was usually asleep at midday. Being awake and in an argument probably brought the demon lurking in his blood closer to the surface than usual.

"It feels wrong. Let the other guards babysit the tourists. You're the boss. Delegate."

"Yes, Ven. I *am* the boss." Patrick turned back to the window, studying the thousands of swimmers—tourists and locals alike—enjoy a gorgeous summer's day at Bondi Beach. "Which means I can't just bugger off."

Out there in the crystal blue waves lurked danger. Sharks. Rips. Undertows. Blue-bottles...all waiting to catch a swimmer unaware. To bring pain, suffering, maybe even death. He'd be damned if he was leaving those swimmers' fates to chance. His team was good. God knows, Bluey had been swimming since birth. The senior lifeguard's rescue rate was the second highest in the country after his own, but—like Ven—Patrick had an uneasy itch in his gut. Unlike Ven, *his* sense of disquiet had nothing to do with a supposed attack from an unknown "thing" and everything to do with the large number of people enjoying the famous stretch of beach. On a day like today, there were close to forty-thousand souls on the sand and in the water. That equaled roughly forty-thousand possible drownings, shark-attack victims, blue-bottle stings...

Patrick's gut itched again. No matter what threat his brother imagined in his paranoid imagination, he couldn't leave.

But he's not being paranoid, is he? You know exactly what threat—

Shutting down the unwanted thought, Patrick scanned the surf, focusing on a group of Japanese tourists bobbing ignorantly close to Backpacker's Express. If the beach's notorious rip took them into its embrace, they'd be out to sea and two miles south before they even realized they were no longer in Bondi waters. It would take at least four lifeguards to round them up, leaving seven to keep the rest of the beach's visitors safe. Seven men to deal with any emergency on the mile-long stretch. His team couldn't do that without their boss, no matter how good they were.

He bit back a frustrated sigh. Just a typical day at work. Danger and death lurking everywhere. He couldn't pack it all in just because his brother thought he was in danger. Besides, it was the middle of the day. What type of paranormal nasty attacked in the middle of the bloody day? And on a busy beach, no less?

The kind in a black suit, maybe?

He ignored the silent question, turning his attention to the packed surf instead. It was a glorious summer day on Australia's most famous beach. Perfect, in fact. Blue, cloudless sky, clean five-foot waves, warm seventy-one degree water. If said unseen paranormal attack was going to happen, it sure as hell wasn't going to be today. What Patrick would more likely be confronted with on a day like today, what the itch in his gut was probably warning him about, was the possibility of a careless, overconfident tourist taking their life in their hands by not swimming between the flags. *That*, he could deal with on his own. He didn't need his vampire big brother to save a drowning person. When it came down to it, Ven wasn't up to swimming these days anyway, not during sunlight at least. He was known to pick up his old board for a midnight surf or two...when he wasn't trying to protect Patrick from God alone only knows, that was.

Shaking his head, Patrick lifted his phone's mouthpiece closer to his face. "Sorry, Ven. I'm staying put. Either come and get me or go back to sleep."

"Ha, ha, brother. Really funny. Will you bloody well listen to reason for a—"

"I gotta go, mate." Patrick cut him off. "I'll call you when I get home."

"But—"

He pulled the phone from his ear, flipped it shut and threw it on the counter before him with a shake of his head and a wry chuckle. Ven had spent the last thirty-six years thinking he needed to protect Patrick from some unknown entity, and Patrick had spent the last eighteen of those years arguing with Ven the entire thing was unnecessary. Nothing was after Patrick. Nothing. *Nothing* could convince Ven differently however. Thank bloody God the bloke spent his days "sleeping", otherwise Patrick would probably go crazy and shove a stake in his chest just to get some unsupervised personal space.

Who in the hell would be coming after him anyway? A simple lifeguard in Australia?

You know who, Patrick. You just have to—

"You see that group in Backpacker's, Wato?" a slightly raspy voice sounded to his left, cutting the dark thought dead.

Grateful for the interruption, Patrick gave his second in charge a quick nod. "Yeah, I see them."

Bluey handed him a pair of binoculars, concern creasing the sides of his pale blue eyes. “One of them’s flounderin’.”

Patrick took the offered glasses. “Tourist?”

Bluey shook his head. “Don’t think so. Not Japanese, at least. Too big. Too blonde. Forty, forty-five years old, I’m guessin’. Take a look.”

Lifting the binoculars to his eyes, Patrick focused in on the group of swimmers bobbing in the surf’s choppy southern swell. Five people moved up and down with the rolling waves, their heads breaching the deceptive water, sinking below the surface and emerging again. Five people thinking they were safe when they were in dangerous territory. Five people who would need to be rounded up ASAP. Five people—

A man burst upward from the water, thinning blonde hair plastered to a domed skull, sunburnt face distorted in abject fear. He struggled to stay above the inescapable waves, the sea pouring into his open mouth every time he shouted for help. One flabby arm clawed above the surface to wave, once, twice, before he sank below the surface with terrifying speed. Gone.

“Fuck.” Patrick threw aside the binoculars. “He’s under.”

He moved without thought, the act of rescuing a drowning swimmer second nature to him. He’d spent the last fifteen years doing it every day. Ordering Bluey to contact the two guards patrolling the southern end of the beach, he charged from the patrol tower. He snatched up a rescue tube and his board and sprinted across the sand, dodging sunbathers and beach volleyballers on his way to the water. It would take approximately six minutes to get to the man in Backpacker’s Express. By Patrick’s reckoning, five minutes too long.

The high midday sun beat down on him as he ran, the blistering hot sand scalding the soles of his bare feet. He ran, board tucked under his arm, stare locked on the notorious rip, searching the increasing swell for any sign of the sunburnt blonde man. Shit. There was none.

To his left, he saw Grub and Hollywood weave through a crowd of laughing tourists before sprinting into the surf. The two guards threw their boards onto the water and launched themselves through the breaking waves at breakneck speed, heading for the group of clueless Japanese swimmers.

He flicked his stare back to Backpacker's Express, picking up his already punishing pace, hot sand peppering the backs of his thighs in stinging pinpricks.

Time pressed on him, as brutal as the sun. Grub and Hollywood were good lifeguards, but neither had the experience in the infamous rip that he had, and the middle-aged blonde man wasn't the only one struggling in the water. It was a foregone conclusion any number of the Japanese tourists would soon realize they were in trouble and make a scramble for the approaching guards the second they saw them. Once that happened, the drowning man would certainly go under for good. If he wasn't already.

Muscles burning, sweat streaming down his temples and chest, Patrick plowed into the surf. The cool water felt like icy needles on his flushed flesh, biting at his focus. He pushed through the chilling pain trying to cramp his legs, positioning his board and dropping onto it in one fluid move. Plunging his arms deep into the sea, he pulled stroke after stroke, powering his way through the crashing waves.

With every crest he rode, he looked for the blonde man with the sunburnt face. With each dip, his chest grew tighter. He couldn't see him. Which at this point could only mean one thing. He hadn't resurfaced.

Fuck.

"Have you seen a bloke with blonde hair out here? Have you seen—"

Grub's shout rose above the roar of adrenaline in Patrick's ears and he snapped his head to his left, finding the young guard attempting to communicate with a frantic Japanese tourist in a bright yellow Speedo trying to climb onto Grub's board.

"I can't see him!" Hollywood shouted on Patrick's right, pulling himself into a sitting position on his board as he studied the churned-up water around him. He shot Patrick a worried look and shook his head. "Where did he—"

He didn't finish. One of the panicked swimmers knocked him from his board, wailing incoherently as they tried to scramble from the water, fear and shame turning their eyes into bulging discs.

Patrick bit back a curse. He didn't have time for this. The drowning man didn't have time. Ignoring the fracas—Grub and Hollywood would have to handle it on their own—he scanned the choppy waves, feeling the rip's undercurrent pulling at his legs with menacing force. Backpacker's Express was aptly named. It sucked you out to sea. Fast. If he didn't find the blonde man soon, he wouldn't. Not until his body turned up on nearby Bronte Beach, bloated and gray and nibbled on by fish.

He wasn't going to let that happen.

Cutting through the waves, he searched the water, tuning out everything but his gut. Nothing existed. No sound. No smell. Just the cool water splashing against his board and body and the tight itch in the pit of his stomach directing his search. The inexplicable instinct he never questioned that helped him save those beyond saving time and again. The enigmatic, uncanny intuition that repeatedly led him to those sinking into the ocean's cool embrace.

That strange, tight itch in his gut, he paddled his board south.

The water grew black beneath him. Deep. Cold.

He moved slowly, the *thump thump thump* of his heart a soundless tattoo in his chest, a silent beat keeping time with his progress, charting his search. The water sucked at his arms with each stroke he took, the rip reaching for them, hungry and demanding and greedy. He denied the powerful undertow, refusing to be taken in its hold as he stared into the ocean.

Searching. Searching.

His heart slowed, his breath slowed, his existence shrank until it was just him, his board and the merciless sea around him. Knowing death waited on his shoulder, salivating.

Knowing life depended on his instincts. A life waning. Fading.

Heart almost slowed to complete stillness, he searched for the drowning man.

And found him.

Plunging his right arm into the ocean, Patrick grabbed a fistful of blonde hair and pulled, a grunt bursting past his lips as the man's considerable weight snapped at his shoulder muscles. "Gotcha."

Counterbalancing himself against the violent jolt, he hauled the limp body further from the sea, changing his grip until he had the older, unconscious man lying facedown across the front of his board. "Get 'em in," he ordered Grub, nodding toward the still-panicking but at the same time gawking Japanese tourists bobbing in the swell to his left. "And give 'em a lecture."

Shifting his position to accommodate the motionless man's bulk, he began to propel his board back to the beach. His job was far from done and time pressed harder on him. He may have pulled the bloke from a wet grave, but the old guy wasn't breathing. Until his lungs were cleared of water, he belonged to death.

Not for long.

Patrick powered through the surf, ignoring the burn in his shoulders and lungs. A distant part of his mind heard Grub and Hollywood barking at the Japanese tourists. An even more distant part noted Hollywood sounded right and royally pissed off, but his main focus was the beach. Bluey waited there, defibrillator and oxi-boot ready.

When it came to saving a life, Patrick never conceded to death. No matter how long an individual had been underwater.

"*Move it, move it, move it!*" Bluey's roar reached Patrick before he even made it to the sand. Swimmers, sunbathers and gawkers alike fell out of the way, mouths agape, eyes wide as the other man barged through the crowd, orange-red hair gleaming in the ruthless sun, face furious, arms cutting a path through the melee. He met Patrick in the shallows, scooping the still lifeless swimmer up from Patrick's board to fling one limp arm around his shoulder. “Got ’im.”

Patrick wrapped the man’s other arm around his shoulder and, heart hammering, gut tight, half-dragged, half-carried him from the surf.

The moment they passed the waterline, they dumped him onto his back, the crowd gathering around them, gasping as one as the man’s limp body hit the sand.

Before the displaced grains could settle, Patrick dropped to his knees. He didn’t have time to wait for Bluey to pass him a facemask. The *man* didn’t have time to wait. Blood roaring in his ears, he tilted the bloke’s head back, pinched his nose shut and covered the slack, blue-tinged lips with his mouth.

One. Two. Three. He transferred his breath into the man’s lungs, watching his chest rise with each exhalation.

Turning his head, he listened for any sound of inhalation. Nothing.

“Don’t you fucking dare,” he growled, feeling for a pulse.

Nothing.

One. Two. Three.

Again, nothing.

Rising up onto his knees, Patrick placed his palm heels to the centre of the man’s chest, left over right, and pressed. Again. Again. Again.

“He’s not comin’ back, Wato.”

Bluey’s low rumble lifted Patrick’s head. He glared at his second in charge, continuing to compress the motionless man’s sternum. “Yes, he is.”

Returning his stare to the man’s pale, flaccid face, he counted off fifty compressions before clamping his mouth over the blue-tinged lips again.

One. Two. Three.

Nothing.

One. Two. Three.

Nothing.

A hand closed over Patrick's shoulder. "He was under too long, mate."

Patrick lifted his head, returning his hands to the man's sternum as he fixed Bluey with a level look. "Get the paddles ready."

Bluey released a long sigh and turned away, reaching for the defibrillator.

Patrick pressed his hands into the man's chest. Again. Again. "Don't you fucking dare," he ground out, staring hard into the lifeless face. "I'm not gonna let you."

He pinched the salt-crusted nose and covered the slack mouth with his, forcing breath into the man's lungs.

One. Two. Three.

One. Two. Three.

Nothing.

"No," Patrick snarled. He rose higher onto his knees and pressed the heels of his palms to the man's chest. "I'm." *Press.* "Not." *Press.* "Going." *Press.* "To." *Press.* "Let." *Press.* "You."

He dropped his head and forced breath into the man again.

One. Two. Three.

One. Two. Three.

Nothing. Still nothing.

"It's enough, Wato." Bluey's voice sounded far away. "He's gone."

"He's *not* fucking gone." Patrick jerked his head up, glaring at his second in charge. "Give me the paddles."

Bluey looked back at him, pale blue eyes calm, face expressionless. "You're frying dead meat, mate. You know that."

"No!"

He smashed his palm heels to the man's sternum, compressing his chest in rapid succession.

A hideous, wet *glurk* burst from the man's throat, followed immediately by a gush of hot water and sour bile from his mouth.

"Yes, you fucking bastard," Patrick growled, ignoring the gasps and cries around him as he continued to stimulate the man's heart in steady, forceful blows. "Spit it out. You can't breathe with half of Bondi in your lungs. Get rid of it."

Another *glurk*, this one less wet, less fluidy. More water erupted from the man's mouth, spurting this time from his nose as well. A groan slipped from his lips, weak and raw, the sound almost lost in the sudden cheers from the crowd. Eyelids fluttering, arms twitching, the man rolled his head, a shudder wracking through his body before he slumped still again.

Patrick's heart stopped for a second. Shit. He was losing him. Again. "Give me the paddles."

Face expressionless, eyes worried, Bluey held out the defib paddles. Patrick snatched them from him, the violent action eliciting another gasp from the crowd.

"Charge 'em," he ground out, staring at the motionless man's face. A high-pitched whine cut the thick tension as Bluey charged the defibrillator.

"Charged."

"Clear." He pressed the gel-smeared paddles to the man's unmoving chest.

Two-hundred joules shot through flesh, muscle, bone and tissue. Two-hundred joules of electric life.

The man bucked, spine bowing, fingers splaying wide.

Mouth dry, Patrick stabbed his fingertips against the man's neck, feeling for a pulse.

He shook his head. Still nothing.

"C'mon!" Patrick shouted, giving the man's fleshy shoulders a hard shake. "I've got you this far. Fight, damn it."

A movement to his left—slight and almost imperceptible—flickered in his peripheral vision. Long legs. Blue denim. Black stiletto boots. A cold breeze blew against his cheek. A hot tightness squeezed his heart. He felt—

"He's breathing!" Bluey yelled, slapping Patrick's back. "Fair dinkum, mate. You've done it again! He's breathing!"

Patrick snapped his stare to the once-motionless man's face, unable to control a powerful surge of elation at the sight of two—albeit unfocussed—brown eyes squinting up at him.

"Wh...wh...what happened?"

The man's voice was barely more than a rasp, but to Patrick it sounded like a pure song. He grinned. "You tried to drink half the ocean, mate."

The man coughed, a scratchy, wheezy hiccup. "That...was a bit...stupid...of me." Closing his eyes, he pulled a ragged breath, another cough choking the shaky intake before he could finish.

"Take it easy, mate," Patrick cautioned, pressing his fingers to the man's neck again. His pulse was weak but steady. "The paramedics are on the way. Where's your stuff? Towel, car keys, clothes—"

"No, no." The man shook his head, struggling to sit up. His brown eyes flicked around the crowd, almost nervous. "No ambulance. I'm okay."

Bluey squatted down beside Patrick and placed his hand firmly on the man's chest. "Mate, you were dead. Wato here brought you back to life. You need to go to the hospital."

"No. I'm fine. I'm—"

Another coughing fit claimed the man and he dropped backward, lying flat.

"The ambos are here," Grub murmured, popping his head over Patrick's shoulder to nod at the approaching paramedics running across the sand.

Fingers still pressed to the man's strengthening pulse, Patrick shot the paramedics a quick look. Relief coursed through him. Thank bloody God. Maybe they could talk some sense into the—

A woman leant over his shoulder, slim and dressed in snug blue jeans, a New York Yankees baseball cap shrouding her face in shadows. A chill rippled up Patrick's spine and his palms prickled, as if he'd suddenly plunged them into a wasp nest. He felt her gaze skim over his face from behind large, black sunglasses before she extended her arm with absolute confidence and stroked long, slender fingers over the man's fleshy chest.

Absolute terror flooded the man's face, turning his sunburnt skin a sick vomit-orange. His brown eyes bulged. He stared up at the woman, soundless words bubbling from his mouth. His pulse rate tripled. Quadrupled.

And stopped.

Dead.

"What the?" Patrick frowned, ramming his fingers harder to the man's neck.

Nothing.

He jolted to his feet, turning to glare at the woman in the baseball cap.

But she wasn't there. In fact, there wasn't a sign of her on the beach at all.

As if she'd never been there in the first place.

Gut twisting, palm itching, Patrick's frown deepened. Where was she? What the hell was going on?

Fred walked away from the lifeguard, the stiletto heels of her boots not even remotely sinking into the soft white sand. The coastal breeze caressed her face and arms and she pulled in a long breath, enjoying its heat even as the blazing midday sun sucked the moisture from the flesh of the humans—oblivious to her existence—around her. Summer in Australia. Hot. Hotter. Hottest. She was glad she'd ditched the stifling cloak.

Adjusting the sunglasses on her face, she sidestepped a teenage couple making out on a beach towel, casting them a detached yet curious look. He would live for another sixty-five years before dying in a car accident, she would die in five years of advanced skin cancer. Fred *tsked,* noting the gleaming oil smeared over the girl's bare flesh. As if humans didn't have enough to deal with in their short time, they had to go and seek her out any chance they could, all in the name of beauty.

She shook her head, following the waterline away from the commotion still unfolding behind her. The paramedics would not revive the drowned man, no matter how skilled or tenacious they were. All she'd left them was an empty skin-wrapped lump of meat and bones.

The icy tingle in the pit of her belly she experienced after every claiming whispered through her, feeding her magic. It nourished her power, sated the demon within. Today however, it also felt wrong. Not because the soul she'd removed from the mortal coil—Richard Michael Peabody—was a closet pedophile who deserved to die. That very morning he'd raped—for the tenth time—his six-year-old niece while his twin sister attended a doctor's appointment. Fred felt no remorse for Peabody. The human male deserved to have his life extinguished. He most *definitely* deserved the eternal damnation awaiting him. When it came to mortal monsters like Peabody, Fred enjoyed her job. But today, even with the tingle in her core and the sure knowledge of just punishment about to be met, she felt conflicted.

Every soul she claimed, every life thread she severed she did with pride. Her purpose was ultimate. Life could not exist without Death. If she didn't do what she did, humanity would pay the price. That didn't mean however, that she was emotionless. She felt no pity for Peabody, really, who would? But she couldn't help feel sorry for the lifeguard who'd tried so hard to save him.

She'd seen many EMOs at work, but none were as aggressively determined to thwart her work as the lifeguard. It was as though the very idea of losing Peabody assaulted him. Wounded him. Raw energy had poured from him in intoxicating waves as he'd fought to save the vile man's life, almost as powerful and energizing as the sun above.

Uninvited, an image of the lifeguard filled Fred's head and

she pulled in a soft, appreciative breath. Now *there* was a tenacious son of a bitch. Not just tenacious, but damn fine to look at as well. Tall, lean and sinewy with smooth skin kissed bronze by the sun and shaggy blonde hair bleached golden by its solar rays. His eyes were a fierce, piercing green, his nose strong and hawkish, his lips totally kissable even when clenched together in stubborn denial.

A soft beat pulsed between Fred's thighs and she took another swift breath, surprised at the reaction. It had been a long time since she'd been aroused by a mortal. The last—an arrogant but brilliant Roman general with a nose just like her lifeguard and a succinct way with words—had dumped her for a snooty Egyptian queen with an asp fetish.

She turned her mind back to the Australian, remembering the way he looked as he ran from the sea with water streaming over his lean, muscular body, the sun highlighting broad, strong shoulders, snug blue swimming shorts hugging narrow hips. It was a good memory. A potent memory.

The heat between Fred's thighs pulsed again and, despite the warm breezes blowing across the ocean, her nipples pinched into tight peaks. Something about the lifeguard intrigued her. Not just his fierce battle to deny her, but something else. Something different.

She strode along the sand, a detached, professional part of her mind marking those around her for their time, and thought of Peabody's failed rescue. Like the lifeguard, something about it had felt...what? Wrong? No, wrong wasn't the correct word, especially to describe the lifeguard. Yummy. That was a good word to describe the lean Australian with the messy blonde hair. Sexy as sin another one. Well, another three, actually. Unusual however, *was* the word she was looking for to describe his rescue attempt.

But why?

What was it about the sequence of events?

The lifeguard works on the drowning man's body, pounding against the man's fleshy chest with his palms, the sun turning his smooth muscular back to a bronzed sheen. The subtle heat of the day kisses her arms and neck and cheeks as she watches him battle the inevitable. The sound of the pedophile's perverted, weakening heartbeat vibrates through her core, feeding the familiar tingle in her gut as she prepares to sever his life thread... She leans over the lifeguard to touch Peabody and the salty bite of the lifeguard's sweat threads into her being like mist. She turns her head, for some reason wanting to see his eyes, wanting see if they burn with the same fierce determination she feels radiating from him. She looks at him...and he looks at her, his soft breath fanning her face.

Fred froze, the sounds of the beach—seagulls screeching, swimmers splashing, people laughing—sucked away by stunned shock.

He looked at *her.*

He could see her.

That's impossible, Fred. The living can't see you until the very moment you claim them. Not unless you choose for them to do so and you sure as hell didn't choose for this guy to see you today.

But he *had* seen her. He'd looked straight at her, and it was only now, with the post- claiming buzz fading to a soft tingle, that she realized it. He'd seen her.

How in all the levels of hell could he see you?

No, he couldn't. The living *didn't* see her. She prevented it. The Powers prevented it.

Wishful thinking? Maybe your starved libido is making you see things?

Before she could stop herself, she turned and gave the lifeguard a long, hard inspection from across the sand.

He sat beside Peabody's inert body, head buried in his hands, broad shoulders slumped. She'd seen this very pose before. The position of a defeated human. But unlike others in this situation, anger radiated from the man. Anger. Not misery, or self-centered contemplation. Anger. Simmering, tangible anger.

Fred cocked an eyebrow, her sex squeezing in base appreciation. *Who* are *you, Mr. Tall, Bronzed and Brooding?*

Stare locked on the increasingly intriguing man, she tapped into the List of the Living threaded into her very existence, seeking the answer.

But all that surfaced from the never-ending database was a name and date of birth. Patrick Anthony Watkins. Born February 29th 1972.

Fred frowned. "That can't be right. Where's his date of death?"

From the moment of conception, the time and cause of death of every living creature with a soul was predetermined. The Order of Actuality demanded it. From the smallest baby to the leader of the free world, their lifespan was locked in a fixed time frame, imprinted on their very genetic fiber.

All, it seemed, except Patrick Watkins. Which made him a...

Fred narrowed her eyes, regarding him across the busy beach. The sun beat down on those around her, drawing moisture from their pores, turning the heavily populated strip of sand to a wavering shimmer of silver light and color, yet Patrick Watkins remained sharp in clarity. Just Patrick. Filling her vision and her core.

She studied him closely and then shook her head. Well, whatever he was he wasn't a demon. He possessed a soul. She could feel its pure, spiritual presence pouring from him, even from this distance. A blazing white essence of life and humanity so strong it made her blood sing and her skin tingle. Frowning, she tilted her head to the side, looking at him through the darkness of her sunglasses. It didn't make sense. If he had a soul, he should have a date of death. So why was she drawing a complete blank?

And why, in the name of the Powers, was she so damned turned on? Did the man's ambiguity have anything to do with it? Or was it just because he was smolderingly sexy?

Fred shook her head again. She needed answers. And another *closer* look.

Because you want answers, or because you want to check him out again?

The unbidden and way-too-close-to-the-bone thought made her sex constrict in a firm, warm pulse of eager anticipation. She couldn't touch him, but she could look. She could look a lot. She could take her visual fill of him because the living *could not* see her. No matter what her foolish mind insisted it saw.

A tense pressure welled in her chest and, turning away from the sight of Patrick kneeling beside the empty pedophile's body, she released a long, dragged out sigh.

It was a sad fact of her existence she could no longer ignore. She, Death, the Grim Reaper, *El Muerte*, Cronus, Azreal, the Fourth Horseman of the Apocalypse, had become a Peeping freakin' Tom.

Gritting her teeth, Fred stormed along the high-tide line, fighting like hell to ignore the damp tightness between her thighs. "Fantastic. Fucking fantastic."

One hundred tall, thick candles materialized into spontaneous existence, illuminating the dark, cavernous room with a cold, flickering light. It washed the black stone walls pale yellow, throwing writhing shadows against the hard surface and casting a weak glow over the slim man in a black business suit where he stood before a massive, bone-framed mirror.

He studied the room—*his* room—in the reflection of the glass. It suited him. A room worthy of the First Horseman. An entity of the Highest Order could create whatever personal environment they desired within the Realm and his space was *exactly* how he desired it to be. A room of sick death and sick life. A room symbolizing his stature and premier position.

In the centre stood his bed, constructed by over a thousand

human bones once white and raw, now blackened by eons of waxy smoke. He had taken many a sacrificial virgin's purity on that bed, all whimpering at his power and inescapable strength. He had taken more than one demon slut as well. She-demons who knew who he was, knew, unlike his disrespectful colleagues, how important he was. She-demons who recognized his potential and wanted to taste his seed and bear his spawn.

He let his gaze slide from the bed to the towering throne standing on a raised dais under a large hanging candelabra. His prick grew stiff at the sight. Both throne and candelabra where made from human bones, just as the bed, but unlike the bed and candelabra, the bones of the throne were stark white. Each humerus, femur, tibia and skull still ripe with living marrow and tissue. The throne was older than time, but he made certain it defied time as well. It didn't take much to infuse each bone in its construction with an incantation to preserve its rawness. To touch each one was to touch a bone freshly torn from a living being's body, still slick and sticky with blood and fluid, still thrumming with that on which he fed the most—dying life. Whenever he sat on the throne, which he did often, the pain of the personally selected humans whose lives were forfeited for its creation seeped into his being, making him stronger.

Whenever he fucked on the throne, his seed destroyed the female impaled on his shaft and his orgasm decimated an entire region on the surface of man's world, striking every living creature down with disease, swarms of insects destroying all plant life and crops. Whenever he fucked on the throne it was as though he and he alone wielded the force of the Apocalypse itself.

The Powers had commanded he cease such activities, ordering him to tow the line. He was growing impatient with them. He was growing impatient with them and their timeline and their preordained hierarchy. Who were they to decide what *he* did and when he did it? Did they forget who he was? What he would bring about?

Returning his stare to the mirror, he studied his reflection, pursing his lips as he did so. He was short for an entity, he knew that. Short and thin, without the typical ostentatious tail and horns and over-developed muscles so favored by other first-order entities. No one would ever accuse him of using steroids, that was for certain. His blue eyes were pale and watery, his dark hair lank, his flesh pale and dull. "Sallow" was a word he'd heard muttered often by his brethren to describe him. "Sickly" and "weedy" two more adjectives used loudly and without secrecy by one of his number in particular.

His eyes narrowed as he let his thoughts turn to the last Horseman. Death. He drew her image into his mind, remembering all too easily her condescending rebuke of the proposal he'd suggested. A partnership of greatness. Not just a sexual one, but one to undo the very Fabric, to destroy the Order of Actuality completely. A magnificent, malevolent duo to bring about the very end of existence. A *duo*, not a quartet. Two Riders, not four.

She'd laughed. At both his sexual advances and his proposition. Laughed at him and told him to grow up and get a life. "Seriously, you don't still believe in that old wives' tale, do you? Do you see my black horse anywhere? Or my pale one, for that matter? Do you see me strutting around in a pair of chaps getting ready for the big assault?"

Curling his fingers into fists, he thought of Death and the Powers and how *all* would suffer from his wrath.

"I am Pestilence," he murmured, smoothing his left palm over his hair as he stared at his reflection in the giant mirror. The flames of the candles flared brighter at the sound of his name and the organ between his thighs grew stiff with dark anticipation. "I am the First Horseman of the Apocalypse. The one who brings disease and suffering incarnate. The one who destroys the world of man's crops and stock, their weak and young and feeble. *I* am the one who will bring the end, the one who will bask in the glory of the Apocalypse. Me and me alone." He gazed at his reflected form, cock hard, blood thick and fast in his veins. “And *nothing* or no one can stop me.”

His reflection stared back at him, human façade just the way he wanted it to be. Deceptive. Misleading. “No one,” he repeated, hot impatience eating at him, cold confidence feeding its hunger. “Not even him.”

His reflection stared back at him.

And, with barely a shimmer, turned into that of the lifeguard’s.

Chapter Two

Patrick threw his keys on the sideboard and swung the door closed behind him. What a day.

He dragged his hands through his hair, pushing the image of the dead man—Richard Peabody—from his mind. As with all drownings on Bondi Beach, the police had grilled him and his team for two hours after the failed resuscitation. Before that, the inevitable and always heart-wrenching conversation with the victim's loved one had occurred—in Peabody's case, a sister whom arrived at the beach just as the paramedics were loading his still-warm body into the ambulance.

He'd finished the day counseling his team who, like himself, took losing a swimmer hard, before jogging home, the tragedy replaying in his mind over and over again in a vivid, inescapable loop. And every time he experienced it again he saw the woman in the New York Yankees baseball cap with the concealing black sunglasses and leg-hugging jeans.

The woman who seemed to have disappeared into thin air.

Scrubbing at his face with his hands, Patrick made his way to the kitchen and grabbed a beer from the fridge. He opened the bottle and turned to the window above the sink, studying the black strip of the Pacific Ocean barely visible above six dark blocks of rooftops and twinkling streetlights. What a bloody day. He took a pull from his beer, closing his eyes as he did so.

Immediately, the woman in the baseball cap slammed into his head, exuding poised confidence and surety, like she had every right to be there.

Patrick's balls grew tight in his shorts and his dick twitched in a base, primitive response.

"Fair dinkum, Patrick." He shook his head, his voice thick in his throat. "You can't be horny about a hallucination."

"Do you have any idea how bloody uncomfortable your sofa is?"

Patrick jumped, the sound of his brother's irritated growl directly behind him almost making him drop his beer. He turned around, scowling. "Don't *do* that, you rotten bastard."

Ven gave him a toothy, decidedly evil grin. "That's what you get for hanging up on me today." Eyes a shade lighter than Patrick's took him in, the inspection so quick anyone else would have missed it. Patrick however, had been the subject of his vampire brother's scrutiny for close to two decades now, not to mention the eighteen years prior when Steven was still human. Those sharp green eyes missed nothing.

He held out his arms, returning Ven's sarcastic grin with one of his own. "As you can see, I'm still alive." He took another mouthful of beer before frowning at his brother. "And what the hell are you doing sleeping on my sofa? What's wrong with your coffin?"

Ven yanked open the fridge and withdrew his own beer. "You know, I think the coffin jokes got old about seventeen-and-a-half years ago." Twisting open the bottle, he flipped the small metal top at Patrick, who snatched it midair and tossed it into the sink, scowling. "And I wouldn't have traded my soft, king-size bed with its thousand thread-count silk sheets for your crappy sofa if I'd known this was the thanks I'd get for being worried. Seriously, brother, when *are* you going to get rid of that thing?" He raised the bottle to his mouth, his Adam's apple working in his throat as he drained its contents.

Patrick cocked an eyebrow. "Thirsty?"

Ven shook his head as he wiped the side of his mouth with the back of his hand, a glint of white fangs flashing from behind his wet lips. "Hungry. But I wanted to check on my kid brother before I got a bite." Concern flittered across his perpetually twenty-seven-year-old face. "What took you so long? I'd have come looking for you hours ago if it wasn't for the sun still being up."

Taking a mouthful of beer, Patrick studied his brother. Did Ven need to know about his day? Should he tell him about the woman in the sunglasses who may or may not have been there?

If you don't and she really was *there, some kind of paranormal nasty in tight jeans with killer curves, and Ven finds out he'll tear you a new backside. You know that, don't you?*

Steven Owen Watkins was nine years old when Patrick was born. According to their mother, he'd greeted the arrival of a baby brother with a lop-sided grin and the adamant proclamation *he* wasn't changing any nappies. Eighteen years later Ven had been killed in a side street in inner-city Sydney by an unknown assailant when both he and Patrick were attacked leaving a pub after celebrating Patrick's birthday.

It came as a bit of a shock to Patrick and their parents when six hours later, Ven walked into the family home, dropped onto the sofa and said, "Can I have some Vegemite on toast, please, Mum. I'm starving."

Since then, he'd lived the typical life of a vampire, if there was such a thing. He had a bevy of willing "feeds", all female, all gorgeous. He slept the days away in his king-size bed, haunted the dance clubs at night and generally enjoyed the new, rather unusual stage of his existence in the same way he'd enjoyed his completely usual life—laid-back with a sardonic bite.

Except, that was, when it came to Patrick. There was nothing laid-back about his attitude and relationship with his baby brother. From the minute he'd laid eyes on Patrick—barely two hours old—Ven had taken it upon himself to protect him. From what, Patrick didn't know. Neither did their parents. It wasn't until Ven's death and, subsequently his completely unexpected transformation, that the threat was given a name. "*Something.*"

"Something" was out for Patrick. Something "bad", and Ven

had made it his mission to keep his kid brother safe, regardless of how many times Patrick told him he was being crazy.

Tonight however, Patrick couldn't deal with another lecture about being exposed. "I've had a shit day, Ven. I'm not in the mood. I'm alive. You should be happy."

"I am happy, brother. I've got a stiff bloody neck from that evil sofa of yours, but I'm happy. That still doesn't change the fact my gut tells me you were in danger today."

Patrick rolled his eyes. "Here we go."

"Don't 'here we go' me." Ven pointed a finger at him, a sudden flash of iridescent yellow in his eyes as his demon reared close to the surface. "You know what I'm talking about and I'm getting fed up with you pretending otherwise. Jesus, you can see the future, mate. *I* saw you pick up the television remote control from the side table without moving a muscle."

"I can*not* see the future," Patrick snapped, a dull red heat twisting in his chest. "I made a lucky guess as a kid about who was going to be the next prime minister and you turn me into some kind of freak."

"You also knew when and where Mum and Dad were going to die, the date and time of the attempted assassination of the Canadian deputy prime minister, and who was going to win the 1986 Soccer World Cup final."

"I was a dumb kid talking out of my arse."

"Well, that dumb kid's arse sure knew a lot." Ven's eyes flashed yellow again. "And you still haven't explained the remote control to me. Even after all these years."

Patrick scowled, turning away from his brother to stare out the kitchen window at the deepening night. He couldn't explain the remote. Not to Ven. Not to himself.

Confined to an armchair with a broken leg after a particularly nasty pushbike accident, the then twelve-year-old Patrick had wanted to change the channel on the television. The cordless remote, a new and wholly remarkable invention that young Patrick was totally enamored with, was on the lamp table beside him. Almost in his reach. Almost. All he needed to do was twist slightly at the waist, raise his butt an inch or two from the chair and lean over the padded armrest to retrieve it. An impossible task thanks to the thick, heavy cast covering his right leg from hip to toe.

To this day, Patrick had no idea *how* the remote came to be in his hand. He remembered a pulling sensation in his gut, a prickling heat behind his ears and then Steven's stunned "Bloody hell, brother! How'd you do that?" as the device slammed against his palm.

The remote he couldn't explain. But he wasn't having that conversation now.

Finishing his beer, he turned back to his brother. "I'm not talking about this, Ven." He flicked his gaze over the other man, noticing a stretched tightness around his eyes. "Go feed. You look half-dead. Oh, wait a minute, you *are* dead."

Ven bared his teeth, fangs partly extended. "Funny bloody bugger, aren't you." Folding his arms across his chest, he leant back against the edge of the kitchen bench and crossed his ankles, a wicked glint in his eyes. "Amy's been taking yoga lessons lately." He licked his lips at the mention of his favorite "donor". "Not only has it made her blood taste like pure ambrosia, her flexibility is now phenomenal. The other night she did this thing where she wrapped her thighs around my neck and I fed from her—"

"Stop, stop, stop!" Patrick raised his hands in protest. "Do I look like someone who wants to hear about your sex life?"

Ven grinned. "You look like an older version of me and *I'm* definitely the kind of person who would want to know about *your* sex life, so...yeah. You do."

Patrick shook his head, trying not to laugh. Ven was right on at least one count. They *did* look alike. True, he now looked the older brother, being thirty-six and inflicted with mortality while Ven was an eternal wrinkle-free twenty-seven. But apart from that—and the fact Patrick's skin was tanned by the sun and Ven's tan had faded somewhat—they looked very alike.

Both tall and lean, both broad shouldered from years of swimming and surfing, both square jawed with a nose slightly too large for their face. Obviously, two brothers. One a lifeguard, one a vampire. One alive, one undead. Just your typical Aussie family unit.

Patrick shook his head again. "I'm going to bed. Unlike you, I have no sex life to speak of and, as I said before, I've had a shit day and I need some serious shut-eye." He put his empty beer bottle in the sink and crossed the kitchen floor, pausing for a moment in the entryway to give Ven a serious look. "If you're going to hang around for a bit, can you do me a favor?"

"I'm *not* doing your bloody ironing!"

Patrick grinned. "But you do it so well."

He turned and walked from the room, snatching the empty beer bottle Ven threw at his head without slowing his stride.

"Freak," Ven chuckled behind him.

"Good night, brother," he replied over his shoulder with a grin, heading for his bedroom. "Have fun."

He runs. Along the deserted beach, the wet, compacted sand crunching beneath the soles of his jogging shoes with every pounding footfall.

His heart thumps in his chest, his neck and ears. A steady beat surging blood through his veins. Each breath he pulls floods his being with renewed life, filling his lungs through his nose, the fresh tang of the ocean biting into his sinuses.

The high sun shines down on him, bleaching the empty stretch of beach of all color, a glaring ball of cold energy.

He runs, heart thumping, sweat trickling down his temples, into his eyes. He feels alive. He feels totally at peace. The beach stretches before him, a never-ending strip of isolated beach.

"Patrick."

The soft voice whispers behind him. He spins about,

frowning at the empty beach.

Jogging backwards, his frown deepens. There is no one there.

"Patrick."

The wind calls his name. He turns back to his original direction, blood, no sweat streaming down his face.

She stands before him. A woman in a...hooded cloak...and baseball cap, face shrouded by shadows.

The wind lashes his face and he raises his hand, protecting his eyes from the wild, swirling sand. He blinks and continues along the deserted beach, feeling fine.

"Patrick."

A woman stands on the beach. The woman with the baseball cap. She looks at him and smiles. He trips over a...body... No, a piece of driftwood. The sand bites into his face, tiny grains of raw glass embedding in his sweaty flesh. Staggering to his feet, he looks for the woman on the beach and sees only sand.

No water. No land. Only sand.

And bodies?

Dead, blotted bodies. Oozing pus and bile and ichor. Flesh decaying, blistering in the merciless, icy sun. Dead, bloated bodies piled atop each other, blank eyes staring at him.

Run.

The word slithers into his ear, a serpent of sound and texture. He spins, looking for the speaker. And sees the bodies. Stirring.

Run.

The snake writhes in his head. His gut clenches, his skin prickles. He stares, frozen, as the rotting, putrefying bodies move as one, a rising, rolling wave of decay. Growing higher. Higher. Blocking out the sun. Curling over him. Dead, decaying corpses all staring at him as they come crashing down, drowning him in—

"RUN, PATRICK."

A scream shatters the silent, still air and Patrick stumbles, frowning as he looks around the empty, deserted beach. Sweat trickles into his eye and he swipes at it with the back of his hand. Nothing. Just the beach and the rolling waves and the quiet. He begins to jog again, chuckling at his own foolishness. He must be hearing things.

The sand crunches under his feet, a relaxing sound that echoes his heartbeat. He smiles, enjoying the day. The sun warms his flesh, turns the sweat beading on its surface to hot bubbles of salty water. He runs, feeling fine.

He runs. Faster. His...scream... No, his smile growing.

He runs and... Oh God, it's here. It's here. It's found you. It's found...

The sun runs with him. The cold, white sun that reflects off the bones crunching under his feet. The bones of the dead left in his wake.

He runs.

And it chases him, its hand reaching for his heart, reaching and squeezing and crushing and killing him. He runs, and it runs after him. Gaining. Gaining. Until it is right behind him, ready to tear him apart, ready to tear him into a thousand bloody—

Patrick jerked awake, his heart smashing against his breastbone, his sweat-soaked sheets tangled around his legs. Christ. Not again.

He sucked in a long, shaky breath, flicking his gaze around his darkened room. Yes, it *was* his room. Not a deserted beach.

Raking his fingers through his hair, he sighed, forcing his heart to slow. A dream. Just a dream. The same dream he'd had for as long as he could remember—running along the beach. Dead bodies. Being hunted by something unseen. Something dark and sick—but a dream all the same.

No. Not all the same, Patrick. This one was different somehow. This one had—

He frowned into the darkness. The woman. The woman in the baseball cap from the beach. Letting out a frustrated breath, he rubbed his face with his hands. Fair dinkum, he must be losing his mind. Not only had the recurring nightmare been more vivid, more *insistent*, his messed-up psyche had gone and incorporated the mysterious woman from the beach into his dream.

Patrick shut his eyes and bam! There she was. Face still shadowed by the peak of her cap, eyes still concealed by large, black sunglasses, long black hair tumbling over straight, fine shoulders. The woman who may or may not exist. The woman making him—

Something touched his chest. A feather-light caress that felt like cool fingertips stroking his bare skin directly above his heart.

He leapt from the bed, smashing his fist against the light switch barely a second after his feet touched the floor.

And saw the woman from the beach.

Standing beside his bed.

Looking at him.

Fred noticed three things straight away. Patrick Watkins was looking directly at her, he was stark naked and he was semi-aroused.

By the Powers, he's huge.

"Who the hell are you?"

His deep, angry growl made her jump. She stared at his face—his *face,* Fred, his *face*—her mouth dry. "You *can* see me!"

"Of course, I can see you. And I saw you at the beach today." Sharp green eyes narrowed. "What the fuck did you do to my drowning victim?"

Fred clenched her jaw, giving the human before her a level look. "For your information, your drowning victim was a pedophile."

A shimmer of disgust ignited in Patrick Watkins' dark green eyes before he clenched his own jaw. "Mr. Peabody was alive until you touched him."

Fred cocked her head to the side, trying like hell to ignore the fact that the man seemed to have forgotten he was naked—and still partially erect. *Ignore it? How do you ignore something that impressive?* "Yes, I must say, you did a very good job resurrecting him from his initial passing. But it was his time and no interference, no matter how skilled or stubborn, would have saved him."

Patrick's eyes widened. "Interference? His time?" Anger flared in his unwavering stare. "Who the fuck are you? The Grim Reaper?"

Fred inclined her head slightly. "Just call me Fred."

"Well, *Fred.*" Patrick took a step toward her, the anger in his face growing dark. Menacing. "*I'd* saved him. I don't care how bloody sexy you are, or who you think you are, he was alive until you touched him. What the hell did you do to him?"

Fred's heart stopped for a split second, before pounding triple-time. Sexy? A grin stretched her lips and a wild flutter erupted between her thighs. He thought she was sexy.

He also thinks you're a murderer.

She pulled a face, crossing her arms across her chest. Her nipples brushed against her forearms, sending a little jolt of damp electricity into the pit of her belly and she bit back a curse. How was it possible this one mortal male made her so horny? "I really can't explain it all to you," she snapped, irked by her body's irrational response and Patrick Watkins' not-so-irrational agitation. "Just know Peabody is in a *much* more deserving place now he's gone."

Patrick cocked an eyebrow. "So, what? You're a vigilante?"

Fred ground her teeth. "As I've already said, I can't explain it."

"Try. Before I call the cops."

Fred couldn't help herself. She burst out laughing. "The cops?"

Black anger flashed across Patrick's face. "Look, love, you've got exactly twenty seconds to give me an answer, or I'll knock you on your arse, tie you to the bed and let the authorities deal with you when they get here."

A hot, wet wave of sinful pleasure rolled through Fred at the idea of Patrick Watkins tying her to the bed. Damn. She'd never gone down that path of sexual gratification before, but the Australian lifeguard made her body fantasize about *all* sorts of things it hadn't before. All of them very, very wicked. "Patrick Watkins," she said, unable to stop her gaze roaming over his naked body. "I would like nothing more than to see you try."

Another wave of fury—and something else far more primitive—charged his expression. "Okay. If that's the way it's going to be."

He moved. Much quicker than Fred expected. Much quicker than any human should. One moment he stood glaring at her from beside his bedroom door, the next he was slamming her against the wall, his fingers locked around her wrists, his hips rammed into hers.

Immediate and absolute pleasure tore through her. Dark, intoxicating, submissive pleasure. Her sex constricted, her breath caught in her throat. She'd never been handled so. Even her Roman had treated her with kid gloves, like he'd been too scared of her to truly show how much she'd aroused him. Patrick Watkins however, knew no reason to be scared of her. And it made her sex flood with cream.

By the Powers, she wanted to fuck him and be fucked *by* him.

The licentious thought whipped through her head and, before she knew what was going on, her jeans, boots and t-shirt vanished. Leaving her just as naked as the man pressing her against the wall with his hard body.

He froze, his fingers digging into her wrists, his cock grounding against her belly. "What. The fuck. Is going on?"

Christ, she felt amazing. Even as Patrick's mind struggled to process the unreal shit currently tormenting it, his body reveled in the firm but lush softness of the woman pressed against it. Whoever Fred was, *whatever* Fred was, she felt like sin.

And as a result, *he* felt on fire.

He stared at her, stared into eyes the color of blue ice. Without the concealing sunglasses, her eyes were almost hypnotic, framed by thick black lashes and a face almost impishly beautiful. She was undeniably, incredibly sensual in a mysterious, exotic way and his cock grew stiffer. It liked what it saw—and felt—a lot.

His erection nudged her belly and a soft moan slipped from between her lips. She licked them, flicking the tip of her tongue over the soft, full swell of her bottom one before catching it with white, even teeth. He watched, enrapt. A surge of heat flooded his balls at the simple seductive action and his cock twitched again, growing longer and harder. It pushed against the firm flatness of her stomach, insistent. Eager.

Jesus, Patrick. What's wrong with you?

The woman's eyelids fluttered closed for a second, another moan—softer and longer—sounding in her throat before those arresting eyes of hers returned to his again, holding his stare as she pushed her hips forward.

Her smooth thighs slid against his, the curve of her sex rubbing the root of his shaft. The thick ebony curtain of her hair tumbled over her bare shoulders as she lifted her chin a little, almost daring him to...what? He sucked in a sharp breath, tasting her subtle musk on the air.

An insane urge to crush her mouth with his surged through Patrick and he frowned. "Who *are* you?"

"I told you." Her voice was a husky murmur. "Call me Fred."

Her breath fanned his lips in a whisper of warm air. Her eyes challenged him from behind a few tousled strands of her hair. He could feel her heart beating against his chest. Could feel the hard points of her nipples rubbing against his flesh. She shifted under his weight, her crotch aligning with his in perfect symmetry. His cock—the most honest and truthful organ of a man's body—jerked. Engorged with blood and undeniable desire. Thicker and harder than ever before.

Something deep and long repressed ignited within his core. Something hungry and powerful. Closing his fingers tighter around Fred's wrists, he growled.

And she captured the wild sound with her mouth.

Her tongue plunged past his lips and he met it with his own, lashing and battling the wonderful invasion. She tasted of secret spices and cool allure. He should be pushing her away. He *should* be calling the cops *or* the men in white jackets, but there wasn't a force strong enough in the world capable of tearing his lips from hers at that very moment in time. He thrust deeper into her mouth, wanting to explore its delicious sweetness.

Pressing his body harder to hers, he raked his hands down her arms, scoring a line along the subtle dip of her waist, over the curve of her hips and back up to her ribcage. The full swell of her breasts were compressed against his chest and he brushed the backs of his fingers along their sides, drinking in her moan as he continued to kiss her. She shifted beneath him, maneuvering in his hold until he felt the dampness of her arousal stroke the base of his throbbing cock. His head spun and his blood turned hot. She wanted him. As much as he wanted her.

Refusing to break the kiss or contact with her lower body, he captured her breasts with his hands. Their heavy weight spilled over his squeezing fingers, sending a ribbon of liquid power into his groin. Jesus, none of this made any sense. In fact, he was probably still dreaming, but what a dream. If his mind really was unhinged, he was more than happy to go along for the ride. As long as this woman—Fred—was in the passenger's seat, his to hold and kiss, he'd spend the rest of eternity in a padded cell.

A low, raw growl in the back of Fred's throat sent another surge of lust straight to his cock. She writhed against him, fighting his hands on her breasts even as she wrapped one long leg around his hip. Immediately, the soft heady musk of her desire filled his breath and his pulse quickened. Bloody hell, this was insane.

She rolled her hips, sliding her spread sex up his rigid cock, painting its length with her cream. Hot, wet pleasure crashed through him. He jerked his mouth from hers, staring hard into her pale blue eyes.

"Anytime, Patrick Watkins."

The ambiguous invitation slipped from her lips. He didn't need to ask what she meant. The heat in her body, the scent of her desire told him.

Dragging his hands from her breasts, he grabbed her hips, yanking her arse from the wall and sinking his fingers into her butt cheeks. Without preamble, he hauled her from the floor and spun about, throwing her onto his bed before she could utter a sound of resistance.

She slammed against the mattress, ink-black hair fanning around her head like a dark halo. He stood at the foot of his bed for a moment and gazed at her. Pale, flawless skin, firm, toned muscles, full, high breasts, small dark nipples, soft black pubic hair shaped in a shallow crescent. The familiar silhouette held his attention and his heartbeat quickened, his cock growing painful with fresh blood at the sight.

Crescent? Like a scythe?

"Do you like it?"

Her question raised his head and he met her stare. "Yes."

Without breaking eye contact, he placed his right knee on the bed between her legs. His cock felt like a rod of steel, so erect the edge of its distended head bumped his abdomen with every move he made. He shifted his weight onto his bent knee, smoothing his palms up the bed until they were beside Fred's waist, leaning slightly over her body as he raised his left foot from the floor.

She watched him with ice-blue eyes. Unreadable eyes. Her breath came short and shallow through parted lips. He slid the outside of his left knee along her inner calf, a slow, deliberate journey toward the junction of her thighs and its mesmerizing crescent, inching her legs further apart as he did so. A soft, almost inaudible whimper sounded in Fred's throat and her eyes fluttered closed.

Jesus, she is gorgeous.

The thought whipped through Patrick's head...a split second before she opened her eyes and gave him a smoldering look. "No offense, Patrick Watkins, but this is taking too long."

With inhuman speed, she jackknifed her body. Her long firm legs locked around his thighs, her arms wrapping around his shoulders. Before he could react, he was on his back, pressed flat to the mattress, Fred straddling his hips. "I really want you to fuck me," she stated, lowering her body closer to his as she threaded her fingers through his and held his hands locked beside his head. "Right now."

Patrick stared up at her...and the door slammed open, the sudden crack of wood splintering against drywall like an explosive shot.

Ven stepped into the room, his light green stare locked on the bed. "What the hell's going—" He froze, and Patrick saw recognition flood his face. *"You!"*

In the space of a heartbeat, he transformed. From a good-looking, slightly pale man, to a terrifying, malevolent creature. He lunged straight for Fred, knocking her off Patrick in one blurring leap, his hands locking around her throat, fangs extended, eyes burning baleful yellow.

He smashed her against the wall, white plaster dust showering down on them both as he shoved her high off the floor one handed, bringing her face level with his own. "What the fuck are you doing to my brother?"

"Jesus, Ven!" Patrick scrambled off his bed. "What the hell are you doing?"

Ven swung his head around, fixing Patrick with a very demonic glare, his yellow eyes an inferno of icy rage. "I told you something was after you, brother."

Patrick blinked, stunned disbelief killing the powerful sexual hunger in his blood. “What? This woman?”

Fred squirmed in Ven’s hold, her fingers digging into his wrist. “Hey!”

Ven shook his head, the demon fully surfaced. “This woman isn’t what she looks like, brother.” He turned back to Fred, baring his fangs with a low, menacing hiss Patrick had never heard him make before. “This is Death.”

Fred bared her own teeth—white, even teeth that looked like they would cost a fortune at a cosmetic dentist. “I prefer Fred, fang face.”

Something punched Patrick in the gut. At least, it felt that way. He swung his stare between his vampire brother and the mysterious woman from the beach.

“Death?” he said. For the first time in his thirty-six years he did not want to listen to what his gut was telling him. “As in the Grim Reaper? Musty old cloak, rotting bones and antediluvian scythe?”

“Hey!” Fred said again, sounding far more indignant than she should, considering her situation.

He ran his gaze over her, not questioning his brother’s actions at all, just his motivation. If Ven believed the woman was a threat, he wasn’t going to argue—yet. After all, she had killed Peabody with just a stroke of her fingers *and* her clothes had seemingly vanished without a trace, but Death? “I don’t mean to rain on your parade, Steven, but have you *looked* at the woman you’re holding?”

“I *saw* her, brother.” The vampire turned to stare at him, the knuckles of his fingers growing whiter as his grip tightened around Fred’s neck. “The night I died. As I lay on the filth-strewn ground with you desperately trying to revive me, I saw her. She took my soul.” He turned back to Fred, pressing her harder to the wall, his fangs grazing the high angle of her cheekbone with each word he growled. “And now she’s trying to take yours.”

Fred rolled her eyes, and for the first time Patrick noticed she didn't seem overly fazed by Ven's strangulating grip. "I'm not trying to take his soul, you moron. I was just..." A soft pink blush flooded her cheeks and she faltered.

Ven glared at her. "Just what?"

Patrick stared at them both. The whole scene was surreal, like something from a late-night television program aimed at teenagers, yet with a bigger budget for the special effects, and tangible, potent sexuality beyond their adolescent experience. The paranormal he could swallow. He'd given up disbelieving in spooks and demons when Ven had walked into their parent's home six hours after dying, but his overwhelming, powerful and completely undeniable sexual response to the woman Steven claimed ended his life? How could he be so aroused so quickly?

He flicked his gaze to the naked woman still pinned to the wall by his brother and a tight tension pulsed through his cock. Bloody hell, what was going on with him?

Snatching his boxer shorts from the nightstand, he yanked them on, scowling at Ven and Fred who were scowling at each other.

"Just *what*, Death?" Ven growled again, knuckles growing whiter still.

Fred squirmed, the pink in her cheeks growing a deeper shade of red, before she lifted her chin in a clearly defiant angle. "I was just checking him out."

Patrick raised his eyebrows at her. "Checking me out?" An itch began in his gut and he frowned. "You mean..."

Still imprisoned in Ven's demonic grip, Fred closed her eyes and shook her head. "This is getting ridiculous," she muttered.

Her eyelids snapped open, revealing eyes a blinding pure white. She spread her fingers wide and suddenly, as if he were a rag doll, Ven went flying backward across the room, slamming into the far wall with a solid thud.

"*Ooff.*" The grunt burst from Ven's mouth, the first sound of discomfort and pain Patrick had heard his brother make since he'd become a vampire. He watched him drop to the floor before turning his stare back to Fred.

Or should that be Death?

She stared back at him, eyes ice blue once more, a black pair of leather pants, black biker boots and a black Bob Marley t-shirt covering her body the moment she rammed her fists to her hips. "I *mean,*" she growled, "I was having what you Australians call a perv. I saw you on the beach and thought you were worth checking out again." She flicked a look at Ven, now stumbling to his feet, Patrick noted, with a stunned and very pissed-off expression on his face. "Of course, I didn't know you had a pet vampire guarding you."

"I'm his *brother,*" Ven snarled.

"Or that you could see me," Fred continued, ignoring Ven. "And while we're at it, how *can* you see me, and why *is* fang face leaping to your protection like an overzealous fox terrier?"

Fred folded her arms across her chest, fixed Patrick with a hard look and then turned her attention to his brother. She narrowed her eyes, studying the vamp closer. He wore his human face again, almost a mirror of Patrick's but slightly paler with less life in the seams around his sharp green eyes. She remembered him. His soul had fought the taking with more strength than she'd ever encountered before. Those with a powerful reason to stay attached to the mortal coil always did, but this one's soul, Steven Owen Watkins' soul, had resisted the claiming like the world itself depended on his existence.

She remembered being impressed by his strength and tenacious stubbornness. Two traits he obviously shared with his brother. The night of his claiming came back to her in a flurry of shadows and senses. She'd arrived as he lay stretched on the grimy concrete sidewalk, blood oozing like thick red paint from his neck through the fingers of the young man leaning over him, a man she'd paid little attention to at the time but now realized was her lifeguard eighteen years ago.

A deep squirming sensation unfurled in the pit of her belly and she ran the tip of her tongue over the edge of her teeth.

Fang face was pretty damn fine, even more so for the simmering demon lurking in his blood, almost as fine as his human brother, but something felt wrong. Something didn't gel.

She slid her gaze from Steven, to Patrick and back to the brooding, irritable vampire again. Her spine tingled, a soft tickling itch at her tailbone that made her worry. When *that* part of her spine tingled, the place where her spine became her tail when she was in her demon form, it was a warning of mischief in the Realm. That part of her spine had tingled the time the fallen star had tried to alter the spiritual status quo, that part of her spine had tingled the time the serpent started up its conversation with Eve, and it tingled now.

Why?

What was it about the Watkins brothers that set off her internal warning system? How could these two men, okay, this one man and this one vampire, have any impact on the Realm?

"I've had enough of this, Death." Steven took a step toward her, his pale-green stare shimmering yellow anger. "Time to tell us what you're really doing here."

"It's been fun, fang face." She grinned, ignoring his demand. She flicked another quick look at Patrick and the tingle in her spine exploded into an undeniable spasm of sensations, some of them downright delicious.

He stared back at her, a flash of ambiguous color seeming to shimmer through his deep-green eyes.

Who are you, Patrick Watkins?

She touched her tongue to her lips, tasting him still...and transubstantiated herself from his bedroom. Something was not as it was meant to be, and she needed to find out what it was. Now.

Ven raked his fingers through his hair, staring hard at the empty spot in Patrick's bedroom only seconds earlier occupied by Death, before turning to glare at his semi-naked brother. "I hate to say I told you so, brother—"

"No, you don't."

"But I told you so," he went on, shaking his head. He crossed the room to the tallboy under the window, yanked open the top drawer, snatched out a white t-shirt and threw it at Patrick. "Well, at least I know who's after you." He watched his brother pull the item of clothing over his head, forcing aside the driving urge to grab Patrick and shake him. "What I *don't* know is *why* you were lying naked on your bed under the Grim bloody Reaper? I'm telling you here and now, the sight of your erect dick will scar me for life."

Patrick gave him a dark look. "Don't you mean will scar you for undeath?"

"Ha ha. There you go again with the lame undead jokes, but it's not going to work this time." He folded his arms, fixing Patrick with an equally dark glare. "You've got some explaining to do, little brother. What the hell was going on?"

Patrick didn't say a word. Not for a long moment anyway, and for a second Ven thought he would need to give his brother a kick up the arse. Until Patrick released a harsh sigh and dropped onto the side of the bed, looking up at him with unreadable eyes. "I don't know what's going on, Ven. I wish I did."

Ven frowned. "Maybe we should begin with how Death came to be stark naked and straddling you like a rodeo rider on a prize bull?"

Patrick flashed him a cold grin. "Thanks for the simile, Ven. I keep forgetting you were a journalist before becoming a hellish monster."

"Still am a journalist, brother. Just freelance now." He dropped onto the bed beside Patrick. "How else do you think I pay my bills? You don't become an instant millionaire the second you become a hellish monster, you know. I still have an electricity account, a water account, a phone account, a cell phone, a—"

Patrick raised a hand. "Yeah, okay, I get the point."

"But *I'm* still missing one. The point about you and Death

naked?"

"I woke up and she was in my room. We argued about Peabody, I grabbed her and suddenly she was naked."

Ven raised his own hand. "Wait a minute, I'm missing half of that conversation. Who the bloody hell is Peabody?"

Patrick let out another harsh sigh. "A drowning victim today. I'd resuscitated him. Fred touched him. He died."

Ven shot his eyebrows up. "Fred?"

Patrick shrugged. "Fred. I'm still not convinced she's what you say she is. Come to think of it, I'm not convinced this isn't still a dream."

A tightness pulled at Ven's unbeating heart. "Dream? What kind of dream?"

Patrick's eyes closed and he pulled an irritated face. "Fuck. Not this again."

"You're still having those nightmares, aren't you?"

With another, much more violent muttered curse, Patrick rose to his feet. "Leave it alone, Ven. I've had a gutful. Whatever it is you think I am, I'm not."

Hot anger shot through Ven and he stood, glaring at his brother. "How many times have I saved you from dying, Patrick?"

"Jesus, not this again!"

"How many times did I save your life before my death? How many times did I pull you from the surf after a freak wave dumped you under? Wiped you out? How many times did I grab you from the road after you somehow stumbled off the curb into the pathway of a bus, or a truck? How many freak accidents have I saved you from, brother? How many? It seems to me I've kept you alive on more than one occasion when some force has been pulling as many strings as possible to see you dead."

Patrick didn't respond. Ven studied him, trying *not* to be angry. His brother had spent his life struggling with something inside him, something he didn't want to acknowledge or release. But it was there. It wasn't just his denied ability to see events in the future, nor the way he'd moved the television remote control without touching it. It was something Ven couldn't explain. Like Patrick was important. More than important. On a level of existence he couldn't understand or vocalize. He'd sensed it as a human, he'd felt it as vampire. Whatever Patrick was, he was more than he thought, more than he wanted and quite frankly, Ven had had enough of his refusal to see that. His kid brother needed to face it. Especially now that Death was interested in him. "Not to sound churlish, Pat, but I died protecting you. The vamp that attacked us outside the pub was not after me. It was after you. There's gotta be a reason for that."

"He was hungry. I was the weaker target. That's all."

Ven shook his head. "That's bullshit, and you know it."

Patrick shot him a silent look and Ven couldn't miss the stubborn glint in his eyes, or the bunching tightness in his jaw. His shields were coming up. As they did every time Ven raised the issue.

Biting back an inhuman growl, he stormed across Patrick's bedroom, heading for the door he'd so recently barged through. "Fuck this," he threw over his shoulder as he crossed the threshold. "I want answers."

And there was only one creature he knew who could provide them.

It was time to face Death. Again.

Chapter Three

Amy Elizabeth Mathieson lay stretched on her bed, gazing up at the ceiling. She ran her hands over her ribcage, down her waist, across her hips, noting with pride the toned muscles and complete absence of fat. She worked hard to stay in shape, spending hours in the gym, even more in Pilates and yoga classes every week. If she didn't, who knows what vacuous bimbo with a vampire fetish may lure Ven away from her.

Sliding her fingertips up her torso, the sound of Kings Cross's nightlife wafting through her open window like background music, she traced a slow line over the swell of her bare breasts, circling the nipple on each until they puckered into hard tips.

A shot of heat stabbed into her pussy and she closed her eyes, releasing a soft, hitching sigh. She wanted to feel Ven's fangs on her nipples. He'd never drawn blood from her there, no matter how often she'd suggested he could. He'd bitten her once or twice, but never with his fangs. Never to feed. What would it feel like for him to do so? To suckle her blood from the tiny wounds he made as he massaged and cupped and squeezed each heavy curve of flesh?

Her pussy fluttered at the thought and she whimpered, arching her back a little to press her thighs together.

Opening her eyes again, she studied the small black cracks marring the white plaster of her ceiling. They looked like tiny varicose veins.

The comparison made her think of her own blood and she lifted her hand to her neck, fingering the pulse beating just below her ear. Ven's preferred spot to bite.

For three years, she'd been his primary feed source. Almost every night he came to her, made love to her, drank from her. Not just her blood, but her juices as well. He made her come with his mouth and his teeth and his cock and fed on the product of each. Her blood *and* her cream.

The burn of his penetration—both fangs and cock—was something she didn't want to live without. It consumed her. The nights he didn't come to her, she lay waiting, her body on fire, trembling, aching for the pain and the pleasure he brought upon her.

She was a good feed. She knew that. Always there for the vampire when he needed her, never saying no to anything he suggested—and when the mood took him, he suggested some pretty kinky things—offering herself to his every whim and desire. Just as a loyal and loving pet should.

Amy released another sigh, this one not so ragged. Loving. What a hideously dangerous word. A word fraught with pain and complications. How had she let herself fall in love with a vampire? A vampire who'd once been a surfboard-riding journalist, of all things. A smoothie both with his body *and* his words.

If she'd known what he was when she'd first met him—during a nighttime beach volleyball game at Bondi where he and his brother were wiping the sand with their opponents—she wouldn't have asked him out for a beer.

Who are you kidding, Amy? The idea of vampires has turned you on since you first saw Brad Pitt as Louis de Pointe du Lac.

A shiver rippled through Amy and she rolled her eyes. Ven made Brad Pitt's vampire look like a reject from a bad TV show. That he hadn't revealed to her he *was* a vamp for close to a month after that first post-beach-volleyball beer only made his appeal all the more intoxicating. She'd been well on her way to falling for him as a human, his dry sarcasm making her laugh, his smoldering green eyes making her burn and his tender, attentive lovemaking making her melt. When he'd finally revealed her fangs to him, his eyes almost nervous, she'd wrapped her arms around his broad shoulders, bowed her neck and whispered *yes, oh, Lord, yes,* without hesitation or fear.

Three years later and here she was—in lust, in love and intoxicated.

Pressing her fingertips harder to her neck, she licked her lips. She'd asked Ven to "turn" her the last time he'd come to her. She'd practically begged him. The rapture she felt whenever his fangs punctured her neck, the deep, steady burning sensation through her body as he drank from the twin holes... Fuck, she couldn't go without that. Even twenty-four hours was almost impossible to bear. If she were a vampire too...

A shudder wracked Amy's petite frame and she let out a gasp. An eternity of that drawing burn was too exquisite to ponder. The idea almost made her come there and then.

Rolling her head to the side, mouth dry, sex throbbing and wet, Amy looked at the clock beside her bed. She frowned.

Nine-sixteen p.m.

Ven should have been here by now.

Her gut clenched and she licked her parched lips, closing her eyes for a moment. She ached for him. A desperate ache low in the pit of her belly.

Rolling from her bed, she stood and crossed to the window, parting the flimsy gauze curtains to stare out into the night. He rarely entered her home that way anymore. Her open invitation allowed him much more freedom to come and go. But every now and again when he was in a playful mood, she'd hear her name whispered and there he'd be, perched on her windowsill, four stories above the ground, grinning at her with that cheeky, sarcastic glint in his pale eyes.

Tonight didn't seem to be one of those nights.

Amy gazed at the busy street below, watching tourists and locals alike move about the Cross's main drag, some pausing to listen to the strip-club hawkers, some popping in and out of the various twenty-four-hour stores, some giggling at the hookers teetering along the sidewalk in stiletto boots and leather thongs.

There was no sign of Ven at all.

Her sex constricted with denied need and she frowned. Two nights, now. Two nights that he hadn't come to her.

She gnawed on her bottom lip, rubbing her palms up and down her bare arms as she did so. The ache in her core grew stronger and her pussy constricted again. God, he wasn't coming.

Maybe he's hurt?

The chilling thought shot through Amy's distraught mind and she sucked in a sharp breath. The paranormal world in Sydney existed in shrouded secrecy, only known to those within it. Territorial demons, vampire hunters, weres, dark elves, shit, even other vampires—all existed side by side in a tenuous concord, all presenting a very real threat to that concord and each other. And from what she could gather, most either targeted Ven or avoided him like the plague.

"That's it," she muttered, turning from the Ven-less windowsill. She crossed back to her bed, grabbed the cordless phone on the nightstand and punched in his cell phone number, hands trembling, pussy constricting. She needed to know he was okay almost as much as she needed to feel the burn of his feed.

"G'day, you've reached Steven Watkins. Leave a message and I'll get back to you."

Amy quickly punched a key on the phone, cutting the connection. She could leave a message, but she didn't want Ven to think she was desperate.

But you are *desperate, girlie girl. Your whole body aches, your cunt feels thick and heavy, your muscles weak and trembly. You* know *what you want. You* know *what you need.*

She closed her eyes, chewing on her bottom lip before snatching up her jeans and a skimpy black shirt from the end of the bed. Damn it. Damn him. She yanked them over her naked legs and torso, muttering senseless sounds of contempt the whole time.

She *did* know what she needed, what she craved and hungered for. She needed to feel the burn so fucking much it hurt. And she knew where to go to get it.

She just hoped to God Ven never found out.

Ven stepped out of St Vincent's Hospital ER and stormed along the crowded passageway toward the exit, the glaring fluorescent bulbs above him bleaching his already pale skin to a ghastly white. He weaved his way through waiting patients, worried family members and exhausted interns alike, shutting the potent, tantalizing stench of fresh blood permeating the air from his mind. He was hungry, bloody hungry, but feeding wasn't the priority at the moment. Finding Death was.

He'd been to just about every hospital, morgue and seedy twenty-four-hour pub he could in the last two hours, hoping to catch her scent. She wasn't at any of them and nor had she been, not even the Tudor Hotel, inner Sydney's most dangerous, high-mortality-rate pub, despite the fact a drunk Irish tourist had been stabbed in the neck and died during a brawl over a spilt bottle of Guinness no less than fifty minutes ago.

Wherever Death was, she wasn't lending a hand to the expiration of the newly dead within a twenty-mile radius.

Meters from the hospital's exit, he stopped and pulled in a deep breath, tasting the three-a.m. air, hoping to detect even the faintest trace of the Grim Reaper.

The rich, cloying stench of blood filtered through his nose, over his highly tuned olfactory nerves and his mouth flooded with hot saliva. Christ, he was hungry.

He ground his teeth, forcing his fangs to retract and the demon within to back off.

His stomach growled, a wholly human physical reaction to denied sustenance and he bit back a curse. This wouldn't do. He would need all his strength when he found Death—the dismaying memory of how easily she'd thrown him off back in Patrick's bedroom was still too fresh to ignore—and unless he fed soon, he'd be weaker than an asthmatic kindergartener.

He pulled his cell from his back pocket, flipped it open and then snapped it shut. Amy would be more than willing to accommodate his hunger right at that moment, but what he needed was a quick, sharp, no-questions-asked feed. In and out in less than ten minutes.

He had two options.

One, he could "charm" his way into the local cop shop and take his pick of any of the scum incarcerated in lock-up. Two, he could hit the Pleasure Pussy Nightclub on Kings Cross's main drag and take his pick of any of the human females willing and wanting to give themselves to one of Sydney's underground "creatures".

His saliva glands exploded again at the thought.

Growling with frustrated impatience—he *really* didn't have time for this—he sprinted into the shadows of the hospital's dimly lit car park and folded space.

There really was no other way to describe the process by which he moved around when in a hurry. He thought of where he wanted to be, pictured it, pictured an impossible fold in reality bringing his current location and his desired location together and then—with a blurring of his surroundings and a white-hot surge of energy through his body—he was there. He knew he physically traveled the distance between the two spots, but *how* still eluded him. Sometimes he had recollections of flying, the night air kissing his face as the lights of the city streaked beneath him, other times he recalled sensations of sprinting across the ground on what seemed like four feet, each covered in glossy black fur and tipped with sharp, hooked claws. He never questioned the mode of transportation. What mattered was that he got where he wanted to be fast. It had saved Patrick's life more than once from some unexplained "accident".

And hopefully it would again tonight, although he had to admit, Death in the flesh could never be called an accident.

A vivid and all-too-clear image of Death in the flesh popped uninvited into Ven's head. The very naked flesh. A dark tension coiled through the pit of his stomach and a twinge of unexpected hunger that had nothing to do with blood shot through his cock.

He growled. He most definitely didn't have time for *that.* Besides, the bitch had taken his soul. What the bloody hell was he doing being turned on by her?

Forcing the way-too-enticing image of a naked Grim Reaper from his mind, he replaced it with an image of the filthy but hardly used alley behind the Pleasure Pussy Nightclub.

His cold skin began to tingle, his blood began to burn. He pictured the hospital car park and the alley coming together, like a piece of paper being folded in two. He drew the image into his mind and then he was moving, his hair rippling back from his temples and forehead, lashing behind him as he ripped through the black night sky.

The lights of Sydney blurred to a kaleidoscope of glowing lines below him, the scents of the city assaulting him as he passed through them. He increased his speed until, with an abrupt jolt, he stood in the alley.

Immediately, he was attacked by the stench of stale beer, vomit, old blood and even older semen. The alley, it seemed, was the perfect place to finish an act of carnal sin started within the nightclub, whether that act be murder or sex.

Raking his fingers through his windswept hair, he walked out of the filthy alley onto the infamous Darlinghurst Road, Kings Cross's main drag and Australia's premier home of sex, drugs, hookers, pimps and five-star restaurants.

Strip-club hawkers, curious tourists, harried locals, barely dressed whores and overly dressed businessmen moved past him, most of the women and quite a few of the men giving him decidedly interested glances. Even while human he'd been considered good looking, but since his transformation...suffice to say, he had *no* problems finding companionship whenever he wanted it.

Funnily enough, since meeting Amy Mathieson, he hadn't needed or wanted to go looking for it. The petite photographer satisfied all his desires. That didn't stop his allure to the living however, and tonight was no exception. More than one human sized him up as he pushed past them. One tall, willowy blonde in skintight black latex pants and a blood-red bustier disengaged herself from the arms of a man dressed in a U.S. naval officer's uniform and sashayed her way up to him, her smoldering blue eyes promising all sorts of fun. She stopped directly in his path and, without hesitation, placed her palm completely on his groin. "I'm yours if you want me."

"Hey!" the sailor barked behind her.

Ven gently closed his fingers around her slender wrist and lifted her hand from his dick. "Not tonight, love. I'm in a hurry."

The woman pursed her lips. "Pity. Would've been a freebie, too."

Chuckling to himself, Ven turned away from the hooker and walked the few steps to the Pleasure Pussy's entryway. A short, stout hawker with wild, bloodshot eyes shouted from the sidewalk, regaling anyone who would listen with a censored-for-human-ears list of the delights they would find within. He flicked Ven a quick look, inclining his head in a slight nod of recognition. The Pleasure Pussy was one of a few undercover nightclubs catering to Sydney's non-human population, a high-end strip joint serving a plethora of beings a range of delicacies while gorgeous dancers who may or may not be human entertained those in the dark, shadowy booths.

Ven didn't frequent the joint that often. He didn't need to anymore, but the hawker still recognized him for what he was.

A tight fist of disquiet squeezed Ven's still heart. For some reason, he was *always* recognized by Sydney's underground otherworld.

Squashing his unease, he pulled in a steadying breath. Now was not the time to—

A subtle, delicate scent filled his being, almost hidden by the overpowering odor of beer, sex and sin hovering in the air. A scent of mysterious spices and menacing secrets. *Her* scent. Death was here. In the Pleasure Pussy.

Not caring about who saw him move or how many gasps his inhuman speed caused, Ven shot past the hawker into the dim, smoky nightclub.

He came to a fluid halt just inside the entry foyer, scanning the smoke-filled club with eyes already adapted to the dark light. Humans and non-humans alike moved about the cramped floor space, all enjoying themselves in various stages of conversation, copulation and consummation. Vampires fed from willingly offered necks, demons of all rank and ethos mingled with various species of weres. The distinct musky odor of lycanthrope filtered into Ven's breath, threaded through the almost gagging stench of brimstone and ancient blood. Somewhere in the shrouded mix of patrons, a *molekh* obviously enjoyed itself. Ribbons of sickly-sweet pheromones wafted through the heavy air like delicate bands of iridescent light.

In the centre of the club's arena, a semi-naked couple—the female petite, gorgeous and human, the male tall, stunning and fae—danced on the extended stage, their lithe bodies gleaming in the single golden spotlight tracking them. They writhed and pressed against each other, removing the skimpy items of clothing they wore, piece by piece in time to the slow, somehow dirty music.

Ven watched them for a second, their carnal act sending a stab of wet heat into the pit of his stomach. It reminded him how hungry he was—on every level. He turned from the show, narrowing his senses on the subtle hint of spices drifting to him from somewhere toward the back of the building. She was in here, *waiting* for him. He could taste it in her almost-intoxicating scent.

Stepping deeper into the nightclub, he relaxed his hold on

his demon a little, the release amplifying his preternatural instincts tenfold. Death's distinct scent slipped through his nose, past his lips and over his tongue like cool, sweet mist. It pulled at his very core and, with a sudden surge of dark excitement, he saw her sitting in a shadowy booth to the rear of the arena floor, a half-empty margarita glass in her right hand. She watched the couple's performance, a nonchalant expression on her perfectly beautiful face. Her pale skin appeared almost luminescent in the booth's muted light.

He destroyed the distance between them in half a blurring second, dropping onto the padded bench directly opposite her without word or warning.

"Hello, Steven." She took a sip from her cocktail, her attention never wavering from the couple all but copulating on stage.

Ven glared at her, struggling to keep his demon—now both excited *and* agitated—in check. "Stay away from my brother."

Death took another drink, her ice-blue stare riveted on the strippers. "Your brother is not what you think he is."

He snorted. "You don't think I know that?"

She raised one dark, exquisitely shaped eyebrow and gave a soft, unconvinced sound, her gaze following the movement of the strippers with attentive focus.

Ven couldn't suppress his growl. "I know I'm only young for a vamp, and you're what...older than God? But stay the fuck away from my kid brother. If you touch him again I'll—"

"This is a very good show," she cut him off, lifting her glass toward the writhing pair before her. "I like the use of the serpent. Nice symbolism, if a touch clichéd. Not sure I appreciate the comment about my age, mind you. It's not nice to insult a lady like that."

Hot anger tore through Ven. "Jesus, Woman! I'm threatening you with a considerable amount of pain here and you give me a live porn critique and lessons in etiquette?"

"Well, it's a very good show. It makes me horny." Eyes the

color of an ancient glacier turned to him. “And I know it makes you horny too.”

Another wave of anger crashed through him, all the more scalding for the disgust her statement brought. She was correct; the strip show *did* make him horny. But that wasn’t why he was there.

“What are you doing here?” he demanded, suppressing the urge to squirm in his seat. Fuck, how did she make him feel like a bloody hormone-crazy teenager? “Don’t you have souls to take?”

Death turned back to the stage show and took another sip of her margarita. “I rarely get to take in live theater these days, and I had time to kill while waiting for you. What better way to pass the hours than to check out one of your favorite haunts.” She chuckled, the sound low and throaty and having an immediate effect on his dick. “Haunts. That term has so much more relevance when associated with someone as dead as you.”

“I’m not dead,” he growled through clenched teeth, his body still recovering from her far-too-sensual laugh. “I’m *undead.* There’s a difference.” He grabbed a bottle of beer from the tray of a passing waitress and took a mouthful before giving Death a narrow-eyed glare. “And how the fuck do you know where I like to ‘haunt’?”

She raised an eyebrow, a grin playing at the corners of her mouth. “Still insisting you can imbibe human food?”

Ven took another mouthful. “It’s beer, not food.”

“From what I understand, to you Australian men, it’s the same thing, isn’t it?”

“Great. Insult my gender and nationality.” He drained the bottle, placing it on the table between them with a little more force than he’d planned. She was getting to him. A lot. “So tell me, while you’re camped out here checking out the skin show, the world goes without death? No one dies while you’re getting your thrills?”

She laughed, that throaty chuckle again sending a jolt of wet heat straight into his balls. “God, no.” She favored him with an easy grin. "About one-hundred and fifty-three thousand, four-hundred and six people die every day, give or take a few. That's roughly a little over one hundred a minute. I have a whole staff of underlings to take care of the simple stuff."

Unable to stop himself, Ven frowned. "So what do *you* do, Death? I distinctly remember you strutting about over my body as I died. What? Today a religious holiday?"

"I do not strut, thank you very much, and please, call me Fred." She finished off her margarita and gently placed the empty glass on the table, fixing Ven with a very pointed look. "I tend to the more complicated claimings. If someone is meant to die and something or someone is interfering with that, I step in. Example—the kiddy-rapist your brother saved at the beach was fated to die by the Order of Actuality. If I hadn't intervened Patrick would have resurrected him and the Order would have weakened." She leant back in her seat, stretching her arms along the edge of bench. Ven studied her, unable to miss the upward thrust of her breasts the casual position caused. They were a perfect size, her breasts. Not too big, not too small. Just the perfect handful. He swallowed, feeling an invisible pull on his gut he hadn't experienced since becoming a vampire. Plain, simple, old-fashioned desire.

"Trust me," she suddenly said, making him jump. He snapped his gaze to her face, relieved to discover she was watching the fornicating dancers on the stage once again. "Where Peabody is now, is a much more deserving place for a pedophile."

She studied the performance in silence for a moment, allowing Ven to take in the exquisite beauty of her profile. Smooth, rounded forehead, turned-up nose, full, bee-stung lips, long, swan-like neck of the creamiest alabaster. His mouth filled with hot saliva and his cock grew thick in his jeans, pressing against the snug, restricting denim. He bit back a groan. Damn it, what the bloody hell was he thinking?

What was he doing being turned on by the Grim bloody Reaper?

He glared at her, wanting to get away from her as soon as possible, wanting to yank her against his body and fuck her senseless just as quickly.

You are in trouble, Steven. Big trouble.

The dark thought shot through his head just as Death turned her gaze away from the stage show to fix him with an unreadable stare.

"Tell me, Steven Watkins, why do you need to protect your brother? Who do you need to protect him from?"

The sudden reminder of his brother sent an icy shard of guilt into Ven's gut. He scowled at Death, letting his demon rear closer to the surface. "You."

Death shook her head, her piercing blue gaze refusing to let his go. "I don't want to claim Patrick." She tilted her head, a tiny grin curling her mouth. "Well, not in that way. His ass is gorgeous. And his chest." She made a low, whimpering groan in her throat. "Oh."

Ven pulled a face, an unexpected jolt of something ominous twisting through him. "God. Do you have to?"

Death cocked an eyebrow, her unreadable eyes growing even more ambiguous. "Jealous?"

Ven blinked, that same dark jolt twisting deeper into his gut, turning into a heavy churning sensation he now recognized. Death was correct—again. He *was* jealous of her response to Patrick. A feral growl worked its way up his throat and his demon stirred in angry disgust. He'd *never* been jealous of Patrick. Ever. Even when Pat had won the Bondi Beach Charity Triathlon, an event he himself had competed in for more than ten years, the idea of being jealous never entered his mind. Patrick was his brother and he loved him unconditionally. There had never been a need for jealousy.

And yet here he was, green with envy over Death's lustful interest in Pat when he should be dealing with her deadly interest in him instead.

He scowled, forcing the unwanted, traitorous emotion away

with a sharp breath.

The scent of secret spices and subtle, feminine arousal filled his nose and a ravenous surge of hunger—both blood and sexual—immediately roared through him, making his cock pulse and his fangs extend.

Death's blue eyes shimmered to pale ice. "I can feel the hunger in your veins, Steven."

He curled his fists and glared at her, refusing to acknowledge the desire gnawing at his control. "What do you want with my brother, Death, if not to take his life?"

She chuckled a silent laugh, obviously humored by his tenuous resolve. "That's not the question that needs to be answered, fang face."

"What is, then? Will he go to the prom with you?"

Death leant forward in her seat, her gaze locking on his with fierce curiosity. "*How* can he see me? If he is just a mere human—albeit a fucking sexy-assed one—how can he see *me*? No one sees me unless I chose for them to do so, no demon, no demi-god, no entity beyond the Powers. No one. And yet, Patrick did. How?"

The enormity of her statement made Ven's already ice-cold blood run colder.

A smile played over Death's lips. "Told you he isn't what you think he is."

"So what is he, then?"

She gave the slightest shake of her head, her midnight-ink hair tumbling around her shoulders, her eyes unreadable again. "I don't know. But I'm going to find out. One way or the other."

Hot, red anger flooded through him. He leant forward, staring her hard in the face, his nose almost touching hers, his fangs extending to lethal points. "Stay. Away. From my. Brother," he whispered, letting his demon turn each word into a guttural promise of pain.

Death's lips parted, enough for the tip of her tongue to

touch her bottom lip. "Or what?" she whispered back.

Ven moved without thought. His mouth crushed hers. Hard. Brutal. She froze for a split second before kissing him back with a savagery that equaled his. Her tongue plunged into his mouth, flicked at the insides of his lips, the daggers of his fangs. The wholly erotic caress was electric. His pulse tripled immediately, an explosive detonation of mortal response he'd not experienced for eighteen years.

He jolted to his feet, his body thrumming with blistering energy, his cock throbbing with rapacious need.

Death stared back at him, her eyes wide. Shocked.

Ven ground his teeth, the sweet elixir of her saliva still on his fangs. "Stay away from my brother," he growled, his confused mind incapable of commanding his mouth to say anything else. He turned and stormed through the club, struggling to sheath his fangs and his demon.

The hunger surged through him, devouring him, made the battle to keep his human façade almost impossible. He pushed through the crowd at the club's entry foyer, his every breath filled with the tauntingly delicious stench of human blood and sweat leeching from those around him.

Bursting out onto the street, he clenched his fists, fighting for control.

Focus on your anger, Steven. Think about how hideously you've just betrayed your only brother. That should cure your depraved hunger.

The thought brought no relief. Instead of guilt and rage dousing his lust, his demon grew closer to the surface, powerful and insatiable. Craving blood and sex with such voracious, predatory force, he almost locked his arms around a nearby hooker there and then, his fangs growing longer, readying for her sweet coppery blood to gush from her jugular and flood his throat with vital life.

He barged through the busy sidewalk, rigid cock pulsing, ragged breath shallow. If he inhaled the human-tainted air too deeply, he would lose control and be lost to his demonic needs.

With a growl, he shoved his hand into his back pocket and ripped out his cell phone, flipping it open and punching in Amy's number in feverish haste. He needed to feed. He needed to fuck. Now. At the same time. He needed to sate his hunger before he did something foolish. Something—

A hand closed over his fingers, snapping his phone shut with a soft click. A cool, pale hand with long, slender fingers tipped with blunt, blood-red nails.

He jerked his head up, dragging his stare from his now-closed phone to the woman standing before him, her lush, lithe body encased in skintight black silk and leather, her pale, pale blue eyes shining with confused desire.

Without uttering a word, she lifted her hand from his phone and placed her palm to his chest, directly over his still, unbeating heart.

A wave of heat rolled through him, so hot and pleasurable he bit back a cry of exquisite pain. His cock—already ramrod stiff—flooded with fresh blood and lust and he growled, the sound so far from human he felt the pedestrians around them tremble with subconscious terror.

He didn't give a flying fuck. How could he? When Death stood before him with her hand on his lifeless heart, making him feel more alive than he'd ever felt.

"I've just thought of something, Steven Watkins." She studied him, eyes smoldering. "*You* saw me in Patrick's bedroom as well."

Ven's throat grew tight. He stared at her, his fangs lengthening, his cock throbbing.

"How did you do that, fang face?" she asked, her dark eyebrows pulling into a puzzled frown. "Tell me."

He stared down into her face, anger, guilt, confusion and desire roaring through him.

Desire as ravenous as his hunger took possession of his body, his mind. Working through his body like an inferno, igniting in his groin, burning through his belly, up into his chest, his unbeating heart, his mind.

"Tell me," Death whispered, leaning closer. Her eyes shimmered again. From pale blue ice to an infinite, iridescent white. The eyes of a demon more powerful than existence itself. "Or kiss me."

He did as commanded. He kissed her. Unable, unwilling to deny his desire any more.

The inferno devoured him, and before he could plunge his tongue past her lips the pure, primeval rapture of the kiss consumed him and nothing else mattered. Not humanity, not existence.

Not even Patrick.

Chapter Four

Amy held her breath, watching the vampire—*Raz, Amy. He calls himself Raz*—brush aside the stray lock of her hair falling over her shoulder. The deep predawn shadows of the alley made his face almost indiscernible, but his eyes were impossible to miss. They glowed with iridescent yellow greed, a greed she felt all the way in the pit of her belly.

She tensed, ready for the agony and ecstasy of his fangs. The pain would consume her first, followed by the pleasure, the rapture of the feed.

And if he kills you?

Her body trembled at the thought, but she ignored it. She didn't care. She needed to feel this now. She couldn't wait any longer.

Ice-cold fingers traced the line of her jugular down from her jaw to her collarbone, the path they took followed by a tongue both wet and cold.

"You smell delicious," the vampire murmured, grazing her flesh with his teeth.

Another tremble shook Amy, this one a surreal mix of sexual craving and abject terror. "I've been told so," she gasped, struggling to keep her voice even. She'd never offered herself to a vampire other than Ven. She just wished this one would hurry up.

There was a heavy pause, a tightening of his arrogant, overly familiar grip on her arse, and then he pulled back, his yellow stare drilling into her with almost contemptuous humor. "Really?" He grinned, his fangs glinting in the dim alley light. "By whom? I assumed I was your first?"

Amy shook her head a little, the fire in her belly and her sex threatening to devour her. Oh, God, would he never bite her? Would she never have release? "No. My...my boyfriend is a vamp."

It was a little lie. Ven had never called her his girlfriend, but she'd been his main feed for three years now. They went to the movies together, swam in the beach at night together, made love on the sand...surely that's exactly what she was? His girlfriend? And if Raz thought she had a vampire boyfriend, he would be less inclined to drain her. Wouldn't he?

She swallowed, her mouth suddenly dry even as her pussy grew wet with dark, impatient craving.

The vampire's grin stretched wider. "Really?" he repeated on a chuckle. "And what would his name be?"

Amy shivered, her sex contracting in denied anticipation. The aching need in her body was beginning to undo her. "Steven Watkins," she ground out, breath quick, eyes squeezed shut. "Now, shut the fuck up and bite me, damn it. I didn't come here for a conversation."

Raz stiffened for a moment, his lips still on her neck. "Steven Watkins?"

She nodded and for a glorious moment, she felt his tongue touch her neck, just above the point where her pulse beat like a trapped moth. Her breath caught in her throat in a hitching whimper and she braced herself.

"The vampire that surfs by moonlight?"

"Yes."

"Tell me more about him. Now."

The low command vibrated through her neck and she groaned, her nipples pinching tight, her fists curling tighter. "Why?" she moaned, pressing her hips against his cold body. "Does it matter?"

"That depends." He touched the curve of her shoulder with his icy lips. "Do you want me to bite you?"

Hot frustration rolled through Amy, bringing stinging tears to her eyes. Her body shook, the need to feel the burn so powerful she could hardly think. "He's just a vamp."

"So why are you here?" Sharp fangs dented her neck. A little. "With me?"

"Because he didn't come to me tonight...or last night, and..." She bit her lip, humiliation almost dousing the craving. Almost, but not at all.

A cold tongue traced a lazy circle around the little dip at the base of her neck. "And?"

A shudder rocked through her. "And I can't wait any longer."

The vamp tugged her hips harder to his and another, more primitive shudder claimed her. He was aroused. Very aroused. *Oh, Lord, forgive me.*

"Why hasn't he come to you? Did you do something wrong?"

Amy shook her head, trying to rub her neck against his open mouth. Fuck, how much longer? She couldn't take it anymore. "No," she groaned. "He has a younger brother he needs to protect. Sometimes he goes to him instead."

Raz became very still. "A brother?" The fingers on her arse curled harder into her butt cheeks, the lips on her neck softly nibbling her flesh. "Tell me his name."

"Patrick."

Ven's brother's name burst from her lips before she could stop it. A wave of unease rolled through her, tight and cold, but she ignored it. What did it matter if a vampire knew Patrick's name? It wasn't like he was anyone important, and Ven spent so much time looking after him, even if the vamp at her neck *did* decide to go after Patrick, he'd fail.

The unease in her belly twisted into a knot at the thought and for a split moment Amy wished she could take it all back.

What was she *doing* here? Why did the vamp want to know about Ven and Patrick?

She shifted, trying to move away when she felt sharp fangs graze her skin.

Hot pleasure rushed through her. Oh, yes!

"Steven and Patrick Watkins?" Raz murmured against her neck.

Her pussy contracted and she leaned closer to him. "Yes."

He made a humming sound, fangs pressing harder to her flesh. "Hmmm. Good."

That sense of unease rolled through Amy again. She stiffened...and he bit her.

Her orgasm, explosive and tainted with dark guilt, shot through her. Clamped her cunt shut on a nonexistent dick.

The burn spread through her body, wicked fingers of wonderful, terrible heat scalding their way to her craving core.

Oh, yes, yes!

Her newfound "friend" she'd all but thrown herself at in the Pleasure Pussy not but forty minutes ago, sucked at her neck, his fangs gouging deeper into her throat, his tongue rasping against her flesh.

She closed her eyes, letting the burn devour her. It was the single most painful yet exquisite sensation she'd ever experienced. There were no words to describe how it felt. None that she knew of, anyway. All she knew was the need to feel *this* never left her anymore. She needed it more than breath. Every second of every minute of every day she felt the craving. It consumed her. Like the raw energy of a cyclone—forceful and undeniable. Magnificent. Lord, why had she wasted so many nights waiting for Ven to come to her when she could experience the burn any time she wanted.

Why had she waited when it felt so...so... "Fucking good," she moaned, pressing her legs together as the product of her climax dribbled down her thighs.

Raz chuckled, the soft sound vibrating through his lips, his fangs, down into her centre. "As good as your boyfriend?"

The question filled Amy with fresh guilt and she squeezed her eyes shut, blocking out the sight of the grimy, trash-strewn back alley in which they stood, shutting out the faint pink smear of dawn coloring the dark sky above them. Ah, she didn't want to think about Ven. Not now.

But the vampire wouldn't let up. He seemed to draw pleasure from the acrid guilt in her soul, fed from it as enthusiastically as he fed from her neck and there was nothing she could do to stop him. Not while *his* pleasure allowed hers to be.

"Tell me, my sweet little Amy," he continued, lifting his lips from her throat. Amy cried out, sinking her nails into his icy-cold shoulder in an attempt to hold him to her. Pale red eyes regarded her from behind stubby black lashes. "Tell me what Steven Watkins would think about you being here with me." His lips curled into a sly grin, his tongue darting out to catch a drop of her blood lingering at the corner of his mouth. "Tell me what his human brother would think of it." He lowered his head a little and blew a fine stream of air onto her wet, blood-seeping neck. "Where are they now, Amy? Shall we go find them before the sun rises completely? Shall we let them watch our little show?"

A soft whimper slipped from Amy's lips at Raz's murmured suggestion and an image of Ven watching another vampire feed from her flashed through her head. A sinful thrill shot straight to her still-contracting sex and she shook her head. "No." Her voice was husky. "The sun is almost up. Ven will be sleeping."

Raz pressed his lips back to her throat, touching the weeping puncture wounds there with the tip of his tongue. "And his brother?"

Amy shivered, her heart pounding, her flesh tingling. "At work." She shifted, pressing closer to the vampire. "He is a lifeguard."

Raz's tongue flicked from one wound to the other before he lifted his head to stare into her eyes. "A sun lover."

She laughed, a nervous little hiccup of sound. “Yes. You could call him that.”

Raz’s eyes flashed brilliant vermillion. “Yes,” he murmured. “I could.”

His lips parted again, as if to return to her neck, and Amy braced herself for the agonizing rapture of his continuing feed. She needed it still. What he’d given her so far was wonderful, glorious, but it was not enough.

But instead of suckling her throat, Raz kissed her flesh with cool, wet lips and straightened, removing his arms from her body.

“No!”

She hadn’t meant to shout. Nor sound so desperate. She bit at her lip, her body already screaming with furious denied want.

“Do not fret, my sweet little Amy,” he purred, red eyes glinting. He stepped back into the protective safety of the narrow alley’s nighttime shadows. “I will give you more tonight. Much more.”

Amy’s pulse quickened. More.

A long finger extended from the deep shadows to touch her cheekbone, her lips. “Tonight I shall feed from you until your orgasm drains you of your very will to live.” He paused, and his hand withdrew from her face. “As long as you give me something in return.”

Her body all but writhing from Raz’s declaration, Amy nodded, searching for him in the darkness. “Yes. Just name it.”

His chuckle floated from the alley—before her, behind her, above her, she couldn’t tell. “In time, sweet Amy. In time.”

His words fell over her like a silken promise. She groaned in protest and impatient anticipation, turning on the spot, looking for him. But he was gone, leaving her with nothing but the agony in her neck and the greedy insistent want in her sex.

A cold ripple of guilt slipped up her spine, singed at the edges by her desperate, consuming need and she shivered.

Oh, God, what if she couldn't give him what he asked for? What would she do then?

You'll give it to him, Amy. No matter what it is, you'll give it to him. If he asks you to kill your mother, you will. And you know it. For the burn he gives you, you'll do whatever he asks. Whatever.

The horrifying thought ate its way through her head, down into her chest to the pit of her stomach, and she whimpered.

Because it was true. As horrible and hideous as it was, anything the vampire asked of her, she would do. Anything.

After the pleasure and pain he'd given her this morning, she was close to no longer caring.

The beach is deserted.

Except for the woman standing at the far end, near the houses rising from the eastern point. Still, quiet houses bereft of life and light. The sun sits high on the horizon, a burning ball of angry orange fire that casts the beach with a cold, vomit-yellow glow.

He runs along the sand, the tiny grains slicing into his feet, his stare fixed on the body on the high-tide line near the flags.

He needs to reach him before the woman does.

Heat surges through his muscles and he increases his speed. He's taken too long already. If he doesn't reach the body soon he'll never revive—

He kneels beside the body, staring hard at the lifeless man, searching for a pulse. Nothing. Peabody is—

The woman steps up to him, her striking blue eyes watching him as he punches Peabody's motionless chest.

"He's dead, Patrick. You're too—"

Late. The day grows late. He runs along the empty beach, watched by empty houses. A body rolls listlessly in the slush waves on the sand before him. Tumbling over and over, snatched by the waves, dragged back into the surf and then spewed up onto the wet sand once more. He starts to sprint. Shit. How could he have missed—

The sand bites into his knees as he drops down beside Mr. Peabody. The man's eyes bulge from his white, bloated face, as if he's seen—

Death leans over his shoulder.

"Patrick."

Her voice is soft. Seductive.

"Leave him be. I am here for—"

"You."

The voice, a guttural growl, makes Patrick stumble. He looks around the empty beach, searching for the speaker, his heart thumping hard. He knows that voice. Like he knows his own name. It belongs to—

Pestilence.

The shadows reach for him, the cold sun sinking behind the flat line of the ocean, painting him in sick red blood. He swallows, turning back to the patrol tower. He had paper work to do before heading home. He has to write the report for Peabody's—

Resurrection.

The sand slices into his knees, like a million diseased fire ants devouring his flesh. He looks down at the man lying on the ambulance stretcher, his fat, black tongue poking from bloated lips, his eyes closed, his skin still wet from the sea.

"He is gone, Patrick. Let him be gone."

Death whispers in his ear and his cock throbs, desire burning through him in a wave more powerful than any he's ever surfed.

"Time to acknowledge who you are so you and I can continue what we started in your—"

He looks up from Peabody and his stare falls on a man casting no shadow on the sand. A small, thin man with lank, dark hair and glowing yellow eyes. A small, thin man in a black suit, watching him. Staring at him with malevolent hate and fury.

"You are not going to stop me, lifeguard."

The man's whisper shatters Patrick's eardrums. He slaps his hands over his ears, dropping his head to his chest, teeth grinding together.

And watches Peabody open his eyes.

The corpse looks up at him with bulging, empty eyes and before Patrick can move, Peabody's hands wrap around his throat and fingers of ice sink into his neck.

"Time to die, Patrick Watkins."

"No!" Patrick snapped bolt awake, sucking in breath after ragged breath. He looked around his bedroom, the pale, weak light of predawn filtering through the curtains, turning the furniture into a collection of indistinct, looming shapes.

He raked his hands through his hair and flopped backward onto the mattress. Jesus. What a nightmare.

Staring blankly at the dark ceiling for a moment, he fought with his hammering heart, forcing it to steady.

Okay, two nightmares in one night was just not on. This is what he got for going back to bed while Ven went off hunting Fred.

An image of the woman insisting she was Death popped immediately into his mind, destroying the residue ghosts of his nightmare. He ground out a groan of frustrated disbelief. He saw her all too easily, naked limbs smooth and firm, belly toned, breasts high and round.

His body stirred, the terror of his dream forgotten.

Another groan rumbled in Patrick's dry throat and he threw himself off his bed, his feet hitting the floor with a thud.

Normality seemed to be unraveling around him. He was turned on by a woman who may or may not have murdered a man with just a single touch of her fingertips, who called herself Fred and somehow turned up in his bedroom in the middle of the night. A woman Ven insisted was the Grim Reaper, who was almost half his brother's size yet strong enough to fling him across the room like he was a rag doll.

A woman capable of making her clothes *and* herself disappear before Patrick's very eyes.

Normality unraveling.

Like it had before.

Frowning, he crossed to the cupboard and snatched his work clothes from the top drawer. He wasn't going to think about that. He'd pushed that particular "unraveling" to the back of his mind and that's where it was staying. No one knew about it, not even Ven, and it served no purpose thinking about it now. What he needed to do *now* was get dressed and get to work. It may be only—he shot the clock beside his bed a quick look—five a.m., but it was the middle of summer. The sun was beginning to break the horizon and that meant there'd be swimmers and surfers already hitting the waves in the faint predawn light. Swimmers and surfers who needed to be watched over. Protected from danger. From…

Pestilence.

Patrick's chest squeezed tight at the unexpected thought and an image from his dream smashed through his head. A man in a black suit who didn't cast a shadow on the sand. A familiar man.

"Stop it," he snapped, his frustration turning into self-contempt.

He yanked on his shorts and left the room, tugging his shirt over his head as he went. He wouldn't let normality unravel again. Not again. He'd barely recovered the last time it had happened.

Maybe Ven is *right? Maybe you are something—*

"Jesus bloody Christ, Watkins, stop it! You're a lifeguard. That's it. You're not some goddamn savior of the human race."

The jog to work passed in a blur of denied memories and denied images. Memories he didn't want to dwell on, memories of strange occurrences he'd never told Ven about, strange "accidents" he couldn't explain but almost cost him his life.

Memories of a shadowless man on a deserted beach. Staring at him. Wanting him dead.

Images he *wanted* to dwell on a lot, too much. Images of the mysterious woman, images of her naked, stretched out on his bed, waiting for him to join her, waiting for him to make love to her until they both climaxed, screaming each other's name.

The crunch of sand on concrete under his feet snapped Patrick from his torment. He blinked, his attention turning to the empty car park around him and the dawn-quiet stretch of beach before him. He was at work already?

He looked at his watch. 5:07 a.m.

Patrick frowned. Shaking his wrist, he brought it up to his ear. The battery must be flat. He'd left home at 5:05.

The soft, almost inaudible *tick tick tick tick* of tiny mechanics slipped into his ear and he frowned again, dropping his arm. His watch, it seemed, was working fine.

Normality unraveling, Patrick?

Refusing to acknowledge the squirming tension in his gut, he took the stairs up to the patrol tower's door two at a time and let himself into the building. He'd punch in and then hit the water. Perhaps all the swimming required to check out the surf's conditions would clear his head. After that he'd work through the morning's paper work, pitch the safe-swimming flags and then call Ven. His brother was probably settling in for the day by now, and he wanted to touch base with him.

To ask if he'd found Fred?

Squirming tension twisted through his gut again, lower this time. Almost in his groin. He bit back a groan. His brother had most likely spent the night chasing a paranormal Peeping Tom and all Patrick could think about was the deranged woman herself? 'Struth, he needed a swim. He only hoped the surf was still cold.

It wasn't. But despite its pleasant temperature, it achieved what he wanted it to. As he swam out past the shallow sandbar of the beach's eastern end, any thought of the mysterious woman, the shadowless man, the memories he'd long denied vanished, replaced by the calm meditation of stroke after stroke after stroke.

The outgoing tide pulled gently on his body as he moved through the water, not too strong but there all the same. The waves were small and peaky, barely more than six feet, a leftover from the larger southern swell out beyond the shark nets. This would be the ideal patrolled swimming area for the morning. He rotated in the surf, treading water for a bit as he triangulated his position with the patrol tower back on the beach, committing to memory his location and where exactly he would erect the flags.

Turning back to the open sea, he headed toward Backpacker's Express, the undercurrent growing stronger the closer he swam to the rip. Even still, it was a mild undercurrent. Perhaps the infamous, dangerous strip of water was playing nice for a change.

Swimming directly into its pull, Patrick uprighted himself, treading water to gage the rip's real strength. He smiled, feeling the current pull at his body with little force. Unless there was a major change in conditions the rip was unlikely to claim any unsuspecting victims today, which meant he and Bluey and the rest of the team might have a relatively relaxed day. Well, as relaxed as any day on a beach populated by over forty thousand people, the majority of which were overseas tourists who'd never set foot on a beach before, let alone—

Something grabbed his right foot.

Hard.

And pulled.

He went under the water, his whole body tugged a good five feet or so below the surface. Cold, salty water surrounded him. The grip on his ankle grew harder. More insistent.

He kicked out, trying to dislodge the—

The what? Seaweed?

Icy fingers sank into his ankle with what felt like needles

puncturing his skin.

Patrick kicked again, dragging his arms through the water in an effort to release the hold on his leg and reach the surface. Jesus, his lungs felt on fire.

What's got you? What dragging you down?

He didn't have time to ponder an answer. Whatever it was, it was pulling him deeper.

Cold water pressed against him, filled his nostrils. He blew out a burst of precious air through his nose, the released bubbles churning past his face in a chaotic storm, surging for the longed-for world above.

Fuck, he needed to breathe!

He kicked again, opening his eyes against the briny ocean, desperate to see what had him. Seaweed? Fishing net? Shark?

The dark, dawn water revealed nothing. He could barely see his thighs, let alone what gripped his—

Something grabbed his knee. Something stronger.

Cold terror roared through him. He sucked in a gasp and icy-cold water poured into his lungs.

Christ. He was going to drown and he didn't even know what the fuck had him.

Focus, Patrick. Focus.

A wave of powerful calm rolled through him, quelling his crippling fear. He kicked, his foot and shin striking something dense and solid below his waist, his trapped leg thumping what felt like a body.

The water churned around him in angry agitation. Became hot. Hot.

He lashed out, picturing his foot smashing against whatever held him.

Something pierced his knee. Nails? Claws? Teeth? A surge of absolute rage ripped through him, hotter than the heavy water pressing against him. He kicked again, the unformed image of his assailant shuddering with the savage force of his blow.

Christ! He needed air! He needed to breathe!

Another kick. Another mental attack.

The hands on his ankle and knee slipped. The water displaced around him, a sudden surge of icy temperature engulfing him from below. He struck out again, dragging his arms through the water, pulling himself toward the surface even as he attacked whatever held him. Picturing its unseen form reeling from each delivered kick.

Air! I need—

He drove his free leg downward, his heel striking something solid and fluid at once.

Another violent surge of icy water rushed past him and suddenly he was free.

He forced his arms and legs to swim, pulling his body up, up, up toward the surface.

Air. Jesus, air!

He broke through, sucking in a long, deep lungful of sweet, dawn air. It filled him with stinging life, charged him with furious energy. He swam, propelling his body toward the beach with powerful, rapid strokes, the empty stretch of sand taunting him with its safety. With every kick of his legs, he felt fingers brush his ankles, tearing his flesh. Trying to snare him again.

Forcing calm into his core, he pictured himself swimming faster. Faster than humanly possible. Moving through the water like a seal fleeing a hungry killer whale. Cutting through the water like a hot blade through butter.

His arms and legs burned, his muscles ached. His lungs felt on fire. But still he swam, his unseen attacker trying to grab his legs, trying to pull him back under. Drown him. Kill him.

Devour him.

Time's up, lifeguard.

The deafening whisper tore through his head and Patrick let out a roar. *NO!* His expelled breath bursting from his mouth in an explosion of furious bubbles.

He pushed himself harder, faster through the increasing

waves, growing closer to the beach and the safety of dry land.

Fingers lashed at his kicking feet, but he stayed out of reach. Just.

The sandbar smashed into his chest before he realized he was in the shallows. He shoved his feet into the sand, pushing himself up out of the water to dive over the natural barrier separating the ocean from the beach. Struggling to his feet, he ran through the knee-deep water, stare fixed on the patrol tower, the rising sun's faint rays reflecting from its polarized windows in shimmering, blinding silver.

He ran through the water, ungainly at first, but growing faster, more sure-footed the shallower it became. He ran, heart hammering, terror turning to molten rage with each pounding footfall, until he was on the beach, the sand sticking to his wet flesh, a prickling second skin he'd never felt so happy to wear.

Staggering further from the lapping waves chasing him up the beach, he turned, staring back at the ocean behind him. Fists clenched, ready to fight. Ready to continue what had begun in the water. Ready to destroy...

Nothing.

Peaceful waves rolled toward the shore with relaxing ease. Nothing burst from their smooth formation. No monster of the deep, no creature from the ocean's floor.

Patrick sucked in breath after breath, chest rising and falling in rapid succession, studying the sea closely.

Nothing except a seagull skimming the surface out over Backpacker's Express, a lone windsurfer away out in the distance and the rising sun peaking over the horizon in a blinding white slither of light.

He fell to his knees on the sand, shaking his head. What the fuck had just happened? Was he going insane?

He ran a shaking hand though his wet hair, the matted strands clinging to his fingers like seaweed.

Jesus. What was going on?

A seagull squawked behind him. The sound harsh. Frantic.

Patrick closed his eyes for a moment, steadying his breathing. *In your mind, mate. Just in your mind. Time to pull your finger out and get back to work.*

He pushed himself to his feet, turning to shoo the seagull away.

And saw the sand shift.

Tiny individual grains rolled over each other. Moving. Coming together. Building. Forming...

Patrick's mouth went dry. *Jesus, it's a monster.*

Muscles locked frozen. He stared at the rudimentary arms sprouting from a torso thick and dense and massive, at the hands forming on the end of each one, hands with talons both long and hooked. The sand shifted, like it was alive, a bulge the size of a head spewing from the formation. A head with a gaping maw and sunken, lifeless eyes.

A head that swiveled about until those lifeless pits came to rest on Patrick.

He stared at it, his blood roaring in his ears.

A monster. Looking at you.

The hideous thought unlocked his muscles and he lunged.

Straight for the sand creature.

Ven fisted his hands in Death's hair, the cool, silken strands like molten ribbons threading through his fingers. He growled, plunging his tongue deeper into her open, willing mouth.

She tasted so fucking sweet, those mysterious, secret spices flavoring her scent a thousand times more potent on his tongue. Savage desire surged through him. Controlling him. His demon, his *true* self, felt her phenomenal, infinite power and reacted to it, roaring so close to the surface his fangs grew longer and his forehead furrowed. His demon felt the terrifying entity that was Death, but *he* felt a *woman.* A warm, lush woman with smooth womanly curves and soft womanly bits.

He deepened the kiss, pressing his hips forward. His cock, engorged with blood and stiff with lust, ground against her groin. Fuck, he wanted her. Bad.

Removing one hand from her hair he grabbed her arse and jerked her hips closer to his, tugging her head backward with his other until her neck bowed into a glorious, exposed arc.

He tore his lips from her mouth and placed them on her throat, sucking at the warm, muscled column directly above her pulse. He could feel her indisputable power beneath his tongue, a latent current of utter supremacy that made the tiny hairs on his body stand on end. He'd never felt anything like it. It was raw. Ancient. Timeless. Undefeatable. He knew, before even puncturing her flesh and drinking her blood, he was already addicted to it. To *her*.

A hand fisted in his hair, brutally hard, whether to pull his head away or hold him to his neck, he didn't care. He opened his mouth, ready to pierce the wonderful column of flesh, sinew and muscle. Ready to partake of the glorious, frightening power flowing through the veins within.

"Fuck, Steven, what are you doing to me?"

Death's strangled question sent a ripple of liquid heat through Ven's core. Fed his lust and his hunger. Mouth filling with saliva, cock rigid, blood burning, he tore his lips from her neck, wanting to see the desire he was positive smoldered in her eyes before he fed from the desire in her veins.

Needing to see it and know it was for him and him alone.

He lifted his head. And stopped.

Everyone around them was motionless. No. Not just motionless. Frozen. Like the population of Kings Cross had been replaced with statues. So lifelike one could almost swear they were once real. He straightened slowly, staring about himself in stunned disbelief, his grip on Death's hair and arse dropping away. "What the fuck?"

Death gazed up at him, her breath shallow and rapid, her

eyes shimmering white, radiant light. "It's how I get my work done," she said, voice shaky. Her arms still wrapped his body, a confused frown pulling at her eyebrows. "I'm not governed by human and earthly temporal laws." Expression growing more puzzled, she pulled away from him, by a fraction. "You try claiming five souls at the exact same moment and see how well you can do it without stepping out of the time phase." Her hips still pressed to him, she studied his face, her frown growing deeper. "Why...how...how are you making me feel...?" Her eyes shimmered white light and a soft hitching breath caught in her throat. "I...?"

A surge of unadulterated hunger roared through Ven at the somehow primitive sound, so forceful and heady he almost sank his fangs into her jugular immediately. He was so fucking hungry on every level, and she was so fucking delicious and potent and willing...

Fresh saliva flooded his mouth and he almost moved. Almost.

White eyes flickered to pale, ice blue. "Steven?"

He sucked in a deep breath, forcing the intoxicating taste of her scent from his mind as he stared down into her face. Hell, he'd thought he'd wanted her in the strip joint, but that was *nothing* compared to this. He'd never wanted a woman so bad, but she wasn't *just* a woman. She was Death and he'd found her with his only brother in the middle of the night.

No matter how much he wanted her, how ferociously he hungered for her, he still couldn't betray Patrick. Death had come to his kid brother in the middle of the night and Ven still didn't believe it wasn't to take his soul.

Staring into her face, his body screaming in denied pleasure, his demon screaming in denied release, he slowly lifted his arms and wrapped his fingers around her wrist. "Return me to real time, Reaper," he growled, removing her hands from his hair and lowering her arms to her side. "Now."

She studied him, her frown fading, her forehead smoothing. A strange, ambiguous expression crossed her flawless face and then she stepped backward, eyes unreadable, chin tilted. "I'm beginning to wish I'd never met the Watkins brothers," she stated before, with a soft sigh and a shake of her head, she vanished.

Ven blinked.

People walked and pushed and hurried past him, hookers and tourists and businessmen alike. Pushing past him as if they'd never been frozen in time. Darlinghurst Road was once again a living, breathing strip of sin. He looked about himself, doing everything in his power to remain calm. He was hungry and confused and angry as all hell and Death had just played him for a fool.

He glared at the pedestrians before lifting his head to the sky. Shit. It was almost day break. He needed to get home, no matter how hungry he was, no matter how horny he was, before he became a charred hunk of ash.

He began to draw an image of his home high on the Bondi Beach hills into his mind when a voice almost tore his head apart. Patrick's voice.

Fuck! It's trying to tear me in two!

Chapter Five

The creature swung its massive head, staring at him with pupiless eyes. Its maw stretched wide, revealing jagged teeth formed by tiny grains of sand, glistening with moisture in the rising sun's faint light. Teeth, Patrick didn't doubt, more than capable of tearing into his flesh with hideous ease.

He didn't halt his sprint. Whatever it was, it wasn't fully formed yet. That meant it was vulnerable. He hoped.

He smashed into it, driving his shoulder into its gut. Millions of grains of sand bit into him in a million pinpricks of scalding heat and he let out a loud roar. He heard a wild squeal shatter the quiet of the beach, felt the scream of furious pain deep in his soul. Before his mind could register the unreal fact his shoulder was sinking into a writhing, animated mass of sand grains, he burst through it, like a desperate man barging through a living dust storm.

He stumbled to a halt on the other side, spinning about to stare at the creature, disbelief and dismay making his gut churn.

It was reforming. Bigger. Wider. Almost half the size of the patrol tower, blocking out the sun's infant rays, shrouding him in its cold shadow. Its head swiveled toward him, sightless eyes drilling into him with terrifying intent, its mouth stretching wide to reveal teeth more jagged and pointed than before.

Patrick swallowed. "Oh, fuck."

The creature lunged at him, a hideous pillar of living sand

and sea. It smashed into him, its fingers sinking into his chest and hip as it drove him backward.

He lost his footing, his heel dropping into a hollow in the beach, and he stumbled, arms flailing in an attempt to keep his balance. If he fell he was done for. There was no way he could beat this thing on his back.

The creature roared, the deafening screech of triumph punching at Patrick's ears. Yet even as he fought franticly with his traitorous feet, even as he grabbed at the thing's arms, he knew the sound was only in his head.

Claws of sand tore at his chest, his hip, ripping into his flesh. The creature lowered its face to his, sand blasting his cheeks and forehead as it screeched again. It sank its talons deeper into his body and began to pull.

Fuck! It's trying to tear me in two!

A surge of raw fury ripped through him. He glared up into the face of the sand monster, into the sunken pits of its eyes. "Fuck you, you bastard," he growled, curling his fingers into its dense, writhing arms. "The beach is closed."

An image exploded in his head—the creature detonating into a billion grains of sand, each one scattering through the air on a furious gust of wind. He drew on the power of that image. Let it fill his entire being, the way he let the feel of the surf fill him when he searched for a missing swimmer.

Cold calm flooded through him. Turned his fury to icy resolve.

He gazed at the creature, pictured his fist stabbing into its mammoth chest, saw it exploding into a feeble, pathetic puff of individual sand grains. Saw each and every one of those grains scatter to the winds.

He stared at the creature...

And lashed out with his mind.

A piercing wail burst from the thing's mouth. It reeled back, arms flailing, mouth gaping in obvious pain. A violent shudder wracked through its impossible body before, in the space of a heartbeat, it shattered, each grain of its formation whipping away on a sudden coastal gust.

Gone. Just like that.

Patrick dropped to his knees, sucking in breath after breath, his whole body on fire. Trickles of blood painted crimson lines over his skin, blending with his sweat. He stared at the ground, struggling to breathe. Jesus. Had that really happened? Had he really just fought a friggen' sand monster?

"How the hell did you do that?"

The shocked male voice snapped Patrick's head up. Throat tight, blood roaring, he gazed at his brother standing on the sand beside the patrol tower. Directly in the bright dawn sunlight.

With Death standing right beside him.

Fred gaped at Patrick, not entirely convinced she'd actually seen what her eyes told her she had. Had he just destroyed a *nikor*? Had he? And if he had, with what?

All about him, swirling about on the suddenly violent wind, were the remains of the aqueous demon, the tiny particles of sand and even tinier particles of seawater scattering in the turbulent air. Aqueous demons were impossible to kill in the water and damn nigh impossible to kill on land. As long as they were close to their dwelling they were almost invulnerable. Yet she'd just witnessed Patrick Watkins decimate one with...what? She returned her stare to him, her heart hammering so hard she felt sure it was trying to escape her body.

She'd heard his furious snarl in her mind the second she'd arrived back in the Realm, her sex still squirming with unexpected pleasure from Ven's savage kiss, her head still spinning with confused conflict. She'd had time to notice her reflection in her mirror—to note the troubled white glow in her eyes and the swollen bruising on her lips—and then, bam! Patrick's voice had roared through her head, sharp with rage and fear. *Fuck. It's trying to tear me in two!*

Instantly and without thought, she'd locked her very existence onto his location and transubstantiated, arriving in the world of man just in time to see him destroy the aqueous demon with nothing but a stare.

That can't be, Fred. No one can destroy a third-order sub-demon without a weapon. Even if it is *a water demon on land.*

She watched him study the minute particles of the annihilated *nikor* whirling through the air around him, his expression revealing nothing. He gazed at the floating grains of sand before, with a silent groan, he collapsed to his knees, head hung low.

A fierce, intense wave of concern crashed through Fred, an utterly alien emotion she'd never experienced before. She frowned. Concern? For a human?

But he's not *human, is he Fred? He can't be. Not if he can destroy a sub-demon with...with...*

With what? His mind?

She didn't care. Patrick, whoever, *whatever* Patrick was, was hurt. He needed help. He needed care and she wanted to be the one to give it to him. Wanted it more than she'd ever wanted anything in her infinite existence. There were questions to be asked, but she would ask them later. Starting with—

"How the hell did you do that?"

The sound of Ven's shout smacked into Fred with almost as much force as Patrick's earlier roar and she jumped, spinning to her left to stare at the man standing but a few feet away from her. Or should that be *vampire* standing but a few feet away from her? A vampire fully exposed to the new day's streaming solar rays.

The dawn sun painted him in a warm golden glow and for the first time, illuminated by natural daylight, she noticed the strawberry-blonde accent to his shaggy hair, the faint smattering of light brown freckles across his hawkish nose.

And then the obvious hit her and her mouth fell open. He wasn't burning to a screaming, vaporized crisp.

He was a vampire. He was standing in the sun. How could he *not* be burning to a screaming, vaporized crisp?

Like an explosion of fire ants, her tailbone erupted in a violent itch, the very same ominous itch that forewarned trouble in the Realm, and she choked back a gasp. Well, almost choked back a gasp. A soft hiccup of breath sounded in the back of her throat, barely audible even to her ears, but it was enough to make Ven spin in her direction.

He vamped out instantly, the beautiful dawn light illuminating his demonic features in stark, unavoidable detail. *"You!"* he snarled, and if she hadn't been a creature of myth herself, Fred would've missed the instant coiling of finely honed, paranormal muscles as he prepared to lunge at her.

But she didn't miss it. And neither did his brother.

"Steven!" Patrick yelled. "Stop it!"

The vampire seemed to freeze, his stare—locked on her with deadly, menacing intent—flaring bright red for a split moment, before he turned back to Patrick, his human façade flowing over his features once again.

Fred studied his profile, and then swung her gaze back to Patrick. A groan of dismayed realization vibrated up her throat and bit back a curse. Her sex remembered all too easily the erotic electricity of Ven's demon-tainted kiss, but her heart, her very core, throbbed with a smoldering heat she could not name nor fathom whenever she thought of his brother.

Oh, no. This can't be happening.

"What are you doing here, Fred?"

Patrick's deceptively calm voice made her jump.

She looked at him, mouth drier than the sixth level of hell. "Umm."

He cocked an eyebrow, his eyes green mirrors that revealed nothing. "Umm?" Blood still trickled over his sculpted body, tiny rivulets that reminded her with harsh reality he'd just fought and *beaten* a *nikor.*

"I heard you," she blurted out. Her answer made her flush

and she ground her teeth, frustrated and embarrassed. Damn it, once again, he was making her flush like a schoolgirl.

"You what?" Ven snarled.

Fred swung a quick look at the vampire before turning back to Patrick. "I heard you. In trouble." Her cheeks grew hotter. "So I came."

"Why?"

"A very good question, brother," Ven growled. "Especially since she'd just spent a considerable amount of effort trying to keep me where I was."

Fred started. "What?" Did he really think she'd been trying to distract him while an aqueous demon attacked his brother? "Wait just a damn minute. I'm not the bad guy here, okay?" She jabbed a finger at Ven. "*You* shouldn't be standing out in the sun without turning into a char-grilled drumstick, extra crispy, and *you*—" she turned her scowl on Patrick, wishing to the Powers her heart would stop squeezing whenever she looked at him, "—just pulverized a *nikor*, a third-order sub-demon, to dust with no weapon I can determine." She crossed her arms across her chest, giving them both a long glare. "So don't be making out I'm the only one here with answers to cough up."

The same puzzled frown pulled at Patrick and Ven's foreheads, and Fred would have burst out laughing at the almost comical sight if she wasn't so pissed off. With them and her stupid, stupid libido and stupid, stupid heart. Usually her emotions and sex drive were in perfect sync. It had never been otherwise, despite an eon of lovers, both demon and human. What was she now doing wanting both of them? She didn't need this. Not with her tailbone itching so goddamn violently.

"How *did* you destroy that beastie, brother?" Ven asked, his earlier concern returning to his eyes. "Cause the Reaper's correct. I *didn't* see you wielding a gun or a sword or even a bloody big broom and yet the sandy bastard is no more."

"How come *you* haven't turned to a pile of dust, Steven?" Patrick shot back, clearly not interested in answering. "And what do you mean, she'd just spent a considerable amount of effort trying to keep you where you were?" He narrowed his eyes. "Where were you exactly, and what kind of effort?"

Fred flicked her gaze from one brother to the other. Uh oh, she didn't like where this was going. "Listen." She stepped between them, holding her arms out to the side. "Far be it for me to interfere with a family squabble, but the beach at daybreak is not the place to discuss this. I've claimed more than one soul jogging along the sand at this time of day, I know how busy this place is going to get any moment now, and quite frankly, we're already starting to draw a crowd."

She let her gaze slide to the few early-morning risers walking or jogging past them, their expressions curious, almost troubled. Uncomfortable. They'd only be seeing two men arguing—she was not visible to anyone except Ven and Patrick—but it was enough to make her edgy. There was something much larger than she first thought going on here, something that made the battle of Jericho seem like a schoolyard fight, and for some reason, she felt like a sitting duck. Like she was being played.

Someone had sent a *nikor* after Patrick. And there were only a few entities capable of doing so. Four, in fact. And she sure as shit knew *she* hadn't sent it.

Fred curled her hands into tight fists by her side.

Pestilence.

Shooting the crowd, the ocean and the rising sun a harried look, she turned to Patrick. "I'm sorry, but we've got to get out of here."

Steady, indecipherable green eyes studied her. Weighed her up. She waited, knowing she couldn't rush this. She still had no idea who Patrick was, no idea why Steven could withstand daylight, but she knew one thing, the answers to those questions would decide their very fate.

She wasn't the Fourth Horseman, the ultimate bringer of the Apocalypse, because she looked good in black.

When she needed to, she could kick serious first-order demon ass.

"Patrick," she spoke his name, and a ripple of scalding tension warmed the pit of her belly. "Come with me. Now."

"Hey!"

Ven's indignant growl made her turn her head and she grinned at the vampire, sensing his demon rise close to the surface of his control in protective agitation. "You too, fang face."

He bared his perfectly human, perfectly perfect teeth at her, but she was already turning back to Patrick. It all came down to Patrick. Whatever it was, it started and ended with the lifeguard.

She needed him on her side. Until she figured out whose side he really was on.

"Patrick?" she said again.

He studied her, impenetrable eyes never wavering from her face, and then shook his head. Once. "No."

She bit back a growl of frustration. Damn it, that wasn't the answer she wanted to hear. Suppressing the urge to just snare him in her hold and transubstantiate him back to the Realm, she took a step toward him, fixing him with a level stare. "Patrick. Please."

His jaw clenched, but before he could refuse her again, she took another step toward him. "Please." She reached for his hand. "Come with—"

Something pushed her backward. Something she couldn't see but felt with no problems at all. Something hard. Something strong.

"I said no." Patrick's angry voice punched into her, an echo of the unseen force shoving her chest. She stumbled, her boot heels sinking in the beach's soft sand, her arms pinwheeling to keep her balance. By the Powers, what was pushing her?

Her gaze snapped to Patrick's face and she gasped.

He was glaring at her, his expression both angry and lost at once. But it wasn't his expression that shocked her. It was his eyes. Normally a light green, they now burned a dark, dark emerald. So dark they almost appeared black.

Her spine erupted in a violent itch, making her cry out with pain and, yes, fear. What was going on? Without thought, she snatched out for Patrick with her mind, locking him in an inescapable psychokinetic hold. Whether he wanted to or not, she needed answers. It seemed Pestilence wanted him removed from existence for reasons she didn't know and that made her uneasy. She needed to get him back to the—

She went flying backward in a wild, abrupt arc. Struck in the chest again by the same invisible blow.

Her ass smacked the sand first, followed by her palms, elbows and the back of her head. Her teeth snapped shut, sinking into the tip of her tongue and a galaxy of black stars exploded before her eyes.

What the?

Incredulous fury shot through her. She surged to her feet, uncaring of the humans hovering around them. How *dare* he? How dare—

Patrick was gone. Walking toward the car park. Away from her.

"Hey?" She locked her stare on him. What the hell? How could he be walking *anywhere*, let alone away from *her*? "Hey!"

She took a step forward, ready to run after him, prepared to tackle him to the ground if she must, when, in a sudden blur of color, Ven stood directly in her path, eyes glowing yellow.

"You heard him, Reaper." He gave her a cold, menacing grin, the tips of his fangs glinting in the sunlight. "Now, fuck off."

Without waiting to see her reaction, he turned on his heel and followed after Patrick, his tall, lean frame relaxed and, she had no doubt at all, completely ready to tear her apart. "Oh, and one more thing," he threw over his shoulder, not deigning to look at her as he moved with fluid ease across the uneven sand. "Stay the fuck away from my brother."

Fred stared after him, after them both, her tailbone itching, her heart pounding. She watched Ven take two blurring steps, defying space and speed until he fell into place beside Patrick. Watched the two men—so alike from behind she would have had difficulty telling them apart if it wasn't for Patrick's naked torso and sun-kissed skin—move through the car park until they were blocked from her sight by a garbage truck.

She stood still, the early morning sun heating her cheeks, the weight of everything that had just transpired stealing her breath. For a moment, she toyed with the idea of going after them. She could overcome Ven easily enough, even if he could survive sunlight...well, she assumed she could, and as for Patrick...

The thought faded away. And Patrick what? She'd just witnessed him destroy a *nikor* with the Powers knows what, he'd shoved her halfway across the beach without lifting a finger, let alone a fist *and* her attempt to hold him with her mind had failed miserably. Something entirely impossible. No one could escape the grasp of Death, no matter who or what they were. No one.

And yet, Patrick Watkins just did.

Beyond frustrated, she huffed into her fringe. Answers. She needed answers, and standing here, gaping after two annoying, irritating, stubborn and unfortunately sexy-assed brothers wasn't getting them.

With a sharp sigh, she dragged her fingers through her hair and transubstantiated.

Straight into the Realm's library.

The room, one of many all the entities and first-order demons could access at will, glowed with warm light. The squat table lamps positioned on either side of two large leather armchairs illuminated the wall-to-wall bookshelves and open fireplace.

She dropped into one of the chairs and kicked off her boots. A small trickle of sand spilled from each one onto the rug beneath her feet and a wry smile pulled at her lips. Even in the Realm she couldn't escape the Australian lifeguard.

Hah. Escape him? That was the last thing on her mind.

An unexpected image of Patrick—wet from the surf, muscles coiled and pumped with blood—filled her mind and her belly tightened. Damn it, she needed to focus on the situation, not how sexy the Australian lifeguard looked. How was she to discover what was going on if she kept daydreaming about him?

Without invitation, Patrick's brother popped into her head as well, sardonic expression making her sex constrict, pointed fangs making her palms prickle.

She dropped her head into her hands and groaned. She was in trouble. Big trouble and it was all the damn Watkins brothers' fault. How dare they be so damn sexy and mysterious and...and...

Grinding her teeth, refusing to admit to herself just how irrational and childish that last thought was, she conjured the first book from the top shelf and opened it.

It seemed Pestilence wanted Patrick Watkins out of the picture for some reason, but why? Hopefully the answer could be found in one of the books in this room.

Scanning the pages of *The First Horseman and the Case for Human Eradication,* a heavy, pompous and ancient tome, she blew at her fringe in disgust. Nothing. Its author, a second-order seraphim, had been infatuated with Pestilence's power over man's health, livestock and crops, and had spent far too many pages babbling on about why man should be made to suffer. Apart from clichéd ideas and tired rhetoric however, it offered nothing. No mention of Patrick, Steven, a vampire who could withstand daylight, hell, not even a passing reference to Australia or the beach.

She conjured another, this one with the delightfully antiquated title, *How the Horsemen Shall Punish Man.* Honestly, why half the Realm's population hadn't kept with the program and realized the idea of the Apocalypse had been benched eons ago was beyond her.

She skimmed through it, finding nothing but an overuse of words like annihilation and obliterate, before discarding it with a growl.

Forty-one books of the same theme and style later and she wanted to scream. No mention of Patrick or Steven Watkins in any of them. Forty-one books and all she had to show for it was a headache, a growing detestation for the word "thou", and an insane urge to round up the authors and give them all a damn good beating. Seriously, were there no decent writers in the Realm?

Running her fingers through her hair, she pulled another book from the shelf and read its title. *Of Men and Demon.* Catchy.

She flicked through its pages, made, she suspected with a curl of her nose, from cured flesh, scanning each one for anything of—

The brother who cannot walk in the sun shall cast a shadow on the shifting grains of glass, and the shadow shall be of blood.

Fred's heart smashed against her breastbone and she read the sentence again.

The brother who cannot walk in the sun shall cast a shadow on the shifting grains of glass, and the shadow shall be of blood.

The brother who cannot walk in the sun shall cast a shadow? Surely that had to be a reference to Ven, the only vampire she knew of who could withstand sunlight? But on the shifting grains of glass? Grains of glass? She gave the book's cover another look, noting the author. The last Fate. Cautious excitement tingled in her veins. Maybe the old biddy finally sprouted something of significance, instead of the usual cryptic mumbo-jumbo she'd been known for before her unexplained disappearance.

She reread the line, trying to garner more information from it before reading the paragraph before it. A growl rumbled in her throat. Nothing relating to or referencing Ven or Patrick at all. Just forty or so sentences carrying on about the relationship between seraphim and archangels and how they interacted with virgins of mankind's sixteenth century.

The next ten paragraphs after the tantalizing line were the

same. The last Fate really seemed to be hung up on the sex lives of the upper-order angels, describing their mating rituals in great detail and an awful lot of very purple prose.

Fred huffed into her fringe again. It was as though the line about Ven just popped out of nowhere.

She read the rest of *Of Men and Demon* word for word, hoping there might be something else, but there wasn't. Damn it.

The Powers alone knew how many books later, and she was beginning to get well and truly pissed off. Nothing. Nothing! Just a waste of time, an even bigger headache and an entirely rational desire to strangle just about every author in the Realm. Once she'd put them back together after tearing them apart the first time, that was.

She threw the latest disappointment aside and glared blankly into the empty fireplace. "Fuck."

There were ten books left on the shelves. Ten tomes containing the sum total recorded knowledge of the Realm and the world of man.

Scrunching up her face, Fred conjured the thinnest—*Death and Lust in the Time of Genesis*. She cocked an eyebrow. A book dedicated to her. She grinned. This could be, if nothing else, entertaining.

The first chapter was dedicated to her antics before the Powers intervened. She chuckled. The author—anonymous, of all things—seemed to have taken quite a few liberties with the facts. Half of what they'd attributed to her after the Creation she had nothing to do with. To believe the author's account, she'd been a right psychotic bitch.

Making a mental note to discover who "anonymous" was later on, she continued reading. The rest of the book read like a trashy human gossip mag. Hearsay and conjecture making up most of the word count, with the odd illustration—mostly of her morbid cloak-and-scythe persona—thrown in for good measure. Nothing entertaining or illuminating at all.

Damn, damn, damn.

She slammed the book closed...just as a line leapt out at her from the pages.

The Cure shall face the Disease o—

A tingle shot up her spine. What was that?

She jerked the book open, frustration eating at her. Damn it, what page had she been on?

"Somewhere near the back of the book, Fred," she muttered, fanning the pages. "Opposite an illustration of you and the other Horsemen, remember? You curled your lip at the way the artist had depicted you—all dead and gross and male."

She whipped through the book, searching for the illustration. Where *was* it?

Her pulse burst into furious life. There. Tenth page from the last.

Giving the hideous artwork a quick look—*For Pete's sake, male*?—she read through the page of text opposite it, looking for the line that had caught her eye.

Yadda, yadda, yadda, blah, blah, blah. *The Cure shall face the Disease on the shifting dunes and the end shall begin and the beginning shall end.* Blah, blah, bl—

Fred's stare locked on to the disconnected sentence.

She read it again.

The Cure shall face the Disease on the shifting dunes and the end shall begin and the beginning shall end.

What did it mean? It wasn't written in the snarky past tense, adjective-heavy style of the rest of the book, nor was it obsessing about her so-called achievements an eon ago, and it bore no relation to anything else written before or after it.

Fred gnawed on her bottom lip. Who the hell was anonymous? Another Fate? One of the earlier sages now long gone?

She studied the words again. What did they mean?

The Cure. Nope. Nothing.

The Disease. Pestilence. Had to be. He'd never taken a human name, considering himself far too superior to do so, but referred to himself often as the Disease, usually with self-absorbed arrogance.

On the shifting dunes... Hmmm. The beach? Surely. Or maybe the desert?

Fred pulled a face. Damn it. There were a lot of deserts in the world and most of them had been the site of one important event or another.

She moved onto the rest of the sentence.

The end shall begin and the beginning shall end.

What the fuck did that mean?

The end. She chewed on her lip again. Could be the Apocalypse? Or the final episode of *Cheers*?

Frustration, hot and thick, rolled through her and she let out a roar, her inner demon surging briefly to the surface. This was useless.

She stared at the fireplace again. This was getting her nowhere.

Then go see the only element of the equation you know.

Fred groaned. By the Powers, why hadn't she thought of that before? Pestilence was confined to the Realm. All she needed to do was speak to him and she'd get her answers.

A distasteful knot twisted in the pit of her belly at the thought. The last time she'd talked to her colleague he'd made some preposterous offer to become partners in an even more preposterous scheme, trying to sweeten the deal by suggesting they become partners in bed as well.

The memory made Fred screw up her face. She couldn't think of anything worse than sex with ol' sick and weedy.

Nevertheless, she had to see him. He'd sent a *nikor* after a human. That alone demanded some interrogation. The task of assigning an end to a mortal's life fell to her and her alone, not the First Horseman. If nothing else, she needed to give him a damn good dressing down. No one stepped on her turf without facing the consequences.

Putting *Death and Lust in the Time of Genesis* aside, she

returned her boots to her feet and drew an image of Pestilence's place in the Realm to her mind.

A shimmer rippled through her body, a tingle through her being, and then she was there. Standing in ol' sick and weedy's master suite, the stench of disease, burning tallow and rotting bones seeping into her lungs with each breath she took.

Her gaze fell immediately on his throne and a surge of contempt heated her blood. The Powers had ordered Pestilence to get rid of the thing. Not only did it offend Their very existence, it was an affront to the Order of Actuality.

She studied it, nose curling. It was fucking hideous and gross, as well. She'd heard rumors of some of the things he did on it, some of the acts of debauchery and depravity. She shuddered with disgust. How she'd been born of the same source as him was beyond her.

"This is a surprise."

The reedy voice behind her made Fred jump and she spun about, fixing the thin man standing in the doorway with a dark glare. "I thought you were ordered to destroy that thing, sicko," she snarled, watching Pestilence walk toward her.

He looked the same as he always did. Small and scrawny. It was a trick. She knew that. His inner demon was almost as powerful as her own. Almost. Why he chose to inhabit such an offensively weak form was still a mystery to her. It didn't do him any favors. Still, she'd heard he had no trouble getting laid. Maybe the lower-order she-demons liked their men...wimpy?

"Do you often make it a habit of trespassing in other people's private space, Death?" he asked, his pale eyes roaming over her with glowering conceit. "Or is this a treat just for me?" He stopped but a mere foot before her, the sickly sweet stench of his body heat curling around her like fingers of fog. "Perhaps you have reconsidered my previous offer?" He flicked his gaze to the massive bed beside the throne before returning his eyes to hers. "I am ready whenever you are."

A shudder of revulsion rocked Fred and she ground her teeth. "I'm afraid my tastes and your tastes differ some what,

Pestilence." She fought to contain her contempt, remembering why she was there. It wasn't to point out his depravity. It was to get some answers.

His pale stare drilled into her and she struggled with the urge to fidget. Of all her fellow Horsemen, Pestilence was her least favorite. War she could deal with. He knew his place, knew his job and stuck to it. His moral and work ethic were of the highest standards and he knew the definition of personal grooming. He was also a very considerate lover and had a dry wit. Famine was a little irritating, but still likeable. She had a warm personality and a weakness for kittens. She just needed, in Fred's opinion, to eat a little more, and maybe lighten up a bit when it came to places like Zimbabwe. What that country had done to her, Fred could never work out. Still...both the Second and Third Horsemen were preferable to the First. And neither of them had tried to grope her during their last gathering.

Pestilence raised an eyebrow before moving to his throne, lowering himself onto the disgusting piece of excessive furniture with slow flourish. "'Tis a pity. I am sure you would more than enjoy what I can do."

"Guess we'll never know, will we, sicko."

His eyes flared vomit yellow. "Do not call me that."

Fred let out a sigh. She needed to get a grip. Antagonizing Pestilence would get her nowhere. "I saw some of your handiwork in the world of man today," she commented, trying to keep her voice light. "I'm just wondering why you thought it acceptable to send an aqueous demon after a human not slated for death?"

She didn't mention Patrick's name, wanting to see Pestilence's reaction first.

It was not what she'd expected.

He laughed.

"Did I?" His thin chest rose up and down with his deep guffaws. "Oh, that was not my intention." He wiped at his eyes, his lips stretched in a wide smile. "I sent the *nikor* to deal with a water sprite who has been stepping outside her place. It must have got its orders wrong." He chuckled again, fingering the knucklebone of the throne's armrest. He slid his gaze to his bed before returning it to her, giving her a pointed look. "I was a bit distracted while giving them."

Fred narrowed her eyes. She didn't believe him.

"Hmmm." Turning her back on him, she crossed his room, trailing her fingers over the edge of one elaborate bone candelabra. "Tell me, Pestilence," she said, knowing he studied the sway of her hips. "What do you know of the Cure?"

Silence answered her question. Heavy silence, followed by a soft rasp as he shifted in his seat. "The human band? Not much, I am afraid. Their music is not to my taste."

Fred rolled her eyes. He was hiding something. She could hear the delaying tactics in his lame joke and the deception in his voice.

She turned, fixing him with a level gaze. "Really? I thought they'd be just your cup of tea. All dark and gloomy and pessimistic."

The comment drew a hiss from the First Horseman. His eyes flickered yellow again, his nails gouging into the throne's armrest. "You think you are so much better than me, don't you, Death?"

Fred gave him a cold grin. "Of course I do. Now, tell me why you sent a *nikor* after a human today?"

In a blur of diseased air, Pestilence left his throne and stood before her, his thighs brushing hers, his breath fanning her face. He stared up into her eyes, his body trembling with what she guessed was suppressed rage.

"Call it an exercise, shall we? I was flexing my puny muscles." He leaned in closer to her, and she choked back the overwhelming urge to gag.

"Why?" he went on, face twisting with contempt. "What does it matter to the great Fourth Horseman? What does the pathetic human mean to you?"

A tight knot of tension formed in Fred's stomach at Pestilence's snarled question and she faltered. What *did* Patrick mean to her? What *did* it matter? Since when had she become so concerned about the fate of one mere mortal?

Since you first saw that mere mortal on the beach, Fred. Fighting to keep Peabody alive. Doing everything in his power, everything in his soul, to defy you.

A wave of warmth flowed through her and she grit her teeth in dismay. Damn it, she was falling for Patrick Watkins.

"What exactly do you want, Death?" Pestilence snapped, jerking her from the sudden, unnerving realization. "I am growing bored with this visit. Either strip and climb onto my bed or remove yourself from my presence."

Fred snorted, a cold, powerful rage building in the pit of her belly. "Strip and climb onto the bed? I would rather let the hounds of hell mount me than be touched by you."

"You should not say such things, Death." Pestilence's eyes burned. "Not to your equal."

A laugh burst from Fred's throat. Sharp and contemptuous. "You are not my equal, Pestilence. You will never be my equal. No matter how many eternities pass, you will always be a piss-weak little demon with delusions of grandeur."

Pestilence's nostrils flared. He stared at her, eyes bulging, lips compressed to a thin, white line. His hands moved in a blur, curling around her neck. "Your time is over, Death," he stated, the fury in his voice laced with smug confidence. "It is *my* time now."

Thick rows of diseased lice scurried up her throat, over her jaw line. Thick, swarming rows of sickness seeking her mouth.

She felt them pour over her flesh. Felt them slip into the tiny dips at the corners of her lips. Felt them stroke her tongue.

And she laughed, destroying each tiny instrument of Pestilence's disease with a thought. "Is that it?"

She lashed out with her own hands, sinking her fingers

into his throat and lifting him from the floor. "You are the *First* Horseman, Pestilence. *Everything* you are, *everything* that makes you what you are, *I* already am."

His mouth dropped open, his shocked expression almost comical. Not funny enough however, to stop her teaching him a lesson.

She released the cold.

Every atom of every molecule of Pestilence's corporeal existence became ice. Instantly and immediately. Bereft of heat and anima. Deprived of vitality and life. The air froze in his lungs, the blood stilled in his veins. He gaped at her, fear erupting in his eyes.

Fred held him off the floor, watching him. She could not kill him. It was impossible for the Horsemen to kill their own, but they could inflict untold pain and suffering upon their fellow entities if they had the strength. Well, *she* could. She was Death. The Fourth and final Horseman. Everything—including her fellow entities—came before her. *Nothing* came after.

She drew the life from Pestilence's being. Pulled it from his form until he wavered on a blade's edge of expiration, letting him feel the unending, inescapable power of her force.

She held him in a lifeless stasis of icy agony, until the fear in his eyes turned to surrender. And then she released her grip on his neck and dropped him to the floor. "Remember who you are, Pestilence. Remember who *I* am. When *my* time is over, so is *yours*."

And, before she could do something she would regret, before she broke the cardinal rule of the Realm and rendered her colleague null and void, she transubstantiated from Pestilence's space.

Glad to be rid of the stench and sight of him.

Without any answers at all.

Damn it.

Chapter Six

Ven paced his brother's living room, glaring at the floor, the blank television, the clock on the wall...the morning sun streaming in through the wide, open window. He approached the diffused edge of light and stood still, studying the dust motes dancing on the air.

Sunlight.

He hadn't seen sunlight for over eighteen years. He'd avoided it like the plague, scurrying indoors at the first hint of dawn, hiding from its warmth. Missing it like mad.

This morning he'd not only seen it, he'd stood in it. Felt it.

Survived it.

Great. How the bloody hell am I going to go surfing now?

The irritated question came back to him in a sudden memory of sight and sound. They were the very first words he'd uttered the second he'd realized he was no longer human but a monster of mythology. He'd been sitting in his mother's living room, a cooling piece of toast in one hand, two bloody big fangs suddenly in his mouth and the shock had been almost too much to bear.

He had little memory of the actual transformation from man to demon. Just flashes of images, really. Sensations. The stunned look on his parents' faces, the absolute horror on Patrick's the minute he'd walked into the living room.

They'd still been in mourning over his death a mere six hours earlier. His mum was openly sobbing in his father's arms, his dad's eyes red and dry with unshed tears, his kid brother silently staring at nothing.

It wasn't until the first bite of toast and subsequent discovery of his fangs that it hit him. What he now was. And with that bite came the images, crashing over him, dumping on him like a killer wave. Taking him under, pummeling him about and leaving him gasping and shell-shocked. Images of fangs flashing, blood gushing. Images of a hideous creature attacking his kid brother. Images of his own struggle with the vile thing, trying to save Pat from certain death. Images of being held down, mauled. Bitten.

Images of the creature fleeing into the night, a broken beer bottle jutting from the back of its neck, its squeals both furious and scared.

Images of Patrick leaning over him, tears and blood streaming down his face, screaming at him. "Hold on, Steven, hold on."

Images of a woman with pale skin and long dark hair walking towards him down the alley, regarding him with ice-blue eyes as she leant over Patrick to touch his chest with a lingering, gentle caress.

Images of the world fading, of Patrick fading. Everything turning dark, darker.

Those terrible, vivid images dragged him under and he'd stared at his parents and brother in horror, his hand going to his neck, his fingers finding the twin puncture wounds below his right ear.

"Great," he'd muttered. "How the bloody hell am I going to go surfing now?"

The sarcastic, bitter thought had undone him. Something he loved more than life, robbed of him. Taken from him. He was a vampire. No longer able to walk in the sunlight. No longer able to consume regular food. Needing to feed on blood to survive. He'd stared at the toast in his hand, the Vegemite smeared all over its warm, crusty surface filling him with such a bitter surge of nostalgic anger he'd thrown it against his mother's wallpapered wall and stormed from the room, a new, indefinable hunger growing in his gut. An undeniable hunger.

An unspeakable hunger.

Pat had caught up with him, as fast as always, faster than a teenage kid should be able to move, just as he was about to sprint down his parents' driveway.

"Hey!" His brother had grabbed his arm, spun him about.

"Go away, Pat," Ven had growled, trying to shrug him off. "You don't want to be near me now."

"What's the big deal?" Pat had asked with a shrug, his eighteen-year-old face open and completely without guile, his green eyes somehow luminous in the dark night. Glowing with an emotion Ven recognized so very well. Love. "So we just hit the waves at night, that's all."

That had been the end of the discussion. Neither he nor Pat had raised his transformation again, not in a serious way, at least. And his parents, God love them, hadn't either. His mum had come to visit to his home the second night of his new existence, hefting a big bag of black-out curtains she'd made on her ancient Janome, hanging them over his windows as she chatted about the research she'd been doing on the differences between A negative and B positive. And his dad... Well, Steven Patrick Watkins had continued on as he always did. Not speaking two words when one would do, letting his first born son settle into his new "life" with nothing more than a nod and a refusal to stock garlic on the pantry shelves. Oh, and a perverse insistence of shoving any corny B-grade vampire movie he could find in the VCR whenever Ven dropped around.

And that had been the way of things for many years. Ven soon discovered the joys of his newfound physical prowess and made full use of them, feeding only from Sydney's many women eager to become a vampire's feed source, enjoying the other "perks" that came with the willingly offered dinner. One night he'd met Amy Mathieson at a particularly rowdy game of beach volleyball and three years later, he was pretty much a monogamous feeder.

He'd never questioned the "rules", those unexplained, completely annoying rules dictated to him by Hollywood. Don't go out in the daylight—there went the day job. Don't go near garlic—even though garlic prawns had been his favorite meal. Don't try to imbibe human food—again with the garlic prawns. Avoid crucifixes and holy water—okay, no real problem there. Don't get yourself stabbed in the heart by a wooden stake—splinters on steroids to be avoided at all cost. Gotcha. He just accepted those rules as he had his new existence. With a wry grin and dry sarcasm.

Fortunately, being staked to dust had never been a problem. The city's small number of, quite frankly, laughable demon hunters never bothered with him. And as for the rest of the "rules", well, he kept to them, crucifixes and holy water the least of his concerns. His family had never been much for religion and they weren't likely to start any day soon. He didn't think his folks even kept a Bible in the house.

But the images of his transformation refused to leave him, haunting him when he "slept", forcing him to relive the moment over and over again. The fear, the pain, the fury, the bliss of Death's icy touch...and an empty longing for the life stolen from him. A life of light and warmth and sun—surfing or jogging with Pat, fishing from the rocks at North Bondi, sitting on the beach watching the waves make love to the sand.

A life he thought lost to him forever. Until an hour ago.

He studied the sunlight spilling into Patrick's living room through the open window and stepped forward. Directly into it, feeling its warmth paint his body.

He sighed. For some reason he could not explain, he felt disconnected. What did it mean that he could withstand sunlight? He knew it wasn't normal. The way Death had stared at him back on the beach, as if she'd seen a ghost, told him what he could do was not right. So what did it mean?

He raked his hands through his hair, a distant part of his mind reveling in the sun-kissed strands. Luxuriating in the warm flush heating his perpetually cool flesh. "Ah, fuck. What the hell is going on?"

"Enjoying it?"

Patrick's casual question jerked Ven's head around. He stepped away from the window, back into the cool shadows of the living room.

Patrick shook his head. "Don't, Ven. You deserve to stand in the light."

The bitter note in his brother's words made Ven frown. They'd walked home from the beach in silence, both lost to their own thoughts. Patrick had called Bluey and told him he was taking the day off before heading for the shower, leaving Ven to ponder the surreal events of the morning.

Now, his brother stood before him, a towel slung around his bare shoulders, eyes clouded with torment.

"Not the usual start to the day, was it?" Ven smiled, trying to break the tension in the room. He felt odd. Like some vital turning point had passed that he should have been prepared for.

Patrick didn't answer.

Ven let his attention drop to his brother's torso. Numerous gashes and puncture wounds scarred Patrick's chest, some still seeping blood. Ven flinched, the jarring sight filling him with the very familiar wave of protective anger. He welcomed the emotion. It was normalcy, a state that seemed to be rapidly slipping away from them both at the moment. "I'll find the fucker who sent that thing after you, brother. I promise." The vow felt right on his lips. And he would. That was what he was meant to do.

Wasn't it?

Patrick looked at him and shook his head. "I'm done with this, Ven. I've had enough."

Ven frowned. He didn't like the tone in his brother's voice. It was flat. Emotionless. "What do you mean, 'done with'?"

Tossing his towel onto the sofa, Patrick crossed to the window. "All I've ever wanted in my life was to be normal, to help people, to surf and to swim. Four simple requests of whatever supreme force pulls the strings of my existence."

Ven narrowed his eyes. "We cannot choose our fate, brother. Mum and Dad didn't choose to die wrapped around a telegraph pole in a twisted hunk of metal. I didn't choose to become a vampire."

Patrick rounded on him, his face etched in dark anger. "You don't think I know that? Jesus, Steven. I live every day thinking about that. Wondering if their car accident really was that? An accident? Wondering if you'd be a Pulitzer Prize winner now, rather than a freelance journalist if it wasn't for me? I spend every bloody minute of every bloody day, deep in my subconscious where I can't block it out, wondering if the people the most important to me have suffered for what I am?" He turned back to the window, his jaw bunching, his stare locked on the glaring light beyond. "I've had enough."

Ven studied his profile, his throat tight. "What *are* you, Patrick?" he asked quietly.

Patrick stared at the day outside.

A surge of hot anger ripped through Ven. "Y'know, we've been over this time and again. I don't have the answer, just a gut feeling. If there's something you should be telling me, something I should know..."

Patrick didn't say a word.

The demon deep with Ven growled. Impatient frustration roared through him. He rubbed at his face, struggling to keep his fangs sheathed. That he struggled at all in the presence of his brother worried and annoyed him. "I need answers, Pat. I need to know what is going on. I've been pretty laidback about things since becoming a vampire. I think I've taken the whole lifestyle change pretty well, but I'm not going to just keep letting you ignore whatever reason you are here for. For some reason, something wants you dead and it's time you accepted it."

"And that something is Fred? Is that what you're telling me?"

Patrick's softly spoken question punched into Ven's gut like a fist. He sucked in a silent, completely redundant breath, fear and anger flooding through him. He stared at his brother. Stared hard. "Don't fall for her, Patrick. Don't. She's not what you think she is."

Patrick's laugh was short. Harsh. Humorless. "I am getting sick of hearing that. *I'm* not what I think I am. *Fred's* not what I think she is. Shit, even *you're* not what I thought you were."

Hot irritation made Ven clench his fists. His demon growled again, stronger, closer to the surface. "You asked me on the beach how Death had been keeping me occupied? Maybe the question you should have asked is *why* she was keeping me occupied?" He looked at his brother, wanting to shake him. Wanting him to wake up and smell the proverbial goddamn coffee. "While you were being attacked by a demon, good ol' Fred was doing her damndest to keep me away from you."

A light Ven had never seen before flared in Patrick's eyes, and for a split moment fear sliced through him and he flinched, sure his brother was going to hit him.

But Patrick didn't. He turned away, back to the window and the strengthening day. "And her damndest was sticking her tongue down your throat? Did you put up much of a fight?"

Ven flinched again. Both at Patrick's icy words and the knowledge behind them.

"I smelt her on you, Ven."

Ven didn't miss the resentment in Patrick's voice. Or the jealousy. Fuck, things were worse than he thought and he had no idea how to fix it. Save remove Death from the picture.

But you don't want to do that either, do you, Steven? You don't trust her. You don't believe her, but that doesn't stop you wanting her. Wanting her on every goddamn level and then some.

"Don't fall for her, Pat," he repeated, gut churning, chest tight, not knowing what else to say. "Please."

"I'm sick of it, Steven," Patrick said in reply, and Ven could tell by the closed resonance in his voice that Patrick had shut him out. “I’ve had enough of you paranormal lot today to last me a lifetime.”

Cold grief stabbed into him, but from his brother’s dismissal or his own simmering jealousy, Ven could not tell.

And at that very moment in time, he pretty much didn’t care.

“I love you, Pat,” he said, giving his brother’s profile a level stare. “But you’re being a right bloody wanker.”

His demon roared, feeding on the dark emotion behind the insult, surging to the surface. He snatched back control—just—before turning from Patrick. He crossed the living room, stopping briefly at the hallway door. “I’m outta here. I’ve spent the last eighteen years living in the shadows for you. Until you’re ready to acknowledge what’s in those shadows, I’m going to live in the sun.” He turned and walked down the hallway to the front door, yanking it open with such force he heard the nails fixing it to the doorjamb tear from the wood.

He didn’t care about that either.

He stepped through the door, out into the sunlight. He was hungry.

He needed to feed.

It was time to visit Amy.

Before his demon took over and he fed from the only other living blood source near him.

Patrick.

Pestilence sat on his throne, furious. He drummed his fingernails against the gnarled humerus bone fashioned into an armrest. Things were not going to plan. Not at all.

Death was sniffing about where she did not belong. She’d flexed her demon muscle and rubbed his nose in it. The cursed *nikor* had failed to drown the lifeguard. The human had not only escaped its clutches, but decimated it as well. How in the name of all the Powers did a human escape a third-order demon?

He drummed his nails harder against the bone, feeling it splinter a little with each strike. By the Powers, how had it gone so wrong?

According to the last Fate, everything should be different now. Death should have been a sick, diseased shell of her former self, groveling at his feet for his mercy and the lifeguard should be dead, and yet nothing had changed. Nothing! How the aqueous demon had let the lifeguard slip away from him, he'd never know. Because the stupid, pathetic thing had let the mortal kill it! Kill it, of all things.

Incredulous rage ripped through him, turning the saliva in his mouth to sour bile. He curled his nose and spat, the wad of phlegm sizzling and hissing on the cold marble floor like fat on molten steel. He watched the spittle eat into the black rock until there was nothing but a small hole in the floor.

"Fuck." His curse shattered the air, bounced off the walls and came back to him. Empty and hollow. He dragged his hands through his hair, trying to calm himself. So the *nikor* failed. All plans of greatness had hurdles to cross.

And you have had so many.

The thought made Pestilence scowl and he dug his nails, growing longer and more hooked with each passing second, into the humerus bone. He had spent thirty-six years trying to end the lifeguard's life.

Thirty-six years of failure.

It irked him. Considerably.

The problem was he was trapped here in the Realm, while Patrick Watkins was free to move around in the world of man. Until the dawn of the Apocalypse, he was confined to the Realm. The Powers had decreed it so and that was the way of the Order of Actuality. Any attempt he made to end the lifeguard's life was determined entirely on rare, brief windows of opportunity when the veil between the Realm and the human world thinned. So far, during those moments, he had sent a fatal wave of typhoid to the region the boy lived, he had arranged a succubus to infiltrate the lifeguard's school and seduce the adolescent, he had commanded a vampire to end the young male's life on the verge of adulthood, and he had ordered a swarm of locusts to attack the cursed boy's parents' car, forcing it off the road, among other things. All attempts had failed. All. Even the one moment three human years ago, when the veil had been at its thinnest and he had managed to all but transubstantiate to the world of man, finding the lifeguard alone and unprotected by his cursed vampire brother, the chance to kill him had failed. Somehow, somehow, the human had taken him by surprise and he had been flung back into the bowels of the Realm before he could prevent it happening. It was as if the Powers watched over the lifeguard and protected him.

They did not, though. Pestilence knew that for a fact. The lifeguard's existence and importance in the upcoming end battle was known only to him. Sheer luck had brought him such knowledge. Sheer luck he had been screwing the last Fate during one of her increasingly rare moments of insight during which she had screamed out the lifeguard's name and destiny.

Pestilence grinned, the action both bitter and cold. The last Fate had been a pathetic fuck—she had known all his moves before he had the chance to use them, but she had been fantastic at pillow talk. The words had just spewed from her mouth, unstoppable and feverish, a mouth that only seconds earlier had been wrapped around his dick.

She screamed of the one who would be the Cure. Who would challenge the First Horseman. She had moaned and gibbered about the weakness of Death coming *when the Disease finds the Cure*. Of Death's end at the hands of the First. It was all gobbledegook, and yet it all made perfect sense. Most of it, at least. *The sun walker will feed of his own and live* still left him confused, but that mattered little when everything else said so much.

He had listened to her carry on, taking it all in. Watching her as the spittle on her lips turned to frantic foam, studying her without a sound as the foam became drool. The words continued, faster, faster, until, with a final scream—*The Cure will rethread the Fabric*—she'd collapsed in a shaking heap on his bed, eyes closed, face flushed.

It was during that brief moment of silence, he formulated his plan.

He slid up beside her, the last Fate, placed his fingertips to her throat and waited.

What felt like hours but was really a fraction of a second later, she opened her eyes, giving Pestilence a small, shy smile. "Did I zone out?"

He had nodded.

The last Fate's eyes grew worried. "I'm sorry. It's been an eon since that happened. Did I say anything important?"

Pestilence had nodded again. "You could say that."

The last Fate smiled. "I'm glad you were here to hear it. My memory's not the best these days. It'll make it easier for me to report to the..."

The rest of the old hag's sentence had turned into an ear-piercing screech of pain and terror as Pestilence had plunged his fingers into her mouth and poured every disease and pest in his arsenal into her being at the same time. Essentially, filling her up to the suddenly bulging, bleeding eyeballs with more sickness and, well, pestilence than the entire human world had ever experienced.

Disposing her body had been fun. Creative, even.

He chuckled at the thought and tapped the armrest once again, this time with less rancor. The last Fate made a great addition to his throne. In fact, she was more comfortable to plant his backside on now than alive.

Alive.

At the single word, Pestilence's humor vanished. His chuckle turned to a sneer. The lifeguard was still alive. No matter his efforts to the contrary, the cursed human was alive and had achieved the impossible—killing a third-order demon.

A cold thread of fear twisted into Pestilence's chest. Curled tightly around his heart. How *had* Patrick Watkins killed an aqueous demon? According to his source in the world of man, the lifeguard's interfering, irritating, overprotective, impossible-to-get-past vampire brother had finally been otherwise occupied. Nothing should have prevented the mature male *nikor* from tearing the man apart below the surface of the very water he so pitifully and pathetically loved. Nothing.

And yet he still lived. In one piece.

Not only that, Death, the supercilious bitch, had not succumbed when he had attacked her. According to the last Fate, Death would be weak when he found the lifeguard. Well, he had found him. Had a metaphysical lock on him, so why was Death not coughing up a rat-filled lung right at this moment?

Tapping his nails, now dagger-tipped claws dripping disease, against the armrest of his throne, Pestilence stared without interest at his bed and the naked succubus chained to it.

He could not, would not believe the last Fate had been wrong. She had never been wrong in her four millennia of existence. It was not possible she had been this time.

No. Everything she had said was true. He knew it.

But time was running out. Within the next moon cycle the thinning of the veil between his world and the human world would reverse and his opportunity would be lost. He needed to eradicate the problem of the lifeguard soon. Very soon. Otherwise he would be in danger of failing and he would not let that happen. He was not going to let some pathetic, weak, feeble mortal take from him that which he had lusted for, planned for, for the last millennium

He needed to tap his source. Hard.

He needed answers. He needed to know Patrick Watkins' weakness.

Now.

Before his only window of opportunity closed.

He remembered the chill of the wind and the cold, white light of the sun. That was always the first memory Patrick had of the moment in time he'd come to think of as the "event".

The early morning wind gusted across Bondi Beach, uncommonly cold, even for mid-winter, its icy breath cutting into his face, whipping up grains of sand and tearing at the ragged peaks of the crashing waves. The stark, heatless sun bleached the angry surf and empty beach to a washed-out grey, leeching the color from the world, turning it into a monotone of chilly stillness.

Out on the waves bobbed six surfboard riders, Bluey the most senior. They crested each irritable peak, disappeared into the trough and popped up again. Of the six only Patrick's second-in-charge challenged the waves enough to put feet to board. Passion and insanity was always a thin, tenuous line for the die-hard surfer.

Standing on the empty winter beach, the collar of his windcheater turned up in a futile effort to protect his face from the elements, Patrick watched his work mate maneuver onto the arcing face of a six-foot curl. The mad man rode it with all the grace of a dancer...until the wave turned nasty and smashed him into water. A jolt of fear tinged Patrick's startled laugh and he'd cringed, knowing Bluey was fine—no wave yet had bested him—but feeling his mate's pain anyway. A wipeout like that would be spoken of for decades to come. Bluey's pride would take a beating even if his body hadn't.

Turning from the sight of his right-hand man scrambling back on to his board and paddling back out past the breakers, Patrick shook his head. They were all insane. He loved to surf as much as the next bloke, but it was bloody freezing, the surf was a messy bitch and he had paper work to do. Just because it was winter, didn't mean he didn't work.

Slapping at his biceps in an attempt to ward off the chill, he began walking toward the patrol tower.

And stopped.

A man stood on the high-tide line about twenty feet away, neat black suit doing nothing to hide his thin, almost scrawny build. His lank, dark hair fell over his pasty white forehead, brushing at his eyes and Patrick frowned. The Nor'wester was blasting up the beach. How could the man's hair not be moving? And come to think of it, why didn't he throw a shadow? What the hell was going—

The man turned his stare from the surfers out on the waves to Patrick, and before Patrick could blink, the unmistakable hum of a million insects filled his ears and the undeniable stench of dying flesh filled his nose. Thick and cloying.

A soft groan vibrated up Patrick's throat and he gazed back at the man, his gut beginning to churn. Something was not right with the man, the wrongness rolled from him in thick, suffocating waves Patrick could not see but sensed all the same. Something beyond Patrick's ability to understand and yet he understood it all too well. Understood and accepted it with calm terror.

This man was the "something" Ven had warned him about. The "something" chasing him his whole life. The "something" of his nightmares.

This man was—

The Disease.

The title—no other term described the two words—screamed through Patrick's head in a deafening whisper almost drowning out the roar of the insects. The man smiled, yellow, jagged teeth glinting in the cold sun, and a wave of sickness rolled through Patrick. Just like that. One moment he felt fine, the next he wanted to throw up.

The man's smile stretched wider, revealing more teeth. An impossible number. All jagged, all yellow. All dripping viscous saliva.

Patrick's stomach lurched. His flesh grew clammy. Cold sweat beaded on his forehead, his upper lip. He frowned, swallowing convulsively. Fuck, he felt sick.

The man watched him, smile growing, teeth elongating, the very air around him writhing with infection and the tiny bodies of a million locusts. *Yes.*

Patrick sucked in a breath and it filled his being, painted his mouth and the back of his throat with the stench of illness, hideous illness, the illness of decay and putrescence. His stomach rolled. A violent shiver claimed his body. Sweat leeched from his pores, icy beads of opaque moisture stinking of the smiling man before him.

Yes.

The man's smile turned into a smirk, his pale blue stare never wavering from Patrick's face.

Yes.

Patrick's knees buckled. He saved himself just before stumbling to the sand, his body shuddering, burning up. His stomach rolled and churned and flipped, his mouth flooding with sour bile, acrid saliva. Insects crawled all over him, in his eyes, his nose, his ears. Heart thumping, pulse pounding, he rammed his palms to his knees, forcing himself upright. If he collapsed to the ground he would drown in his own vomit. Of that he had no doubt. He had to fight. He had to fight the sickness and the swarm trying to overwhelm him. He couldn't let them overpower him.

The man in the black suit with the lank hair and the yellow teeth continued to smirk, his blazing blue eyes locked on Patrick. Refusing to let him go.

Sucking a shaky breath and a thousand bugs in through his nose, Patrick stared back. He was losing. Whatever fucked-up battle he was in, he was losing. His life spent being chased by something in his dreams, his brother killed for reasons he'd yet to understand, and it all came down to this. This man and his radiating disease and flying insects. This beach. This frozen, icy moment. Fury rolled through Patrick. Fury and fatal understanding. He'd never felt so sick. He'd never felt so weak. Weak. Fuck, he felt weak.

The man's smirk became a grin. A saliva-dripping grin of triumph. *Yessssss.*

Patrick gagged, staring at the man through a curtain of locusts. Incapable of looking away even when his stomach wanted to erupt from his body. God, he wanted to throw up. He was going to choke on the diseased crap his stomach ruptured up his throat and he couldn't stop it. He was going to drown in his own blood-tainted, insect-filled vomit and he welcomed it. At least when he died he would no longer feel so sick, so ill. God, he felt so fucking sick. Jesus, please let him just drown in his vomit so he could—

"G'Day, Wato!" A young boy ran up the beach, surfboard tucked under his arm, his face flushed with joy.

Ricky! Patrick shouted, but nothing came from his mouth, his throat choked with vomit and bile and bugs. *Jesus, Ricky. Run away. Go!*

"The surf's a bitch today," Ricky called, running straight for the smiling, shadowless man. "Knocked me on my arse I dunno know how many times. And didja see what it did to—"

He ran through the man.

Jesus, Ricky! No!

The man's shape devoured the teenager, engulfed his body like hungry fog swallowing a lost lamb.

And then Ricky stumbled from the man's form, eyes wide and blank, skin white and ashen and collapsed to the sand.

"Ricky!"

Patrick's scream finally tore from his throat, thick and raw. He surged forward, plunging to his knees beside Ricky's motionless body, his stare locked on the teenage boy's pale face. "Ricky?"

Blood oozed from Ricky's now closed eyes, streaming down his sweat-slicked cheeks to join the blood seeping from his nose. He shivered, a savage rattling of his body that made

Patrick's chest squeeze.

"Oh, fuck, Ricky?"

Patrick put his hand to the boy's forehead, hissing at the scalding temperature of his flesh. He was burning up. Christ, he felt on fire.

Another shudder wracked through Ricky and he convulsed—once, twice before blood spurted from his mouth, a great gush of blood and vomit that stank of rotting organs and flesh.

Patrick reeled backward, staring at the shuddering teenager. Stared in horrified disbelief as the kid's clammy skin suddenly erupted in weeping, pus-oozing sores. As fresh blood burst from his nose, his ears. As his eyes rolled to white, sinking into his head until they looked like pits of putrefied jelly.

It is beautiful, isn't it?

The hollow voice slid into Patrick's ears and he jerked his head up, glaring at the man standing over him. "What did you do to him?"

The man grinned, yellow teeth shining in the cold morning sun, lank, dark hair motionless in the rising wind.

I gave him perfection.

Deep, bottomless fury roared through Patrick, incinerating the terrible sickness churning in his gut. Explosive heat—*golden* heat—surged through him. Heat so pure it purged his body of the man's poisoned smile and turned the insects to ash. He stood, Ricky's motionless frame at his feet, the wind lashing at his face, and looked straight into the man's smug eyes.

The man raised his arm, reaching for Patrick with fingers tipped in long, hooked claws. *And the Disease shall destroy the Cure and the end shall be begun.*

"No!"

The shout ripped from Patrick's throat. Scalding heat crashed through him, a tsunami of fury and rage and something else so elemental he couldn't identify it. He stared at the man and without knowing how, elevated Ricky's surfboard up from the blood-soaked sand and drove it straight into the grinning bastard's gut.

Without moving. Without touching a thing.

The man—the Disease—lurched backward, eyes bulging, mouth agape. His claw-tipped hands smacked against Ricky's board buried in his flesh, gouging great chunks in the fiberglass. He stared at Patrick, fear detonating behind the incredulous disbelief in his eyes. *How?*

Patrick stared back, something undefinable boiling in his soul.

How? The silent question squealed from the man's gaping mouth, and then a dark scowl contorted his pinched, weedy features. *NO! I will not let this be!*

He jolted forward, arms outstretched, surfboard jutting from his gut.

Patrick lashed out. Golden heat roared through him. Engulfing him. Consuming him.

The man flung backward in a screaming blur.

And disappeared mid-arc.

Just like that. Leaving Ricky's surfboard suspended in the air for a split second before it fell to the sand with a thud.

Patrick stared at the empty air for what felt like a lifetime, his mind gibbering at the man's disappearing act. His blood roared in his ears, his gut churned and then he dropped to his knees beside Ricky.

The boy was not moving. The sand he lay on was red with blood.

Pressing his fingers to Ricky's neck, Patrick searched for a pulse.

None.

Not even a weak flutter.

"What the *fuck*?"

Bluey's gasp jerked Patrick's head up and he stared at the ring of surfers surrounding him, their eyes wide with shocked confusion, their faces as washed out and bleak as the winter sky behind them.

"Fuckin' hell, Wato!" Bluey dropped to his knees beside Patrick, studying Ricky with a quick, skilled eye. "What happened? Have you called the ambos?"

Patrick shook his head. "He just..." He stumbled, not sure what to say. What *did* he say? That Ricky ran through a man who didn't throw a shadow and came out the other side dead? He looked up at the other surfers and asked the question for which he already knew the answer. "Did anyone see the bloke in the black suit? He was standing right here."

Blank faces. Just blank faces.

"Bloody hell, Wato," Bluey murmured, searching for Ricky's pulse. His jaw bunched, his Adam's apple jumping. He ran his hands and gaze over Ricky's lifeless body, confusion etching his seasoned face. "The kid was just on the waves. He was just out there. Laughin' with us. Whingein' about goin' to school today. He didn't look sick. What happened?"

Standing in his living room now, staring out the window at the relentless summer sun already beginning to bake the world outside, Patrick closed his eyes. The cold wind and the white sun was always the first thing he remembered about the event but it was his last words spoken to Bluey before calling the paramedics that haunted him.

"I don't know."

The denial still tasted like poison on his tongue. Three years later and he could still feel the numb guilt those words caused in his core.

I don't know.

He *did* know, but he'd spent the last three years refusing to think about what that knowledge meant. He'd shut it out.

Patrick closed his eyes and leant his forehead against the cool glass of the window. Until today, until the demon in the water and on the sand, he'd refused to "use" whatever abhorrent abilities lurked within him. Not since the confrontation with the shadowless man in the black suit that horrific winter's morning. Three years with no warning, no further contact from the strange man. He wanted to believe it didn't exist. It couldn't exist. Hell, even Ven had started to relax somewhat. Life was normal. *He* was normal. As the days passed, Patrick all but convinced himself the event on the beach, the surreal face-off with the man in the suit—*the Disease*—had been just another all-too-vivid nightmare. Reality cocooned him and he'd all but forgotten it.

Until now.

The appearance of Death, the unseen attacker in the surf, the sand creature on the beach, the arguments with Ven, the man in the suit appearing in his nightmares. Reality was unraveling around him once again, and once again, whatever...power...polluted his being had resurfaced and he could no longer fool himself. He wasn't normal. He'd never been normal.

"So, what *are* you, Patrick Watkins?" he muttered.

The Cure.

The ambivalent words whispered in his head and he pulled in a long, shaky breath. What the hell did that mean?

The cure to what? And if he was the cure, why did he feel so goddamn sick?

Thirty-six years of flashes of the future, knowing things before they happened, and for what purpose? Had it stopped his parents' car inexplicably swerving off the road and wrapping around a telegraph pole? Thirty-six years of moving objects, not just the television remote, without touching them and to what end? Had it saved Ven from dying? From becoming a vampire?

No.

He sighed, the sound angry and desolate. "What in the name of all things holy am I the cure to?"

"I can tell you the answer to that," a low, slightly husky female voice said behind him. "I think."

He turned, his gaze falling immediately on Fred and his stomach clenched at the sight of her, his already unsteady heart kicking up a notch. She stood in the middle of his living room, soft black leather pants emphasizing her long, toned legs, a black INXS tank top hugging her glorious curved torso. She studied him with those piercing eyes of hers, their glacier-blue depths apprehensive and bold at the same time. A searing twist of tension knotted in his gut, making his breath quicken and his groin tighten. What was it about her that made his body flush with a simmering heat? That made him feel like a hormone-crazy teenage boy?

It wasn't just that she was gorgeous—she was, but it was more than that. More than a physical reaction. Every time he looked at her, came close to her, it was as if his body and his soul recognized her on a deeper level, the missing half of his existence he didn't know was lost.

He shook his head and turned back to the window, gritting his teeth. After everything he'd been through today, after all the paranormal shit and the run-in with Ven, here he was getting horny and wistful and goddamn Mills and Boonish at the mere sight of a creature that may or may not be planning to end his life. He was insane.

"What are you doing here, Death?" he asked, not turning to look at her. It was safer that way.

Really? Safer? Then why is your pulse pounding? Why are your palms itchy and your balls throbbing?

A soft sigh followed his question. "I figured if you wouldn't come with me I would come back to you."

"To do what? Kill me?"

Heavy silence filled the room, and for a moment Patrick wondered if Fred had left. A sharp stab of disappointment speared into his chest and he bit back a growl. Damn it, he was fucked up.

"Not to kill you, Patrick."

Fred's whisper caressed the back of his neck and, before he could stop himself, he turned. He gazed down into her eyes, his throat so tight he could barely breathe, his thighs brushing hers, his chest rubbing against her nipples. “To do what then?” he repeated, voice strangled.

She looked up at him, her heat folding around him, seeping into his body. Warming him from the icy embrace of the event’s haunting memory. “This.”

And she went up on tiptoe and touched her lips to his.

Chapter Seven

Ven snarled, pushing through the crowded Kings Cross street. He'd never been so hungry. So pissed off.

So desperate for a pair of bloody sunglasses.

He glared at the hot morning sun hanging low above his head, drowning him in ultraviolet rays. He hadn't needed a pair of sunglasses for over eighteen years. His old pair of Ray Bans were probably at home somewhere, maybe tucked in his underwear drawer along with the boxers he'd stopped wearing the night he'd become a vampire.

At the thought of his transformation, his demon growled, making a push for release. His control was weakening, the hunger for blood gnawing at his core like an insane monster...which it was. An insane, ravenous monster cringing at the daylight.

If he wasn't so hungry, he'd stop and buy a cheap pair of sunnies from a street vendor. But he *was* hungry. Damn hungry.

Shouldering his way through a gaggle of tourists snapping a multitude of photos of God knows what, he made his way for Amy's apartment. She lived above a vegetarian café a few blocks away. If he pulled in a deep breath now, he could almost convince himself he could taste her scent on the air already.

His stomach growled, almost as loudly as his demon.

Fuck, he was hungry.

Unbidden, an image of Death flashed through his head, a

carnal reminder it wasn't just blood he craved. He scowled, hissing at one tourist foolish enough to come too close. The man's sweat threaded into Ven's breath, sweet with salt and minerals. Hot saliva flooded his mouth.

He swallowed, tongue pressed to his fangs. The desire to lunge at the man, sink his nails into his bony shoulders and throw him to the sidewalk surged through him. He could all but feel the warm coppery fluid of the man's lifeblood trickle down his parched throat.

The muscles in Ven's face shifted. The light burned into his eyes. Sound amplified. He could hear the man's heartbeat. Could hear the man's blood flow through his thin, delicate veins, pulsing under his thin, vulnerable flesh. Waiting to be sucked from his neck in deep, long pulls. Waiting to be—

Ven snapped his fists closed, sinking his nails, no, his claws, into his palms. The pain stabbed into his bloodlust and he bit back a growl. Fuck. He was close. Too close to becoming lost to his demon. He needed to get off the street immediately. He needed to lock himself away from the sun, away from the cattle around him until he could sate the thirst in his body with Amy's blood.

And after he'd fed, after he'd gorged his demon on the bright red fluid, he'd sate the other more carnal lust in his body.

Again, an image of Death filled his head, pale limbs bare, eyes smoldering with pure white energy. The demon in her called his and a surge of wet electricity shot through him, making him growl once more.

Louder. More bestial.

A woman hurrying along the sidewalk gave him a startled look. She stumbled, her eyes bulging, and it was only then Ven realized he no longer wore his human façade. He was in vamp mode. The early stages, but vamp mode all the same.

Fuck.

He spun on the spot, taking in the gawking, gaping people around him in the blink of an eye. Their confused fear leeched from their pores in sweet, delicious waves. Their hearts leapt into deafening tattoos, pumping their blood around their bodies in delectable, irresistible rivers of—

Get out of here, Steven. Now. Before you tear open someone's neck and bathe yourself in what gushes from the wound.

The thought made him giddy, and for a dangerous, terrible, wonderful moment, he languished in its evocative power. His stare locked on a tall, slim female dressed in running shorts and a sports bra to his immediate left, the thump thump of the pulse in her neck like a beacon to his hunger. Her skin was golden and warm. He could feel her heat radiating from her healthy perfection from where he stood. She favored a macrobiotic diet. She preferred to drink white wine, not red. The last meal she'd consumed that day had consisted of tofu, egg whites and tomatoes.

Saliva oozed from the glands in his mouth and he touched the tip of his tongue to his fangs. It would be the last meal she ever ate. When he was through with her, she would be nothing but a drained shell, an empty sack of bones and—

Fear and disgust smashed into him and he froze. Jesus. What had he just been about to do?

Feed.

Staring into the woman's shocked eyes, struggling to shut out the delicious taste of her scent in his nose and on his tongue, he dropped down into a crouch. He needed to get away. Before he could no longer deny the monster within and fed on the blood pumping through the veins of those around him.

He leapt upward, launching himself directly to the sky. He didn't care if the humans saw him. Really, who would believe them anyway? A pale-skinned bloke with fangs and yellow eyes, dressed in jeans, biker boots and a white polo shirt defying gravity in the centre of Kings Cross in the middle of the morning?

Pushing through the humid morning air, he drew an image of Amy's small apartment into his whirling, screaming mind and folded space.

Warm, summer wind streamed over his face and bare arms as he moved through the empty space above Kings Cross. He knew he was not man, nor bird, nor beast, but something else. Something like the very wind lashing at him. A black and blonde blur of substance slicing through the sky, indefinable and unfathomable, even to himself, let alone the humans he'd left on the ground.

The feeling of freedom was immense—exhilarating—as was the inexplicable, inherent knowledge he could travel this way for miles if he needed to. This was more than folding space. This was defying physics. Defying existence.

He surged forward, smoke on the air and, seconds later, stood at Amy's door. Hungry. Really hungry.

Dragging in a long, steadying breath, Ven forced his muscles to relax. He needed to reel in his demon. He'd come so very close to doing the one thing he swore never to do after his transformation—feed from an unwilling human. It was the second time in less than sixty minutes that he'd almost done so. First his brother, then the unknown female on the sidewalk. Self-disgust rolled through him and he sank his nails into his palms again. He'd always prided himself on not being the monster fate had delivered him to be. He'd suppressed the urge to tear open the neck of any human nearby and gorge himself on their blood. Shit, since becoming a vamp he'd never attacked or drained anyone, although he had come perilously close to the latter the first time he'd fed from Amy. His grueling control over the seductive pull of his demon was, in his mind, what kept him human. If he didn't behave like a monster, he wasn't one.

Yet even now, standing at Amy's door, his tongue still tingled, his stomach still growled with the imagined intoxicating taste of Patrick's blood. The frustrated, infuriated impatience he felt over his brother's stubborn refusal of the situation made it all too easy for his demon to rise to the surface. Couple that with the ravenous ache in his stomach—damn, he'd never been so hungry—and he was a walking paranormal time bomb.

A time bomb quite capable of tearing a bloody great big hole in his only brother's neck.

Another wave of self-disgust crashed through Ven and he ground his teeth. He *was* a monster. A creature of base, carnal needs. It didn't matter how hard he fought with himself, how hard he tried to convince himself otherwise, the long and short of it was, he was a fucking vampire and less than an hour ago he would have quite willingly drained his only brother of every last drop of blood.

Contempt reached into his chest and squeezed his lifeless heart in a tight fist. Just what the hell *was* he? Man? Brother?

Killer.

The mental whisper sent a dark ripple down his spine. His canines began to elongate, his muscles to burn. Eager to strike.

"No." His growl sliced into the silent hallway and he punched the edge of his fist against his forehead. He wasn't going to succumb. No matter how pissed off with Patrick he was.

Why not? You've spent a lifetime looking out for Patrick. Shit, you've spent your death *looking out for him too, and to what end? He doesn't appreciate it. He doesn't deserve it. Think about what it would mean to succumb to what you really are. You've seen the demon in Death. It calls to you just as surely as your demon calls to her. Think about what you could have, what you could do, what you could* be *if you stop thinking about your brother and thought about yourself instead. Think about who you could be with...*

An image of Death exploded in Ven's head and he slammed his hands to his face, squeezing his eyes shut. No!

Blood roaring in his ears, teeth ground together, demon screaming for release, he turned from Amy's door. He couldn't be here. Not now. He didn't know what he would do if he—

"Ven?"

Amy's voice, brittle with shocked confusion, sounded behind him.

He froze.

And then the sweet, sweet scent of her body slipped into his nose, delicate, salty and honeyed at once and his tenuous hold on his starving demon shattered.

He spun, locking his stare on her stunned eyes as he whipped out his arm and curled his fingers around her neck. "I'm hungry," he whispered, and drove her back into her apartment, kicking the door shut behind him as he did so.

He forced her across the small living room, mindless of her stumbling feet. Her back slammed against the far wall, rattling the small photo frames hanging on it hard enough for one—an image of Amy and her parents—to jump from its nail and fall to the floor.

The glass shattered with a crack, spitting razor-edged shards at Ven's leg, but he didn't care. He had the potent scent of Amy's blood in his nose. Nothing mattered except quenching his thirst and sating his hunger.

He rammed her harder to the wall, his fingers gripping her neck enough to keep her in his grasp, not enough to restrict her breathing. She stared at him, eyes wide and shining with shock. Her flesh felt warm under his palm, the beat of her pulse a wild hammer against his lifeline.

"Ven?" she whispered, voice hoarse. "The sun's up. How can you..."

Smacking the inside of his booted foot against the inside of her naked one, he spread her legs apart and smashed his groin to her sex, bringing his face so close to hers he could feel the air displaced by her eyelashes. "It's a brand new world, love," he growled against her cheek. "And I'm a whole new vampire." He pushed his thick erection to the dome of her pussy, covered only by a thin pair of white cotton knickers. "Can't you feel it?"

She whimpered, pulse quickening into a rapid cadence. The bloodlust roared through Ven's veins at the submissive sound, stoking the burning hunger in his gut and core. The smell of her life force tainted the air with its delicious aroma and he drew it greedily into his being with long, deliberate breaths. It almost drove him insane, it was so tantalizing. His fangs grew longer—longer than they'd ever been while he still wore his human face—and the demon within him snarled. Impatient, furious and aroused.

He thrust his cock to Amy's cunt and bared his teeth, letting her see what was about to pierce her delicate, salty flesh.

Her eyes widened more, fear flashing in their chocolate-brown depths.

A rush of dark jubilation licked through him. She was petrified. He could smell it, not only in the blood in her veins, but in the sweat on her skin. It leeched from her the same way it had leeched from the cattle back on the street—thick and sweet and oh, so delectable.

Ven sank his fingers harder into her neck, taking more of her fear in through his nose. Fuck, it was delicious.

"Ven?"

Amy's voice trembled in his ear, sending another wave of bloodlust straight to his groin. He pulled in a deeper breath, savoring the stench of her fear. Now he understood the appeal of hunted prey. What must the knowledge they were being stalked do to the adrenaline levels in their blood? Why hadn't he realized what he was missing sooner? An angry groan rumbled in his chest and he felt the muscles in his face shift slightly, puckering his forehead into a less-than-human frown. All those years feeding from the willing...Christ! What a waste.

"Ven..." Amy squirmed against him, her nails digging into his wrist. Her thighs pressed his, rubbing and sliding over his legs as she struggled to move beneath his pinning weight. The sound of her cotton-covered arse sliding against the drywall behind her heated Ven's blood even more, the feel of her long nails driving into his flesh making his demon purr with rapture.

"Oh, lord, Ven..." she moaned, "...yes."

The words punched into Ven's chest like a fist of ice and he pulled back, staring into her eyes.

Yes?

Imprisoning her against the wall with his hips and hand, his palm pressed to her frenzied pulse, he drew in a longer, deeper breath.

Fear laced her scent, like aniseed through vanilla, but there was something else. Saliva flooded his mouth and his demon roared. His hunger spiked to a greater, darker level. Amy was scared, petrified in fact, and at the same time more turned on than he'd ever found her before.

The conflicting combination was intoxicating.

Addictive.

Fresh bloodlust swept through him and he narrowed his eyes, not releasing his grip on her neck. Incapable of doing so even if he wanted to. His demon controlled him now. Ravenous and licentious.

Jesus, Steven...what kind of monster are *you?*

"Fuck me, Ven," Amy murmured, gazing up at him with abject terror and desire shining in her eyes. "Fuck me and bite me. I'm yours to use and devour."

His demon growled and Ven felt his entire human facade shift. "You're playing with fire, little girl."

Amy gasped, recoiling from him as far as the wall would let her, which was not at all. She whimpered again, eyes bulging...and then wrapped her right leg around the back of his thighs to force her cunt closer to his cock. "I know."

Flashing her a cold grin, Ven forced his demon back down and thrust his straining erection harder to Amy's sex. She moaned, eyes closing, lips parted. "Oh, God, Ven..."

Lifting her feet from the floor, he shoved her legs further apart with his knees and jabbed his cock—still restrained by the denim of his jeans—to the musk-drenched crotch of her cotton panties. "You want me to fuck you, don't you? Just as much as you want me to sink my teeth into your neck and feed on your blood."

Eyes fluttering open, Amy nodded. She squirmed in his hold, rolling her sex over the bulging shape of his erection even as her pulse leapt into frantic flight at his course statement.

His grin stretched wider and he leant into her more, letting her feel not only the undeniable strength of his rigid shaft, but the inescapable steel in his body as well. "Which will it be first, then? Fuck or feed?"

Amy swallowed, her throat working against his grip on her neck. "Feed."

Her whisper sent a prickling ripple over Ven's cool flesh. He studied her, noting the desperation and euphoric terror in her eyes.

"Fuck, then," he growled.

"No."

Her cry of dismay made him chuckle. And mad. The human in him knew she'd been his willing "donor" for three years because she longed for the rapture of the feed. The vampire in him despised the idea she used him for her own pleasure. Tightening his grip on her neck, he snaked his free hand down her waist to the band of her knickers, hooked his thumb past the elastic and jerked his arm outward.

The soft cotton tore to shreds, stripping Amy's sex of any protection the underpants provided from his appetite. She squealed, bucking against the wall, her fingers scrambling at his wrist, her nipples turning into rock-hard points of flesh against his chest.

The subtle scent of her juices flooded his nose. He plunged his hand into the junction of her thighs, parting her sodden folds with two fingers before impaling her on them.

She squealed again, her hips driving into his brutal invasion, her pulse pounding, her eyes alight with excited fear. The sight stung Ven with contemptuous disgust, but he ignored it, stabbing deeper into her tight, dripping sex until the base knuckles of his fingers ground against the tiny nub of her clit.

"Lord, yes!" Amy cried, writhing against him.

"The Lord has nothing to do with this, little girl," Ven growled, wriggling his fingers in her cunt. The walls of her pussy gripped and squeezed each digit. He could feel the warmth of her pleasure oozing over his hand. He pulled in a breath, tasting her desire on the air as surely as he tasted her fear.

She didn't know what he was going to do next. He could see that plainly in her eyes. She didn't know when he was going to stop his assault, and neither did he.

"Yes," she moaned, closing her eyes to the sight of him.

He stabbed his fingers harder into her cunt. "Look at me, little girl."

His order snapped her eyes open and she quivered, though from terror or pleasure he could not tell and didn't care.

"That's better. You wanted this, Amy Elizabeth Mathieson. To be fucked and fed on by a monster and I will give it to you."

She shuddered, an abrupt orgasm rocking through her. She cried out, her pussy constricting around his fingers, her nails gouging at his wrist.

Ven chuckled, fully aware he was losing himself to his demon and relishing in the release and freedom. This is what it was to be a vampire. This overwhelming sense of power. Of dominance.

Fangs elongating further still, hot saliva coating his tongue and the back of his throat, he yanked his fingers from her cunt, lifted her higher from the floor and spun about. Her sofa sat behind them, covered in large cushions of all manner of fabric. They had made love on that sofa more than once over the last three years. He'd fed from her neck, her inner thigh, the undercurve of her breast many, many times there. But this morning, on the dawn of his new existence, he was going to treat her the way a true vampire treated his food source. The way she wanted to be treated. The way she feared being treated.

He threw her down, tore his fly apart, ripped his jeans from his legs and grabbed her hips, yanking them upward until his cock sank into her soaked pussy, stretching it to maximum.

She was tight and wet and hot. The perfect example of the

human female.

And yet you want more?

Her scared, euphoric cry drowned the unnerving thought, turned his cold blood to liquid mercury. He sank his claws into her flesh and hauled her harder to his cock, ramming its bulging length deeper and deeper into her tightness again and again and again. Fucking her until she came once more.

This time her cries came on a terrified whimper and he smiled, feeling no mirth in his body. Just lust. Hunger and lust. He closed his eyes, not wanting to see the craving need on her face...and saw Death instead.

He came. Just like that. Like a naked flame to dry tinder, the unexpected image of the Grim Reaper detonated a climax so savage he lost all rational thought. He roared, claws digging into Amy's hips, his taste buds believing it was Death's blood he smelled on the air.

His balls grew hard, hot. His fangs sank into his bottom lip. He rode Amy's body and fucked Death in his mind. His desire grew into a creature more voracious than his own released demon.

He knew what he wanted now. Knew it without doubt or question.

And yet she appears to Patrick naked. Straddles him on his bed. Begs him to go with her to who knows where.

The painful realization sliced through his head, severing the wonderful, tormenting image of Death in one swift strike.

Opening his eyes, he glared down at Amy, the sight of her orgasm-contorted face setting off another, more bitter climax.

Still his demon wanted more. Wanted to sink into her sheath and fill her with his cold seed.

Wanted to claim her entirely.

Who? Amy or Death?

He growled at the silent question and turned his stare to the woman lying on the sofa before him. "Is this what you wanted, little girl?" He grabbed Amy's ankle in one fist to yank her closer to him, thrusting his spent cock deeper into her sex. “Is this everything you dreamed it to be?”

She gazed up at him, the pulse in her neck hammering under her flesh with such force he felt it vibrate through her body. His mouth filled with saliva again and he fixed that wild pulse with a drilling stare. That would be the first place he sank his fangs into her body. He slid his attention to her breasts, her belly, her cunt, mentally charting the three-course meal to follow.

Dark, malevolent pleasure roared through him and he grinned, withdrawing his still-hard shaft from Amy’s sex. He dropped to his knees, capturing her cream-slicked pussy with his mouth. Amy’s pussy, not Death’s.

But it is Death’s pussy you want. Death’s you deserve. You are more than a normal demon, Steven and as such should be with—

He cut the thought dead and plunged his tongue into Amy’s slit, delving into her folds in deep, lapping strokes. Drinking her juices and his own dead, lifeless cum.

Lost to the malevolent being within him.

Tormented.

Haunted.

Exultant.

The barely there contact of Fred’s kiss detonated an explosion of wicked activity in the pit of Patrick’s stomach. He pulled in a quick breath and her distinctly mysterious scent filled his being.

It was enough. Enough to push him exactly where his body and his aching, tormented soul wanted him to be. He wrapped his arms around Fred’s back, buried his fingers in the long, thick curtain of her hair and yanked her against his chest, plunging his tongue past her parted lips into her wet, willing mouth.

The kiss was just as wild, just as fierce as their previous, but so much more powerful. So much more right. Her lips fit his to perfection, her tongue equal in ferocity to his own. With feverish longing and unquestionable desire, he invaded her mouth, drank from its sweet secrets. A fire roared through his body and he dragged one hand down her back, cupping her arse with ungentle force to haul her even closer. Her hips pressed to his, the soft hood of her sex ground into his erection through the barrier of her leather trousers and a bolt of scalding tension shot straight into his balls.

He yanked her harder still to his straining shaft, wanting to feel the base pain of brutal contact. Wanting the hungry ache in his cock to spread to the ravenous ache in his core. He tore at the back of her trousers, slamming his hand down past her waistband to cup the tight, firm curve of her right arse cheek. Skin to skin.

Frenzied pleasure burned through him at the feel of his flesh on hers and he tore his mouth from her lips, staring down at her.

Oh, Christ. What was he doing? He was out of his mind!

No, you're not. But you will be if you don't make love to her right now.

As if she sensed the dark turmoil threatening to undo him, she pressed her palms either side of his face and rolled her hips against his. "I know you are confused, Patrick." Lifting one leg, she wrapped it around the back of his thigh until he could feel the heat of her desire. "But don't be confused about this. About us."

The delicate musk of her juices slipped into his nose. He groaned, sucking her scent in as he grabbed her knee and yanked her leg higher up his thigh, spreading her sex wider.

He stroked his shaft, thick and swollen and straining for release, against her heat. His head was giddy, his pulse pounding. If this is how he felt dry fucking her, how would he survive real penetration?

"Is this how you plan to kill me, Death?" The question was a ragged growl as he continued to thrust into her leather-covered sex. "Through denied pleasure?"

A pure white light shimmered in her eyes and she chuckled, tightening her leg muscle to force his hips closer to hers. "Denying you pleasure will never be part of my plan, Patrick Watkins."

Her answer set fire to Patrick's senses. He sank his fingers into her butt cheeks and hauled her from the floor, crossing the room to the large sofa at its center in two strides. She hissed, her pussy rubbing the bulge behind his fly with each step he took, her eyes growing clouded with escalating pleasure.

"By the Powers, Patrick," she panted. "Who *are* you and how do you know *exactly* what I want you to do to me?"

"I'm the man just about to claim you as his own," he answered on a raw snarl, "And right at this point in time, I don't give a flying fuck how I know."

He threw her onto the sofa, her arse hitting the cushioned seat, the backs of her knees slapping against the padded armrest. She scurried backward, stare locked on his face, breasts rising and falling in rapid succession.

Patrick watched her move, watched her position herself for his invasion. His blood roared in his ears, hot, hungry blood that pounded through his body in building power. He reached for his fly, jerking it apart, not caring that the metal buttons tore from the denim. His cock sprang free of his jeans, the cool air of the room scalding its turgid length. Fred gasped and the soft hitching of her breath sent another surge of liquid pleasure into his groin.

He walked around the end of the sofa and stood before her, the distended head of his cock level with her parted lips. He watched the pink tip of her tongue flick out to wet them, her eyes staring with rapt interest at his jutting erection. A sizzling lick of hot knowledge tightened his gut. She would take his length into her mouth. Of that he had no doubt. She would take him into her mouth and bring him to screaming, exquisite release if he wanted her to. He saw her shift on the sofa to do just that, but before she could, he tangled his fists in her hair and tugged her head backward, forcing her to look up into his face.

"No." He shook his head, fighting to steady his shallow breaths.

She frowned at him, a curious little puckering of her eyebrows that told him she was both excited and annoyed by his action. He chuckled, the sound very husky. Death was not used to being denied, it seemed. "That can come later," he promised. "But I want to feel your sex sliding over my cock before I feel your mouth doing so."

He'd never spoken such brazen words before. His heart hammered.

Fred stared at him for a still moment, lips parted, and then slowly, deliberately, raised herself onto her knees, bringing her face level with his.

She pushed her hips forward, a small smile playing with the sides of her mouth. "Gladly."

Her murmur sent off a chain reaction in Patrick's body. His cock jerked, ready to feel the tightness of her sex. His throat squeezed, the thought of the exquisite penetration already stealing his breath and his skin prickled with flushed desire. "Take off your pants."

The order rumbled from his chest, harsh and raw at once.

Fred remained motionless, gazing at him. Silent.

A wave of impatience rolled through Patrick and he opened his mouth to repeat the request...before a shimmer below her waist caught his eye and he watched the snug black leather pants she wore disappear.

He sucked in a sharp breath, his eyes widening. Not just because of the way she'd removed her trousers—he'd seen her do it before—but because of the smooth, firm perfection of her thighs, belly and hips now exposed. He gazed at what she'd revealed to him, fresh hunger flooding his shaft with rigid heat.

The same soft crescent was trimmed into the downy hair on her mons and, like it had before, it held him mesmerized.

"Do you recognize it yet?"

There was a low tinkle of mirth in Fred's question and he lifted his stare from her sex to smile at her. "A scythe."

His answer pleased her. He could tell. Her pupils dilated a fraction and her breath caught in her throat.

He leant forward, not sure why but wanting to catch that little hitching sound with his mouth. Her lips were soft under his and he smiled, dipping his tongue into her mouth in a quick exploration before pulling away from her slightly. Her moan of protest made him smile wider and he tightened his fist in her hair. Just in case she decided to take charge.

He may be playing with Death, but it was his game, his rules. This time, at least.

"Undress me."

Her pupils dilated again at his command, a pure white glow flaring in her eyes for a split second. Without a word, or hint of hesitation, she reached for the waistband of his jeans.

As slowly as she'd raised herself to her knees, she hooked her fingers in his belt loops and pulled his jeans down over his hips. Cool air caressed his butt, his hips. The feel of denim sliding over his flushed skin sent a shiver through his body and his balls tightened, rising up closer to the root of his shaft. He watched Fred's face, not wanting to look elsewhere even as the desire to lower his gaze to her hands and watch her progress gnawed at his control.

An unreadable expression on her face, she coaxed his jeans past his thighs until gravity claimed them and they slid to the floor, bunching at his feet. He shifted slightly, lifting one foot and then the other free, pushing the discarded item of clothing out of the way with a dismissive shove of his toes.

Fred kneeled on the sofa, eyes on his, her hands hovering above his bare hips. The heat from her palms kissed his flesh despite the lack of skin-to-skin contact and Patrick swallowed, his pulse pounding. She waited for him to give her permission to do what he could see in her smoldering gaze she so desperately wanted to do—touch him. Take his cock in her hands. But she didn't, and her control sent twisting ribbons of wet tension through Patrick's body. Jesus, the building pressure in his loins was almost too much to bear now. What would it be like when her hands made contact with his hips?

What would it be like when she held his cock?

The thought sent another jolt of wet electricity through Patrick and he clenched his jaw. "Get rid of the shirt."

Fred's blue eyes glinted white. "Whose?"

"Both."

His blunt reply brought a tiny smile to her lips. She lifted her chin a fraction and the black tank top covering her torso vanished, leaving her naked. Gloriously, wonderfully naked. Her breasts but an inch away from his chest. Her nipples all but brushing the material of his shirt.

Head giddy, mouth dry, Patrick leant towards her, wanting to feel those puckered, pink tips against his, but stopped when Fred shook her head and held up her hand between them.

She placed her palm on his chest, directly above his heart, before sliding it—very slowly—over his own rock-hard nipple, down his ribcage and under the hemline of the loose shirt he wore.

Her fingertips touched his skin first, and a soft gasp burst from Patrick at the featherlight contact. His body stiffened, his breath caught in his throat. He stayed still, frozen with expectation, burning with anticipation as, with barely a change in position, Fred pressed her palm completely against his stomach, just below his navel.

The bulging dome of his cockhead nudged the underside of her wrist, smearing the tiny bead of pre-come on its tip over the velvety softness of her skin and he swallowed again. Would she move her hand down? Or up?

With an ever-so-small grin, she slid her hand upward,

inching his shirt further up his torso until his entire stomach was exposed.

Patrick's cock pulsed, denied attention but stimulated beyond comprehension all the same. Wordlessly, he stared into her face, his heartbeat kicking up a notch when she placed her other hand beside her first and, with a deliberately languid pace, slid his shirt up over his chest, over his head and off his shoulders.

They faced each other. Naked. Almost touching. Their bodies so close Patrick was sure he could feel Fred's heartbeat vibrating through his chest, down into the pit of his stomach and lower. He reveled in the sensation, a connection beyond the physical. With each thump his erection grew longer, thicker, his own heartbeat harder, faster. An image of Fred flashed through his mind—her long legs wrapped around his hips, her belly pressed to his, her nails digging into his shoulders, her cunt squeezing his thrusting cock—and he knew immediately it was the future he saw. Five minutes, five hours, five years in the future he didn't know. God willing, all three.

He pulled in a deep breath, taking her unique fragrance into his soul. Spices, musk and secret power. Jesus, he was addicted already.

The thought drove him to act.

He buried his hands in her hair once more, crushed her mouth with his and jerked her to his body with a force he knew was neither gentle or chaste.

Her breasts flattened against his chest, her mons ground against his cock. She snaked her arms around his back, pulling herself harder into his savage embrace. Her tongue lashed his, a battle of passion and lust where neither was the defeated. Dragging his lips from the invasion, he journeyed her jawline and neck with his teeth, nipping at her flesh in tiny bites that drew a low whimper with each one. He liked the sound. It spoke clearly of the desire and pleasure he met upon her body.

Continuing his exploration, he tasted her collarbone, the little dip at the base of her neck before charting the curve of her shoulder, his fists still knotted in her hair, holding her captive. She tasted so good. Like a hidden mystery on a warm summer night.

"By the Powers, Patrick." Her throaty murmur tickled his lips and he lifted his head to gaze into her face. "This isn't..." She didn't finish, instead she closed her eyes and rolled her hips against his.

The heat of her sex melted into his erection, incinerating the brief flare of doubt her words caused. He jerked forward, thrusting his cock to her mons. She was all softness and hardness and musky heat and he wanted to be buried in her more than he wanted to draw breath.

If he didn't do so soon, he would come all over her belly. Of that he had no doubt.

As if she knew his very predicament, Fred moved slightly on the sofa, shifting her weight so as to spread her legs without breaking contact—even a hair's width—with his groin. The change in position allowed his cock, so hard and swollen it felt like steel, to ram against the wet lips of her pussy, her juices painting his stretched flesh instantly.

He growled, arching his back to shove forward, parting her folds with the rim of his distended cockhead. He stroked back and forth, gripping her hair, staring into her eyes. Fucking her but not. Torturing the tiny button of her clit with each pass, rolling his cock over and along it with each stab until he felt her muscles coil and her pussy weep.

The delicate aroma of her pleasure filled his breath. She sank her nails into his shoulders, eyes beyond blue now, shining with an iridescent white glow that would have made him nervous before but now only made him burn.

Raking one hand down her back, he cupped her arse, squeezed one firm butt cheek with fierce strength before jerking her harder to him. The sudden change granted him exactly what he wanted. Her legs spread wider, her damp folds wider still. He felt her sex suck greedily at his cock and then, with one brutal, savage thrust, he was there—her tight muscles enveloping him, embracing him. Surrounding him.

Fred threw back her head, spine bowing, nails puncturing his flesh. A cry as raw and primitive as any Patrick could imagine burst from her throat, shattering the very air around them.

She bucked into him, took him deeper, deeper, her stomach and breasts and nipples sliding over his sweat-slicked skin, her arms holding him to her with such strength he could feel the tremble in her muscles.

"Oh, claim me, Patrick! Claim me!"

Pestilence watched his fingers glide through the kitten's silky white fur, the creature's soft purr vibrating through its tiny body into his lap. Eyes closed, claws sheathed, it was a picture of pure contentment. He smiled, moving his fingers to its head to gently scratch it behind its ears.

The thing had caught his eye in Famine's bedroom earlier that day, its young body quivering with excitement as it stalked its siblings, its blue eyes wide with determination and purpose. He'd taken it right from under the Third Horseman's pointed, turned-up nose, tucking it under his arm as she'd stared at herself in the mirror, complaining of the excessive weight she'd supposedly put on around her skin-and-bone hips.

Sitting on his throne now, Pestilence considered the kitten's fine bone structure under its downy white fur. How fragile. How extremely breakable. And yet, its teeth were already needle-point sharp and capable of piercing skin with just the slightest pressure from its jaws. His smile grew wider and he stroked the kitten's back. Deceptive. Misleading. Just like him.

He raised his head, fixing the bloodsucker standing before him with a level look. "Tell me more."

The vampire shuffled his designer-boot-clad feet on the marble floor, cocking one eyebrow in a smug show of confidence. Pestilence wanted to curl his lip at the demon's conceit. He'd seen the vampire's ilk before—human-world miscreants thinking they were the Powers' gift to the demon race because Hollywood dedicated so much time to their pathetic existence. Still, *this* vampire was, it had to be said, finally proving to be useful.

"The human female is ripe," the bloodsucker answered. "Desperate for what I can give her. After tonight she will give me anything I ask."

Pestilence leaned forward on his throne, earning himself a sudden acupuncture session from the disturbed kitten's claws. "Hush," he murmured, dropping his gaze to the white fluff ball for a second and scratching its chin. "Go back to sleep."

He returned his attention to the cocky vampire, narrowing his eyes. "And what exactly are you going to ask for?"

"The key you seek."

"Pray tell?" Pestilence murmured, stroking the kitten with languid calm while studying the vampire with an unwavering gaze, "what key is that?"

The vampire grinned, an entirely hideous expression in Pestilence's opinion. "The key to Patrick Watkins' demise."

Cold hope rushed through Pestilence's body but he kept his face indifferent, his body relaxed and loose. After all this time, could it be true? Could the bloodsucker really deliver what he promised?

"Do not think to fool me, Raziel," he warned with an offhanded tone, adjusting the sleeping kitten on his lap. For something so small, it was quite heavy. "Or you will find yourself drowning in cockroaches with a very sick taste in your mouth."

The vampire visibly blanched, his already pale skin bleaching paler at the veiled threat. "I'm not trying to fool you, sire," he gushed, fidgeting on the spot. "The female will deliver exactly what I ask and I will deliver him to you."

Pestilence studied the bloodsucker, letting his lips curl into a small smile. Raziel had been his eyes and ears in the human-dwelling demon world for over two decades, with the sole purpose of finding a weakness to the lifeguard's seemingly impenetrable protection. He raised his eyebrows, daring to dream it was all coming to fruition. "As asked?" he said. "As promised?"

Raziel nodded, extended fangs glinting in the flickering candlelight. "Patrick Watkins' brother will be in your possession by sunup tomorrow, sire. I can assure you." He grinned, cockiness coming back tenfold. "As asked. As promised."

With a great show of elation, Pestilence drew the kitten closer to his stomach and smiled. Steven Watkins. The brother who should have died eighteen years ago. Finally removed from the picture.

Things were looking up.

A chuckle sounded deep in his chest and he lifted the kitten up to his face, rubbing its tiny cold nose to his.

Good.

Very good.

Chapter Eight

Okay, first things first. She'd never felt this way before. Ever. Not even with her Roman general with the hawkish nose and eloquent turn of phrase. What did that mean?

Lying on her back, the warm hardness of Patrick's body pressed to her belly, his legs threaded through hers in the most wonderfully intimate way, Fred studied the ceiling of his living room.

The warm afterglow of her five or so orgasms still licked through her veins, still flushed her perspiration-wet skin. What Patrick Watkins could do with his dick left her mouth dry and her pussy saturated and throbbing and so damn hungry for more. What he could do with his tongue, his teeth, his fingers.

A shiver of dirty delight rippled through her at the memory and she grinned, wriggling a little underneath him. The soft carpet caressed her naked butt cheeks in ways plush pile was never meant to and she wriggled again, letting her body consume the surreal pleasure. She chuckled silently, smoothing her palms over Patrick's relaxed shoulders. How could the man make her come so many times and still leave her so horny that carpet made her hot and squirmy?

"Do you mind?" a low grumble sounded from the vicinity of Patrick's head—somewhere near her armpit—and a delicious little thrill shot through her chest and into her breasts. "I'm quite comfortable here and you've suddenly turned into a jumping castle."

Rolling to his side, he slid onto the floor and settled himself beside her body, resting his head on his elbow to give her a decidedly cheeky grin. “I guess this means I can’t say I’ve never fucked around with Death anymore, can I?”

Fred cocked an eyebrow at him. “Not unless you want me to kick you.”

He chuckled, smoothing his hand along the flat plane of her belly up to the curve of her ribcage, his knuckles grazing the underswell of her breasts. The soft contact sent a little shiver of delight through Fred and she let her eyelids close. “Hmmm. That feels nice.”

She opened her eyes again and gave him a wide smile. Only to find him studying her with an ambiguous expression on his face.

“I guess I probably should have asked you this a couple of hours ago,” Patrick said, his hand still on her ribs, his eyes serious, “in light of what we’ve just been doing, but what’s going on with you and my brother?”

Fred’s stomach knotted. An image of Ven immediately flashed into her head and she swallowed down a sudden lump in her throat. What *was* going on between her and fang face? She released a sigh, a small frown pulling at her eyebrows. “His demon calls to mine. Powerfully, in fact.”

Patrick looked at her, his expression never changing. If it weren’t for the slight tensing in his muscles, Fred could almost believe he hadn’t heard what she’d just confessed. A long moment passed. “Am *I* a demon?” he asked, “Is that why we did what we just did? Is that why I can’t stop thinking about you? Why within ten minutes of finding you in my bedroom in the middle of the night, I wanted nothing more than to bury myself in your sex and make love to you?”

His words made Fred’s heart hammer like a sledgehammer. She’d never been told something like that, especially not in such an open, completely matter-of-fact way. Her mouth went dry, the soles of her feet tingled...and the base of her spine itched. Really itched. “No,” she answered, shaking her head as she rolled onto her side, her belly and hips pressed to his. "You are not a demon. I would know if you were." She paused, letting her gaze roam his handsome, troubled face. "You are something else."

"What?"

She shook here head again, wishing with every molecule of her existence she could give him an answer. "I still don't know."

A low growl rumbled in Patrick's chest and he rolled onto his back, breaking the intimate contact to stare at the ceiling. Sunlight dappled the room, streaming in through the open window and Fred could see him tracking the dust motes dancing on the air, his jaw clenched, his breath even and deliberately paced. She placed her hand on his chest, wanting to feel the beat of his heart under her palm, and swallowed as she felt him flinch slightly at her touch.

"I'm not going to hurt you, Patrick. No matter what Steven thinks, no matter what I am, I'm not going to hurt you."

He didn't answer her, just watched the dust motes. Fred studied his profile, the warm euphoric buzz from their incredible lovemaking taunting her. She wanted to be wrapped in his arms now, but it seemed he'd shut her out.

She chewed on her bottom lip. By the Powers, what did she do now? What should she do?

"Why did you come here, Fred?" Patrick turned his head to face her, that strangely ambiguous expression on his face again. "Because I can't believe it was just to make love to me."

Pulling in a slow breath, Fred considered her answer. What did she tell him? And how much of it would he believe?

Tell him everything, Fred. Whatever this *is, you know you don't want it to end now. Tell him everything. Give him a reason to trust you.*

"I have this...early-warning alarm," she said, keeping her hand on his chest, unwilling to break contact with his warmth. "When something is going down that impacts the Realm—that's my home—my spine itches. Well, to be exact, my tail itches. I don't exist in my demon form, ever," she hastened to add, "Not since about five million years ago that is, but that form and my tail along with it still exists in a plane beyond this realm." She paused, waiting for Patrick to say something. He didn't. "The second I stood in your bedroom, the very moment I saw you asleep on your bed, my spine itched. That told me you were more than just a hot guy I'd spied on the beach." She uttered a short, almost dry laugh and rolled her eyes. "And to think I'd just popped into your room to have a perv."

She looked back to him, waiting for a response. All she got was that same expression.

He's not making this easy, Fred.

He doesn't have to. You're just about to change everything he knows.

"Anyways, ignoring the...desire...I immediately felt for you, the itch in my spine made me nervous. I hate being nervous. I also hate being confused, and I have to tell you, Patrick, since you and your toothy brother entered the scene, I've been confused." She chewed on her bottom lip again, the image of Steven floating through her head at his name. "More than confused. And then Steven found me in the strip joint and we..." she faded to a halt, clearing her throat. "We parted ways, and I'd just returned to the Realm to try and find out what in all the levels of hell was going on, when you called me."

Patrick turned to look at her. "I never called you, Fred."

Red heat flushed into Fred's cheeks as the memory of the moment came back to her. "I heard your voice. Well, your thoughts. I don't know how that is even possible, but I did. I heard your thoughts and knew immediately where you were and what you were feeling—which was pretty angry, I have to say. Angry and, on a different level, scared." She shrugged, trying to pretend to be calm when all she wanted to do was show him just how badly the whole thing had affected her. She should not have been able to hear his thoughts in the Realm. She shouldn't be able to hear his thoughts, full stop. But whatever he was, she seemed to have locked on to him. A connection beyond her understanding. More confusion, more questions to be answered.

"I tuned myself into where you were—and again, I don't know or understand how that can be so—and arrived at the beach in time to see you destroy the *nikor*. No weapons. No help. Just you and the aqueous demon and then a billion grains of disconnected sand."

She paused. Not because she wanted Patrick to say something, but because she needed to contemplate what she'd just confessed. She was the Fourth Horseman. She was Death. The ultimate end. She shouldn't be connected to *anything*.

Looking at Patrick, she suppressed the urge to fidget. What was he thinking?

Aargh! Now would be a good time for one of these impossible psychic connections, don't you think, Fred?

He stared at her, the heat from his body seeping into hers, his unique male scent—earth and sand and summer wind—permeating each breath she took. Tension twisted through her muscles. She clenched her jaw, her pulse growing quicker.

By the Powers, say something, damn it!

"You were in a strip joint?"

The question took her completely by surprise. She burst out laughing, the sound both shocked and exasperated, and wacked her fist against his chest.

"Hey!" He pulled himself into a loose ball, protecting his body with his arms and legs.

Shaking her head, Fred went to slap him again, targeting his naked butt cheek suddenly and wonderfully exposed to her by his defensive position.

Before her hand could connect with his flesh, Patrick moved. His body unfurled, his fingers curling around her wrists to stay her arms, his legs pinning hers to the floor with gentle speed.

She gasped, a sizzling bolt of liquid heat stabbing straight into her sex. Her nipples pinched tight, the pit of her belly tensed. She licked her lips, watching him rise above her slightly, his green eyes holding hers.

They stared at each other for a still moment. Fred could feel the tension in Patrick's body. She held her breath, wanting him to lower his head and kiss her. Wanting him to not. She needed to tell him the rest before they got lost in each other again. She *had* to tell him the rest. But she needed to feel him moving inside her sex as well. Damn, she needed to feel him claim her as his own. Maybe more so.

Oh, Fred...this is so dangerous.

Patrick's Adam's apple worked up and down in a series of rapid jumps before, ever so slowly, he released her wrists and moved away from her, nostrils flaring. "There's more, isn't there," he said, pulling himself into a sitting position and resting his elbows on his bent knees. Barely restrained desire radiated from him in hot waves, as did edgy irritation. "You didn't come here to tell me just that. You know something else."

Her body burning with denied pleasure, her chest tightening with anticipated apprehension, Fred released a sigh. She positioned herself beside him, back against the sofa, knees tucked under her chin. There were two ways she could proceed—cautiously, edging into what she'd found back in the Realm's library, or bluntly. No bullshit, no tiptoeing about.

A rush of annoyance heated her blood and she held back a muttered curse. She'd never been like this before. Indecisive. Hesitant. She felt like a dithering old lady.

Just do it, Fred. Don't muck about. Just tell him.

"You've been written about in the Prophesies."

The moment the words passed her lips she wished she could take them back. Patrick would want a no-nonsense explanation, but she didn't need to scare him off with such a surreal statement. Even she got freaked out from time to time knowing there were entities who foresaw her actions eons in advance.

She shot him a quick look and dismay rippled through her. He hadn't reacted. That frustrating ambiguous expression once again turned his face into an unreadable mask.

"What I mean is," she continued, less aggressive, "I *think* you have been."

He raised one eyebrow. "So I'm famous?"

Fred laughed, an uncomfortable sound that made her cringe. What was *wrong* with her? Anyone would think she was in...

The thought trailed away, leaving a lump in her throat and a numb tingle in her lips. She closed her eyes, suppressing the urge to groan.

By the Powers, no. Not that. *Please, not now. Not until...*

"Fred?"

She started at her name. Giving herself a mental slap, she turned back to Patrick, covering her nakedness in a pair of denim cut-offs and a black tank top as she did so. She didn't know why, but she didn't want to tell him what the future may or may not hold for him undressed. Silly, she knew, but there all the same.

Maybe it's because you're—

Shut up!

Patrick cocked an eyebrow, possibly at the sudden appearance of clothing on her body, possibly at the strange expression she knew she wore. He said nothing however, reaching behind him without breaking eye contact to snare his boxers. He tugged them on and, despite the churning apprehension eating away at her, Fred couldn't help but admire the lean, bronzed strength of his legs and the thick, long strength of his—

Patrick cleared his throat and Fred jumped, heat flooding her checks again. She snapped her attention to his face, giving herself another mental slap. *Focus, Fred.* "Umm..." She desperately tried to remember the last thing Patrick had said. *So, I'm famous?* "Well, possibly," she finally answered, trying to will away her embarrassed blush, "Although the reference is so obscure I could be reading it all wrong."

An ambiguous light flickered in Patrick's eyes. "Let's hear it."

"The first quote I found is about fang face." She frowned. "I think. *The brother who cannot walk in the sun shall cast a shadow on the shifting grains of glass, and the shadow shall be of blood.*"

Patrick didn't say anything.

"I'm assuming the shifting grains of glass refer to the beach, being that sand is used to make glass. I'm guessing the brother who cannot walk in the sun refers to Steven being a vampire who is impervious to daylight." She paused again. "But..."

"But you're not sure whose blood the shadow will be of?" Patrick finished, voice level. He looked at her for a long moment before that same ambiguous light shimmered in the depths of his eyes. "Or are you?"

Fred turned away from him, not really sure how to answer. He already had a pretty good idea of where the conversation was heading. She could see it in the tension in his face, feel it in the tension of his muscles. She watched the day stream into the room through the window, noting the changing shadows on the floor and walls. It must be almost midday by now. She'd been with Patrick for almost three hours—the longest she'd ever stayed in one human's company her entire existence.

And you're in no hurry to leave, are you.

Tugging her legs closer to her chest, she turned back to him.

"C'mon, Death." Patrick's grin was wry. "You can do it."

Mouth dry, chest heavy, she let out a sigh. "I don't know."

His laugh was a wry as his grin. "What's the rest?"

She didn't answer him. She didn't want to.

You have to, Fred. You need to prepare him for what is to come. Whatever that is.

Swallowing, she dug her nails into her knees and pressed her back harder to the sofa, welcoming the pain the pressure caused on her spine. "In a book called *Death and Lust in the Time of Genesis..."* She stopped. Patrick was chuckling softly.

"There's a book called *Death and Lust in the Time of Genesis*?"

She pulled a face at him, exasperated. "Pay attention, lifeguard. In *Death and Lust in the Time of Genesis*, these words caught my attention—*'The Cure shall face the Disease on the shifting...*" She stopped again, fixing Patrick with a hard stare.

His jaw was bunched, so tight she swore she could hear his teeth cracking, his muscles coiled to snapping point.

"What? What did I say, Patrick?" She stared at him, her heart hammering. Something she'd said had gotten to him. What? "Tell me."

He turned away, knuckles white.

Fred scrambled to her knees before him, forcing him to look at her. "Tell me, Patrick." She placed her hands on his fists. "Please?"

A haunted expression flashed across his face, warping the stoic one he'd previously worn. He closed his eyes and shook his head, as if fighting an inner war.

"Fuck," he muttered, fists balling tighter under her fingers.

"Patrick," Fred murmured, moving closer to him. "Please?"

"Tell me who the Disease is, Death. I know you know. I can see it in your eyes. Tell me who he is."

Fred shook her head, the fury in Patrick's eyes almost scaring her. She'd never seen him so angry. She'd never seen anyone so angry. Ever. "I... He..." She licked her suddenly dry lips. By the Powers, why did she feel like the very air around her was alive? Like some force was pressing down on her?

"Who is he, Death?"

She squirmed, the unseen pressure on her body increasing.

"Who is he?"

She pulled in a shallow breath, genuine fear licking through her. This was not right. She couldn't breathe. She couldn't move. Something was happening. Something she didn't comprehend.

She looked at Patrick and saw intense fire boiling in his eyes. "Patrick?" she said, but it came out a croak. By the Powers, what was he doing? *How* was he doing it? "Patrick? Please...stop..."

Patrick's eyes flared hotter. And then he blinked, cold horror flooding his face, and the pressure stopped. Immediately.

Fred slumped, staring at him. Her body ached, as if only having narrowly avoided being crushed. She wet her lips with her tongue again, her pulse a rabid beat in her neck. By the Trilogy, what *was* he?

Patrick stared back at her. Silent. Motionless. His eyes narrowed for a second and then a ragged breath burst passed his lips and he dropped his head between his arms. "Fuck," he muttered again, his voice muffled by the bunched muscles of his shoulders.

"Patrick?" Fred whispered, inching closer. Her heart still hammered, but from unease or concern she didn't know. "Talk to me, please."

He lifted his head and looked at her, his eyes normal again. Normal, but tormented and tortured and as angry as hell. "I know who the Cure is, Fred." His statement fell from his lips in a flat monotone. "And I think I've met the Disease."

"What?"

Fred didn't think her heart could smash harder in her chest, but it did. She gaped at him, more than a little stunned.

"Three years ago," Patrick continued in that same monotone. "At work early one winter's morning, I was watching the surf, freezing my arse off on the beach. I turned around and found a man staring at me. A man in a black suit. A man who didn't throw a shadow."

Just like that, Fred's spine exploded into a scalding itch. A man in a black suit. Her breath caught in her throat. Pestilence.

Patrick's fists shifted under her fingers and he swallowed,

jaw still bunched tight. “He told me *the Disease shall destroy the Cure and the end shall be begun*, just before he killed a kid, an innocent kid I’d known since he was ten years old, right in front of me.”

Fred tilted her head. Patrick had to be mistaken. Pestilence couldn’t transubstantiate from the Realm. Of the Four Horseman, only she could move about the world of man.

It makes sense, Fred. You know Pestilence refers to himself as the Disease often. He considers it a title of importance.

She frowned, her gaze fixed on Patrick’s face. And then gasped. If the Disease was Pestilence, then the Cure was...

Patrick nodded. “Me.”

Fred blinked. How did he know what she was thinking?

Does it matter? You’ve just figured out who the key players are. Now you need to work out what the—

Like a fist through glass, Pestilence’s “offer” of a partnership made over an eon ago came back to her. A partnership in greatness, he’d called it. A proposal to undo the very Fabric.

She swallowed, incredulous shock leaving her numb. The First Horseman was attempting to fuck with the Order of Actuality. He had to be. What else did he mean by “the end”? What other interpretation was there. The end of man. Pestilence was trying to bring about the Apocalypse. On his own.

She pressed her hand to her mouth, staring at Patrick, her skin prickling. How could she have been so stupid? Pestilence had told her his plan an eon ago and she’d laughed at him. How could she have not connected the dots?

Because the dots didn’t involve an Australian lifeguard, Fred.

A frown knotted her eyebrows. That was right. Why was Pestilence trying to destroy Patrick? Why, exactly, was Patrick Watkins referred to as the Cure?

Why him?

And how did ol’ sick and weedy know?

The words of the random prophesy she'd found in *Death and Lust in the Time of Genesis* floated through her head. *The Cure shall face the Disease on the shifting dunes and the end shall begin and the beginning shall end.*

Nothing in that mumbo jumbo told her who would be the victor.

Or whether Patrick would survive the confrontation.

The brother who cannot walk in the sun shall cast a shadow on the shifting grains of glass, and the shadow shall be of blood.

The first Prophesy she'd found in the library, written by the last Fate herself, came back to her and her stomach twisted. *Shadow shall be of blood.* She looked at Patrick, studying her with a silent, unreadable gaze.

Whose blood? Why would fang face cast a shadow of blood? Surely the sentence meant Pestilence would fail? Why would Steven cast a shadow of his brother's blood?

Suppressing a sigh, she ran her hands through her hair and chewed on her bottom lip, giving Patrick a worried look. By the Powers, what did she tell him?

That strange flare danced in his green eyes again and he smiled, the action both lost and accepting. "Hit me with it."

Fred chewed on her lip again, and then jumped in with both feet. "The Disease is Pestilence. The First Horseman of the Apocalypse. He plans to ignore the Order of Actuality, the governing Fabric by which all existence is weaved, and bring about the end of mankind before it is meant to occur."

"Okay."

Just that one word. Not even a blink.

Fred wanted to press her body to Patrick's and hold him. But she hadn't finished yet. She wet her lips one more time, and then continued. "Somehow he has garnered information that must have led him to you. He is the Disease and you are the Cure." She paused, tracing her fingertips over the back of Patrick's hands. "I think he believes if he removes you from the picture the Apocalypse shall begin."

Patrick looked at her, his face like rock, his expression stony. "So," he said, after such a stretch of silence Fred had begun to fidget. "What you're telling me is this guy believes I'm the only thing that can stop him wiping out mankind?"

"Pestilence is a demon. An entity of the first order, not a 'guy', but yes."

"Can he be killed?"

She shook her head. "Not even by me. The Horsemen are timeless. We have no beginning and no end."

"And he's trying to kill me?"

Not wanting to do so, Fred nodded. "Yes."

Patrick fell silent again. He looked past her, out the window again and Fred couldn't help but wonder if he wished to be out on the waves. Away from the surreal nightmare he'd found himself in. Away from her.

A sharp pain stabbed into her chest at the thought. She didn't want him away from her. Not even an inch. Smoothing her palms up his arms, she willed him to look at her.

He didn't.

"I won't let him—"

Patrick cut her off. "I'm not going to hide behind you, Death." He returned his gaze to her face and Fred bit back a gasp at the deep lines etching his face. Tormented, angry lines. "I don't care who you are, *what* you are. I'm not going to hide behind you. If this is what I am meant to do, if I'm meant to face Pestilence I will."

She opened her mouth to protest, to tell him to stop being a stupid, macho male. What came out instead was, "I don't want to lose you."

The confession hung on the air between them. Her eyes widened, her pulse leapt away from her, and then she did the only thing she could do. The only thing she wanted to do.

She leant forward and kissed him.

Chapter Nine

Ven took her from behind. His balls slapped against Amy's cunt as he pumped into her, the bright mid-morning sunlight pouring over his naked chest and face, heating his flesh, making him sweat.

It felt good. No longer fighting the lure of the creature he really was. It felt right. More than right.

He rammed into her sodden sex, filling her again and again, his claws puncturing her hips, his growls puncturing the air.

Amy moaned, laying face first over the back of her sofa, her hands scrambling for a grip on the piece of furniture's faux suede. She begged him to stop. She begged for more. He did the latter, his demon growing stronger with every savage thrust, the monster he truly was in complete and utter control.

Steven Owen Watkins no longer existed.

He stared into the sunlight. Let its harsh rays burn indelible shadows on his retina.

The sun. His enemy no more.

The realization sent a charge of triumphant elation through him and he increased his speed, punching in Amy's pussy with such power he could feel her pelvic bone smash against the root of his shaft. Hot pain stabbed into his groin and he threw back his head, roaring at the pleasure it brought to his body.

The hunger in his gut, the craving for blood, grew wilder, more demanding with each penetration. He welcomed it. The gnawing ache of denied consumption turned the carnal rapture of his copulation with Amy to a dark bliss. It fed his demon and his demon thrived. This is what it was to be a vampire. Domination. Power. Possessing on all levels those weaker than he. First with his body and then with his mouth and teeth.

"I'm coming, Ven!" Amy cried out, not for the first time in the last two hours. "Oh, fucking Jesus Christ, I'm coming!"

A thin grin stretched Ven's lips and he withdrew his cock from her cunt in a sudden jerk. "No you're not, little girl." He grabbed a fistful of her hair, holding her to the lounge. He pumped his erection in his free hand. "Not until I say you are."

Amy whimpered, shoving her arse backward, trying to turn her head to look at him. "God, please, Ven, please!"

Her sobs lit a fire in Ven's core. He closed his eyes, enjoying the bright light burning into his eyelids even as the sun's shadow danced behind them. He'd made love in the sun before, many years ago, before his transformation, but he'd never realized its true beauty until now. The sun revealed all.

It felt exquisite. Heat and fire and molten electricity all at once.

His fangs grew longer still, piercing his bottom lip and his own blood trickled into his mouth, down his parched throat.

His demon screamed with ravenous need, its starvation at breaking point. He had not fed from the vein of a human for over forty-eight hours. The agony twisting through his pleasure was overwhelming. A potent aphrodisiac he'd never imagined possible.

Pumping at his cock in savage strokes, he opened his eyes again and stared at the sun through the window. Pleasure. Pain. Hunger. Fulfillment. He had it all. He needed nothing.

White eyes flashed into his head. The white eyes of timeless power.

Nothing except Death.

A jolt of scalding want for the Fourth Horseman stabbed into his chest, straight into his unbeating heart and, before he could stop it, thick wads of cum burst from his cock. Arcing through the air to fall onto Amy's smooth back.

Ven stared at the splattered product of his pleasure. Watched, fascinated as it dribbled over her sweat-soaked shoulder blade. And still primal desire burned through him. For Death. The woman and the demon.

"Fuck me, Ven. Please," Amy begged, her voice raw and terrified.

"What are you afraid of, little girl?" Ven growled, the ache and want in his core well on its way to devour any ability he still had for rational thought. Until he could claim the one he truly wanted, he would sate his hunger on the female before him. He tugged on her hair with one hand and plunged the middle finger of his other into her pussy. She bucked and pushed back into his hand, whimpering and sobbing even as she tried to grind her clit on his knuckle. "Tell me what you are afraid of and I will let you come."

Her sex squeezed his finger. "I'm scared of you, Ven!" she burst out, voice choked with fear. The very fear he could taste on the breath she exhaled and the perspiration slicking her skin. "I'm scared of you. Scared of what you are." She sobbed. "Scared you won't give me what I want."

Scalding rapture flooded Ven's still-rigid cock. At the very second ice-cold insight flooded his heart.

He was a monster. A depraved creature of depraved lust.

What was he doing?

What does it matter?

Bitter pleasure and baleful power claimed him and he chuckled, the sound low and soulless.

It was time to feed.

He tightened his fist in her hair and jerked her backward, slamming her against his chest. "Are you ready, little girl?" he breathed in her ear, slipping his finger from her sex.

She squirmed, shifting her legs further apart. "Yes." Her answer was hardly more than a whisper.

Ven smiled, saliva rolling down his fangs. "Of course you are." He aligned the head of his cock with her spread folds, lowered his head to her neck and—

The distinct scent of another vampire threaded into his nostrils.

Male vampire.

Fury erupted through him. Incinerating and absolute. She'd been with another vampire. Another vampire had taken what was only his to take. His demon screeched, and Ven yanked Amy harder to his chest.

So be it. If she wanted to be a vampire's food source, he would make her a vampire's food source. He would feed on her blood until there was nothing left in her veins to take. He would drain her dry until she was an empty carcass to be thrown away with the trash.

He opened his mouth. Touched his lips to Amy's bowed neck.

Tasted her fear and sweat with the tip of his tongue. Tasted the mark of the other vampire.

His demon roared. Ready, eager, for the kill. The sweet, sweet kill.

No.

The shout tore through his head. Snapped him frozen.

His shout. His voice. His *human* voice.

Guilt and horror smashed into him. He staggered backward, staring at her. Watching her turn to face him, her big brown eyes wide with petrified confusion.

Oh, Jesus. What had he just been about to do?

"Ven?" She took a step toward him, naked body flushed with perspiration, musky desire wafting to him on the air.

He shook his head, raising his hands as though to ward her off. "No."

She blinked, and in the space it took her eyelids to close, he spun about, snatched up his jeans and folded space.

Fleeing.

From her. From any living soul around him.

The morning sun slammed into him as he sliced through the air. He propelled himself over Kings Cross, particles of existence without substance or form. The monster within him screamed, furious at its denied kill and long-overdue feed. Confusion twisted in his consciousness, almost rivaling the agonizing hunger he felt. What was he doing?

Where was he going?

Patrick.

His brother's name flittered through the red haze of his torment but he forced the notion from his mind. He could not go near Patrick yet, no matter how desperate he longed for the sense of safety and familiarity his brother provided. He was too unstable. Too volatile. Too...

Dangerous?

Monstrous?

Weak.

The contemptuous thought filled him with self-loathing so sharp for a moment he felt himself ripping in two. Human. Demon. Both denied existence. Neither existing without the other.

Jesus, what are you doing?

The lashing of leaves and branches at his face and the strong smell of eucalyptus and seaweed on the air told him he'd reached his destination before he realized he was on the ground. He stumbled to a halt, nostrils flaring, and looked about his surroundings.

An ancient gum tree towered over him, standing at the edge his favorite beach, an isolated crescent of pristine sand and perfect curling waves just south of Bondi Beach. Hidden at the base of a craggy cliff, it was impossible to get to by foot and known only by a handful of the most diehard surfers. So small it had never been charted on any map that Ven knew of, nor named by any town planner. He'd surfed here with Patrick most days when alive. He surfed here most nights since dying.

A gentle offshore breeze blew against his face and he closed his eyes, letting its cool caress calm him.

The beach. Almost his second home. Peaceful. A place where he knew what he was at heart. Just an Aussie bloke who loved to surf.

Taking the comforting smell of the beach into his body, he opened his eyes, scanning the narrow strip and the waves beyond for signs of human life.

None. He had it all to himself.

"Thank the bloody Lord."

Watching a perfect set of waves crash over the beach's shallow coral reef, Ven let himself smile. He felt more relaxed already. Less an evil fiend. Better. He felt better.

Another breeze, this one a little stronger, a little colder, gusted past him and a surprised chuckle bubbled past his lips. 'Struth, he was naked. Where the hell were his jeans?

Spotting them crumpled on the ground amongst dry leaves and twigs a few steps away, he walked over and grabbed them up. The urge to cast them aside, to run down the sand and plunge head first into the breaking waves as naked as the day he was born rolled over him. He looked at the surf, lifted his gaze to the midday sun and back to the surf again. It was tempting. To submerge himself in the water...to submerge himself in a life he once thought lost to him forever.

The waves had no memory. They cast no judgment.

He took one step forward.

Go on. Do it. Let the surf scour away the guilt and contempt still churning in your gut. You know you'll feel better. Almost human, in fact.

Stinging disdain smacked into him, a merciless slap of reality. He scrunched up his face, yanking his jeans up his legs and over his arse. He wasn't human, no matter how much he longed to be so. What he'd just done to Amy in her living room, what he'd just been about to *do* to Amy proved that all too well. A quick skinny-dip in the ocean wasn't going to change the fact he was a vile creature of malevolent myth. What he had to do now was prove to himself he *wasn't* the monster lurking in his veins.

"Fair dinkum, you're one fucked up vampire, Steven Watkins."

He dropped to his arse on the sand, resting his elbows on his knees to watch the waves build and break, build and break in a lulling, perpetual rhythm. The sun peeked at him through the branches of the old eucalypt, painting him in a dappling pattern, and he closed his eyes again, breathing in the perfection of the moment. This was heaven. This was where, when the time came and some little Buffy wannabe staked him in the heart, he wanted to spent eternity. If he tried hard enough, he could almost believe the insidious, powerful hunger devouring him from within was just a case of the midday munchies.

A twig snapped behind him.

In a blur of shifting muscles, he was on his feet, his stare locking on the creature standing under the trees before him.

His throat slammed shut and his fists bunched. *Oh, fuck.*

"What the bloody hell are you?"

He is a q'thulu.

Ven started, snapping his head to the disembodied voice to his right.

A man stood there. A skinny man in a black suit with sallow flesh and lank, greasy hair.

The man smiled at him, revealing rotting yellow teeth.

He is a touch grumpy. I had to bend many rules to rouse him from his slumber, so I do not think this will be pleasant for you.

Ven blinked. Every molecule in his body churned. His stomach, sick from starvation, rolled. His demon screeched and without thought or hesitation, he shifted, letting the very thing he'd fled from mere minutes ago rear to the surface again.

Whoever the man in the suit was, Ven didn't like him. At all.

I must say, I have never been able to locate you, Steven Watkins. Until today, that is. It is surprising to find you standing in the sun. The man pursed his lips, a contemplative expression flashing across his face before he smiled. *I would stay to watch, but the sight of one demon tearing apart another quite frankly makes me feel ill.* Yellow teeth flashed in the sunlight, glistening with thick, putrid saliva. *Ironic, really.* He lifted his hand in a small wave. And vanished.

Throat squeezing tighter still, Ven swung his stare back to the horrific thing waiting amongst the trees. "Fuck," he muttered again.

The *q'thulu* stared at him with dead, black eyes, the thick tentacles of its face writhing and twisting. All seemingly reaching for Ven.

Its thin, puke-green wings flapped once, slapping the tree branches in clumsy aggression. It took a lumbering step forward, a high-pitched keening, like the cries of an ill baby, slipping from its nonexistent throat.

Ven was not deceived.

"'Struth, you're an ugly fucker, aren't you." He dropped into a crouch. "I don't know who the bloke holding your leash is, but it's time for me to go." He pictured an empty car park, *any* empty car park and launched himself into the air.

Only to be slapped back down to the ground by a massive tentacle, the suckers ripping chunks of flesh from his torso.

He hit the sand with a grunt, the bones in his right shoulder shattering on impact. Agony detonated through his back, up into his neck, down his arm. He staggered to his feet, spinning around to see the tentacle responsible for his pain squirm back to its place amongst those spewing from the *q'thulu's* face.

Ven bared his fangs, icy-hot pain stripping through his shoulder as the broken bones knitted instantly. Blood ran freely from the wounds torn in his torso, mingling with the sweat and sand caked on his chest. "That hurt, fucker."

The *q'thulu* lumbered forward, wings battering the trees

around it, displacing the air in decay-tainted gusts. Its lifeless black eyes stayed fixed on Ven, a terrible stare that made his flesh crawl.

Tensing his leg muscles, Ven prepared himself for flight once again.

And was knocked to the ground once again.

"Oww," he shouted. "Stop that." He scrambled to his feet...or at least, tried to. In a whiplash-quick blow, a fat tentacle wrapped around his hip and punched its meaty tip straight into his balls.

A bellow of rage ripped from his throat. He threw back his head, gouging deep furrows into the malicious tentacle with his claws as he fought with the agony exploding in his groin.

The *q'thulu* squealed, the tentacle releasing its crushing grip. He dropped to the ground with a thud, new pain exploding in his body. Fists bunched, fangs bared, he lowered himself into a crouching stance. The creature looked fat and slow, but it moved faster than he did.

How the hell did he kill it?

You just do.

An unknown voice reverberated through Ven's head. Undeniable. Impossible to ignore. A shiver ran through him at its authority, its ascendency. His lifeless heart thumped. Once.

Six thick tentacles lashed out from the *q'thulu's* face, wrapped around the truck of a young eucalyptus tree and tore it from the ground. A squealing cry pierced Ven's ears and then the *q'thulu* threw the tree straight at him.

He leapt backward, just as the tree crashed into the ground on the very spot he'd been standing. Staring hard at the *q'thulu*, he took another step back, searching for even ground. He needed a plan of attack. He could sink his teeth into the flabby mass of pudgy fat that may or may not be a neck, hopefully severing its main artery, but did he really want to? He was hungry, but was he that hungry?

"I bet you taste like calamari, don't you, fat boy?"

The *q'thulu* let out a low, wet grunt, wings trembling, tentacles lashing.

Ven eyed the hideous thing. "Never been a fan of calamari."

He shot forward, aiming for the *q'thulu's* grotesque neck, mouth wide, fangs lengthening. A shimmer of icy heat rippled through him, almost identical to the sensation he experienced every time he folded space. Suddenly his arms were longer and more muscled, his flesh no longer pale but jet black and leathery. He flexed his fingers and found them to be talons larger than an eagle's.

The *q'thulu's* dead eyes rolled. It hissed, its tentacles thrashing on its face.

Fucker's scared, Ven thought, mid-lunge. Seconds before his massive wings—*wings*—thumped once more and he slammed into the *q'thulu's* equally massive form.

A piercing squeal shattered the still air. The *q'thulu* stumbled backward, its tentacles whipping at Ven's face.

But even that was different. He could feel it. Gone was his nose, his lips. The tentacles slapped at him, but it wasn't him they struck. Sinking his talons deep into the thing's flabby shoulders, he pumped his wings, forcing it backward, backward until it lost its footing and fell to the ground.

And even then he didn't let up. He snapped up his legs and sank the talons on his feet into its gut, ripping at its thick flesh, tearing its stomach open as the force from his wings drove it harder into the sandy ground.

The *q'thulu* thrashed beneath him, piss and black ink spurting from its body, its face. Ven snarled, ducking the vile, stinking fluid and frenzied tentacles. "Nasty bugger, aren't you."

Enormous arms struck out at him, but he swatted them away with his wings, tearing into the *q'thulu's* shoulders in punishment for its stupidity. The creature wailed, legs and arms flailing, hot guts spilling from the gaping hole Ven's feet continued to tear into its body.

Calm determination rolled through him. Whatever he was,

he was made for this. The utter destruction of something so vile and evil.

Hooking the talons on his feet deeper into the *q'thulu's* oozing gut, his wings acting as a counterbalance, he released his grip on its shoulders and grabbed two fistfuls of writhing tentacles. He crushed them in his grip, holding its head in a fierce lock. "Hold still, fat boy." He lowered his head to the *q'thulu's* face. "Let's get a look at what I've become."

He stared into its wide eyes, drawing closer, closer until he saw his reflection in their bulging black surface. Saw his serpentine face, his pupiless white eyes, his lipless mouth full of razor-sharp teeth.

By the Powers, what am *I?*

Pestilence dropped into his throne with a thud, his mouth open, his blood roaring in his ears. He gazed blankly at his empty bed, his disbelief robbing him of sight. The lifeguard's cursed brother had killed the *q'thulu.*

Molten-red fury ripped through him. By the Powers, the fucking blood sucker had killed the *q'thulu.* It was not possible. No lower-order demon could kill a second-order demon, no matter how fast or strong or powerful.

"Fuck!" he screamed, gouging his nails into the throne's green bone armrest, feeling the veins in his neck and temple throb. This was not happening.

Drawing his power into his core, he reached through the Veil with his mind for Raziel. A wave of blackness threatened to consume him but he fought it. The "visit" to the beach had drained him more than he had expected, the projection into the world of man like forcing his existence through a wall of solid nothingness. He had taken the risk despite the danger, wanting to see the look of terror on Steven Watkins' face.

Incensed rage smashed through him and he roared. It had

all been for nothing. Nothing!

Sinking his nails deeper into the armrest, he locked his mind onto the sleeping vampire and "jerked" him from his undead slumber.

"I do not care how you do it," he growled into Raziel's head, a cold twist of joy threading through his fury at the sudden fear he sensed in the vampire's core. "I do not care that the human sun is still in the sky, I want the key. The woman. I want the female human brought to me. Now."

Patrick smoothed his hand up Fred's bare back, enjoying the velvet feel of her flesh, the firmness of her fine muscles under his palm. She uttered a contented moan, sliding her knee further up his thigh and wriggling closer to the side of his body. Her soft, full breasts pushed against his ribcage, the tight peak of her nipples brushing the side of his chest in a tantalizing tickle that left Patrick's mouth dry.

"I think I've said this already," she traced lazy circles over his stomach, "but that feels nice."

Patrick smiled and pressed his lips to her forehead, pulling in a deep breath of her wonderful scent as he did so. "You have, but feel free to say it again."

Fred chuckled, rolling onto his body to grin down at him. "Now you know I'm not going to do something as clichéd as that."

He returned her laugh, exploring her back and hips with his hands, letting the tips of his fingers brush the swell of her butt cheeks. "There is *nothing* clichéd about you, Fred."

She preened with melodramatic pride, shifting her hips until the damp heat of her sex aligned with the growing stiffness of his. "I will take that as a compliment."

He laughed again. "Of course you will."

Wriggling about on his body, she let her legs slide either

side of his thighs, supporting her upper body on her elbows as she rolled her hips upward. "Laugh again. That feels *really* good."

A sizzling lick of heat worked its way into Patrick's groin at her intimate position and suggestive request. Holding her arse cheeks in a firm grip, he did as she asked, keeping her pussy atop his lengthening shaft the entire duration.

She murmured her appreciation, eyes closed, lips curled into a cheeky smile. "Mmmm...thank you."

He cocked an eyebrow. "Is that how you're going to thank me?"

She returned her gaze to his face, and he clenched his jaw at the serious light suddenly glowing in her eyes. "Depends." She tilted her head, a frown creasing her forehead. "Are we going to finish our conversation about Pestilence any time soon?"

Patrick bit back a growl. Damn, he thought he'd successfully distracted her from that train of—

"Not even close."

He shot Fred a glare. "If you're reading my mind now, we can just call this off straight away. I don't understand what's in there half the time without someone *else* poking around in there as well."

"I'm not reading your mind, Patrick. I could tell by the look on your normally unreadable face." She placed her hands on his chest, and if he didn't know better he'd think she was holding him prisoner.

Why?

To lecture you?

"As much as I want to impale myself on your very impressive male appendage," she gave him a dirty grin, "we need to prepare for whatever Pestilence has planned. I need to help you get ready."

A heavy beat thumped in Patrick's chest and he turned his head aside. *The end shall be the beginning and the beginning shall be the end.* The Cure and the Disease facing off in what was sure to be a real bastard of a fight. A lowly Australian lifeguard and an agent of the Apocalypse. Yeah, he really wanted to think about that.

And now you're just being churlish, Watkins. Grow some balls, will you. You can't stay here like this with Fred forever.

Why not?

Letting out a sigh, he turned back to Fred, his chest squeezing tight at her beauty. He'd heard it said more than once—usually the last whispered words of elderly swimmers dying on the beach—that Death was a beautiful thing. He understood now. She was. She was also a stubborn pain in the arse.

"You've told me I can't kill him. You've told me *you* can't kill him. Seems to me the battle's already been decided."

"That's not true. You're not listening to me. There are ways Pestilence can be defeated, but only if you are ready." Eyes flashing with frustration, she shook her head, her long black hair tumbling about her shoulders. Patrick pulled in a breath. He wanted to bury his hands in that shiny, silky curtain, tug her face down to his and kiss her senseless, not talk about his upcoming appointment with a man he'd already met once who attacked him with bugs and made him almost throw up with just a look.

Churlish again, Watkins. Grow up.

"Shit," he muttered.

Fred studied him, her eyes shimmering with white light. "Lift me up," she said suddenly, gripping his hips tightly with her inner thighs.

Patrick frowned at her, the unexpected command and abrupt change in conversation throwing him for a loop. "Huh?"

Fred squeezed her thighs harder against his hips and a tendril of unpleasant discomfort ribboned through his hipbones.

"Lift me up."

"Hey!" He moved beneath her, trying to escape the discomfort of her increasingly brutal hold.

Her eyes flashed white again and she lowered her face closer to his. "Lift. Me. Up."

Sharp irritation flared within his chest. He curled his fingers into her hips and tried to shove her from his body. But she didn't move.

"Is that the best you can do?"

Patrick ground his teeth, anger joining his heated irritation. He glared up at her, increasing the pressure of his fingers on her hips. "Get off me, Fred."

She bared her teeth in a dark smile. "Make me."

He shoved at her again.

And again she didn't move.

"Not that way, Patrick." Her expression turned deadly and she squeezed her thighs until a shard of white pain tore through his hip joints. "The other way."

Chapter Ten

Fred stared down at Patrick imprisoned between her thighs and pressed her legs harder to his hips. The sharp angle of his hipbones dug into her thighs, a drilling pain she shut from her mind. She needed Patrick to react. If she had to hurt him, then so be it.

What Pestilence planned to do to him was far worse.

He squirmed beneath her, his fingertips digging into her, his eyes flat. He still resisted moving her with his mind. She could see the dogged determination to shift her physically etched in his face. Along with a bleak contempt she knew was directed at himself.

Whatever Patrick was, he loathed it.

She needed him to embrace it. For his sake and the sake of mankind.

If he didn't Pestilence would achieve the unthinkable.

She crushed his hips harder still, drawing perverse resolve from the unnatural light flickering in his angry glare. He was close. Even as he shoved at her hips with his hands, the force within him surged to the fore.

She hoped.

"What are you, weak?" she goaded, fighting his physical strength. It took all her considerable power to remain planted on his hips and groin. He was strong. Very strong. The muscles in his chest and shoulders bulged, growing ropey and hard before her eyes. At another time, such an undeniable display of his might and vigor would have made her sex constrict and her pulse leap away from her, but at this moment it infuriated her. He didn't need to use his body.

He needed to use his—

Crushing heat gripped her arms. There was a split second where Fred *knew* she was about to be torn in two by inescapable, unseen hands and then, with a sudden invisible, brutal shove on her chest, belly and face, she flew backward. Flung across the room by nothing she could see.

She smashed into the wall, her teeth clicking shut, the breath forced out of her lungs in a loud *oof*, and fell to the floor in a crumpled heap.

"Fred!"

Patrick was on his knees before her, his hands on her bowed shoulders, his eyes flooded with horror before she had time to comprehend her new position or the dull red agony coursing through her body.

She grimaced, struggling into a semi-sitting position and gave him a wobbly grin. "Okay, that kinda went to plan."

"Bloody hell, woman." Patrick dropped back to his heels, his glare returning. "What the fuck were you thinking?"

Fred pressed a hand to her shoulder and worked the joint a few times. Nope. Not dislocated. Just damn sore. "I was thinking to get you pissed off enough to do just what you did. Didn't expect you to throw me into a wall, however."

Patrick's eyes widened and he stared at her, obviously at a loss for words.

She grinned, and then grimaced again. By the Powers, even her face hurt. "So what we need to do now is teach you how to control that. Manipulate it at will."

Patrick shook his head. "I didn't do anything, Fred."

"Yes, you did." She twisted a little, biting back a hiss of pain as she looked at the wall behind her. "And there's a great big dent in the drywall to prove it."

Patrick's stare slid to the cracked indent, his nostrils

flaring as he pulled in a quick breath.

“You know you did that, Patrick,” Fred said, moving—albeit, with considerable care—onto her knees to take his hands in hers. “In the exact same way you destroyed the *nikor* at the beach. In the same way you started to crush me earlier today when you were questioning me about Pestilence.”

“And what way is that?”

Fred shrugged, inching closer to him until their knees touched. “Telekinesis, I would think, but no form of telekinesis I know. Moving something with your mind is one thing, tearing things apart with it, like aqueous demons for example, is another thing all together.”

A look of disgust crossed Patrick’s face and he dragged his hands through his hair. “Damn, I feel like I’ve been thrown in the deep end here.”

“No you haven’t, Patrick.” Fred gazed into his eyes, wanting him to see her belief, her absolute conviction in him. That he was finally admitting he’d done it without looking like he wanted to kill someone was a step forward. Now she just needed him to burst into a sprint. “You may not have even realized it, but I’d wage a millennium of picking up Cerberus’s poo you’ve been using your...power, for want of a better word, your whole life.”

He chuckled at the extent of her bet, a wry sound that made her heart soar. He may have said he wouldn’t back away from this task laid at his feet earlier when his blood had run hot with rage, but now, calmer and more focused, she could hear the acceptance of his laugh. They were on their way. Thank the Powers.

Patrick’s forehead creased into a frown. “Question?”

Fred nodded, itching to begin. She had no idea of Pestilence’s time frame. He may be readying for his assault any second now.

“Why can’t *you* stop the Disease? Surely Death has more clout than a human?” A very cheeky smile pulled at his lips. “Even an Australian human?”

Releasing a sigh, Fred shook her head. "The Horsemen cannot interfere with each other's purpose. We exist separately but as a holistic one. We cannot cancel each other out, nor stop the others' action. The Order of Actuality will not allow an entity to directly impact on one of his or her designs. We, the Horsemen, are set into the Weave. We have our purpose and that purpose is paramount. Even someone as hideously horrible as Pestilence has a supreme place in the Weave. The Powers and the Trilogy would not have it any other way."

Patrick pulled a face. "I figured that's what you'd say."

Fred laughed. Whatever Patrick was, whatever he was to become, he had the most unique ability to make her laugh. His sardonic, dry humor made her feel, of all things, warm and fuzzy inside.

That's cause you're in—

"What I *can* do," she cut the thought short, not willing or able to deal with its implication now, "is prepare you."

He gave her a puzzled look. "These Powers, this Trilogy...surely you can tell them what Pestilence is planning?"

"And tell them what? The Powers are not all benevolent, Patrick. The Realm is not the 'heaven and hell' assumed by human religion. There are those in the Powers who would gladly welcome the Apocalypse and the demise of man." She let out a sharp sigh. "There are benevolent entities who would welcome it also." Cocking an eyebrow, she gave Patrick a pointed look. "The human race has not been entirely well behaved during its time of rule. What you have done to the planet alone some deem worthy of decimation, let alone what you do to each other. There are many arguments already raging for the destruction of the Trilogy's most favored, and I fear not as many voices calling for your support and salvation as there once was. If I were to announce what I think Pestilence is planning, and I must remind you, my theory is all still based on conjecture and the words of a missing seer and an author who preferred to remain anonymous, there is the distinct possibility some entities more powerful than I may decide to choose a side." She frowned and shook her head. "We cannot risk that. Mankind cannot risk that. You are it. The Cure."

Patrick blew out a harsh breath, and Fred thought sure she heard the word "fuck" vibrating on its expulsion.

"Now." She rose to her feet and looked down at him. "Get off your ass and fling something against the wall again. I want to see if I can detect what you are doing. We need to make your 'strikes' as unexpected as possible."

With a low grumble and a roll of his eyes, Patrick climbed to his feet. "I'm getting the definite feeling you're a bossy bit of goods." He brushed his palms on his thighs and scanned his living room. "God help me if I actually walk away from this thing alive," he muttered, studying a particularly large armchair positioned in front of the small television. "How I'm going to handle being told what to do for the rest of my life is beyond me."

A wicked, tight little thrill shot through Fred at his words. The rest of his life... The rest of his life with her. In Patrick's mind, they were together.

Aren't you thinking the same way?

An unexpected image of Steven popped into Fred's head, taking her completely by surprise. She turned her head away, hiding her confused scowl from Patrick's sight. Fang face's demon *did* call to hers, did push buttons Patrick had yet to find. But she couldn't think about that now. Things were tricky enough without the worry of an inconvenient love triangle getting in the road.

The sudden smashing of the television against the far wall made her jump and she spun about, gaping at Patrick who stood a few yards away.

He grinned, the expression both boyish and infinitely old. "Am I allowed to say that was fun?"

Unable to stop herself, Fred laughed. "I think you are."

"Are you sure this is the kind of activity you want to be doing now?" Patrick wriggled his eyebrows at her. "I can think of other much more 'hands-on' training."

The pit of Fred's belly did a little flip-flop. She shoved her hands on her hips, cocking an eyebrow even as her sex throbbed with the thought of Patrick's "hands on" attention. "What?" she said, just managing to keep her voice steady. "You want me to kick your butt around the room?"

He laughed and, without the slightest change in expression or the slightest tensing of his muscles, a cushion launched itself from the armchair now facing a blank wall and flew across the room, whacking Fred in the side of the head before she could blink.

She snatched it from her shoulder as it began to tumble to the ground, fixing Patrick with a glare. "Think you're clever, don't you."

He didn't say anything, but his eyebrows wriggled again.

A rolling wave of warm bliss traveled through Fred. From the top of her head all the way down to the tip of her metaphysical tail. She was happy. Patrick made her happy. Happier than she'd ever felt.

So, don't just stand there grinning like a prize-grade moron. Get him ready to win. So you can feel like this forever.

The last word echoed through her soul and she clenched her fists, locking her focus on the still-grinning Patrick.

She threw herself at him, dissolving her form into a blurring dart of blackness. Slicing through the air as insubstantial as smoke and faster than light.

A wall of rock-hard ice smashed into her. Folded around her. She felt the air she'd just been defying crush down on her.

Too easy.

She didn't know whose voice murmured in her head, hers or Patrick's or some other entity. She didn't want to ponder who may be observing the moment, but it ignited her demon. There was no time to treat Patrick with kid gloves.

With a flick of her metaphysical wrist, she shattered the force pushing down on her. Pestilence would not play fair, so neither would she.

In a shimmer of silver light, she snatched her scythe out of thin air and swung it at Patrick in a blurring arc.

His eyes snapped wide just as the head of its solid wooden staff struck him under the armpit. He careened sideways, his hip smashing into the edge of the sofa they'd only recently made love on, sending him tumbling to the floor in a flurry of arms and legs.

She destroyed the distance between them in a single leap, bare feet planting on the sofa's ridge, her arms already swinging her scythe back in preparation to deliver another blow.

A fist she didn't see smashed into her chin in an uppercut that detonated a galaxy of stars behind her eyes. She flipped backward, scythe falling from her hand, white pain ripping through her chin and jaw. Her feet thumped against the floor, spread wide, taking the shock from her landing just as Patrick leapt to his feet and fixed her with a wide grin from the other side of the sofa.

"This is what some would call dicing with Death."

Fred grinned back. She could detect a steely tone in Patrick's cheek. He was only just warming up. "This is what I call an arse whooping."

He snorted. And, eyes erupting blazing fire, he "picked" her up and flung her across the room.

Her back and arse hit the armchair, and before she could propel herself out of it, invisible bands lashed around her wrists, her ankles, pinning her to the ridiculously comfortable piece of furniture.

She struggled against the unseen hold, her sex instantly wet and heavy with lust. Now was not the time to get horny. *Aaargh!*

Pussy throbbing, pulse pounding, she shot Patrick a quick look.

He stalked towards her. There was no other way to describe the way he moved. Captor to captured prey.

Grinding her teeth, Fred strained against the force on her wrists to no avail. She couldn't shift her hands from the chair's armrests no matter what she did.

Flicking her stare to her fallen scythe on the floor beside the sofa, she willed it to her.

There was a ripple of disturbed air and the most iconic weapon of death whipped across the room—only to be snatched from its journey by Patrick as it shot by his head.

He continued to walk toward her, holding her scythe like he'd been born with it in his hand. Another impossibility connected to Patrick Watkins—no one but Death herself should be able to wield the device.

Eyes burning, he raised the instrument of death and leveled its razor-sharp tip to Fred's eyes.

She held her breath, drawing all her power into her core.

"Time for a time-out," Patrick murmured, dropping the scythe to her breastbone. He hooked the very tip into the neckline of her shirt.

And sliced it open.

It was the first time Fred had ever been disrobed by anyone but herself. Wet electricity shot straight to her sex and she came. Just like that. She gasped, the sudden, powerful orgasm making her shudder, the cool air on her now fully exposed breasts making her already greedy for more.

A low groan of appreciation rumbled up Patrick's chest and his eyes flared brighter. Hotter. "Beautiful. So very beautiful."

Fred gave him a slow smile, the junction of her thighs sodden and pulsing. "Powerful." She thrust out with her mind, shoving Patrick across the room.

He hit the wall with a soft, controlled thud, her scythe dropping from his hand, his eyes locked on her.

The invisible bands on Fred's arm and ankles evaporated instantly and she was on her feet, prowling toward him with deliberate intent, the echo of her orgasm still radiating through her body. She "removed" her shorts with a thought, closing the short distance between them with two steps.

His breath heated her already flushed flesh. His jaw bunched.

She held out her arm and her scythe materialized in her hand.

Patrick's nostrils flared.

Without a word, Fred pressed the flat edge of the blade to his chest and stomach, tip pointing to the floor, and slowly, slowly slid it downward. Past the waistband of his boxers, until its deadly length rested beside the rigid length of his thick cock. "Time-out," she whispered on a grin.

Patrick's nostrils flared again. His lips curled into a slow smile, he opened his mouth...and froze as a violent gust of midnight black smoke shot through the open window beside his head.

"Jesus!" Ven burst out, materializing in the centre of the room, human save for his elongated fangs. "You won't believe what just..." He trailed off, his stare sliding from Patrick to Fred to Patrick again. "Am I interrupting something?"

"Bloody hell, Ven!" Patrick stormed. "It's about time you learnt to knock."

Ven snarled something in reply, but Fred didn't hear it.

Because at the very second Ven formed in Patrick's living room, the iconic hooded robe of the Grim Reaper covered her body. Without any conscious thought or decision from her.

And the base of her spine had begun to itch.

Really itch.

What in all the levels of hell was going on?

Chapter Eleven

Ven tasted sex and sweat on the air. He looked at his brother, a surge of something tight and uncomfortable churning in his gut.

Patrick glared at him, his eyes a dark shade of green Ven had never seen before. "What the hell have you been doing, Ven?"

Crossing his arms across his chest, Ven gave him a dark scowl. "Nothing as exciting as you, it seems, brother." He shot Fred an even darker scowl. "Nice getup, Death. Goes well with your eyes."

"Ven."

Patrick's growl jerked Ven's attention back to his brother and he let out a short grunt. Since leaving the beach and the garroted carcass of the *q'thulu,* he'd been attacked by something far more horrific—guilt. Guilt for what he'd done to Amy, guilt for the way he'd treated Patrick before buggering off. He'd told himself he was going to apologise to both. He hadn't expected to find a half-starkers Patrick with a completely starkers Death hip to hip in Patrick's living room.

Another twisting knot tightened in his gut and he ground back a growl. He had no fucking clue what had just happened to him on the sand, but whatever it was, it was more important than what was going on between his brother and the Grim Reaper.

"Mind telling me what's going on, Steven?"

Patrick's arms were folded across his chest in a mirror of his own pose and a wry sense of comfort threaded into the knot in his gut. His brother.

"There I was," he began, doing his best not to look at Death—what *was* she doing in that getup?—"minding my own business at the cliff beach when I'm attacked out of the blue by some fucked-up squid-faced thing some skinny bloke in a black suit who pops out of nowhere calls a *q'thulu.*"

"Black suit?"

Fred's sharp voice made Ven frown and he gave her a quick scowl. "Yeah. Black suit. Greasy hair. Looks like he hasn't cleaned his teeth in, oh, I don't know, a millennium Anyways, he—"

"Pestilence."

Both Death's and Patrick's growl stop him. He frowned at them, the tightness in his gut returning. "Yes, he was a pest. A bloody great big pest. Can somebody tell me why some drongo with bad hair, a face as ugly as a hat full of arse-holes and even worse dental care turns up at my beach and sets a *q'thulu* on me? And while we're at it, what the bloody hell *is* a *q'thulu*?"

He was ranting. He knew that. His mouth was running off and he'd slipped so far into Australian vernacular he could almost see his high school English teacher crying into her perpetually cold cup of tea. But while he was ranting he didn't have time to think about the obvious connection between Death and Patrick. While he was carrying on like an idiot he didn't have to face the fact he'd become something much, much more than a vampire. Something with more power and purpose than he could begin to comprehend.

Jesus, when had life—sorry, when had being undead—become so bloody complicated?

When the little piece of goods in the black robe turned up in Patrick's bedroom.

Ven snorted, the sound short and frustrated. "Women," he muttered.

Death's eyebrows shot up. "Excuse me?"

He shook his head, stormed across to the sofa and flopped into it. "Nothing." He gave his brother a frown. "I see you got your clothes off again."

Patrick glared. "I see you forgot your manners again."

"By the Powers." Death threw up her hands, the arms of her robe billowing about her head like a black shroud. "Will you pair stop it?" She shoved the hood from her head and scowled at them both. "You're brothers. Behave like it."

An unexpected chuckle bubbled up Ven's throat, its warm mirth taking him by surprise. "What?" he laughed. "You want us to wrestle each other to the floor until someone yells 'uncle'?"

"Or punch each other in the arm repeatedly to see who throws up first?" Patrick offered, giving her a grin so cheeky and goofy Ven wanted to hug him there and then. His brother. No matter who he was standing around half-naked with, Patrick was still his kid brother. Just a little more...special then some.

Like you?

The thought stilled Ven's easy laugh and he frowned, sinking back into the sofa to stare at his feet.

Like him.

"Fang face?"

What was he now? And why him? What was going on?

"Steven?"

He glared at his feet, a dull ache in his gut the first reminder since leaving the beach he still hadn't fed. Well, whatever he was, that hadn't changed. He still needed to feed. He closed his eyes, letting his thoughts turn to his hunger for a moment before biting back a curse. He still needed to feed on blood. Human blood. So much for being a better standard of monster now.

"Steven!"

Patrick's shout jerked him out of his reverie and he pulled a face at his brother. "What?"

"I said, what happened at the beach? What did Pestilence say? What did he do? What's this *q'thulu* and did you kill it?"

"Pestilence—stupid bloody name—rattled off some crap about breaking rules and then disappeared up his own—what?" He turned his glare on Death, who was staring at him with such intensity his skin felt like it was being trampled by a swarm of ants.

Her eyes narrowed and she tilted her head to the side. "There's something different about you, fang face."

"Yeah. I almost had my butt sucked off by a squid monster, which, by the way, was not as erotic as it sounds."

Death shook her head again. "No, that's not it." She moved from Patrick's side to stand before him, staring down at him with eyes no longer blue but an iridescent white.

He gazed into those eyes, feeling the force, the power of their infinite depths. A shiver rippled through him, cold and hot at once, and before he could move, she reached and placed her palms on either side of his face.

"Hey!" he yelled, indignant, ignoring the ironic fact only two hours ago he wanted nothing more than to have her hands all over his body. "What the hell are you—"

He didn't finish.

With a sharp hiss, Death jerked her hands from his head, fingers wide, eyes wider. She took a step backward, staring at him with something close to horror on her face. "By the Trilogy..."

Her stunned murmur faded away.

Ven gaped up at her, his heart hammering, his mouth dry. "What? What did you feel?"

"Tell me what's going on, Fred?" Patrick appeared at her side, and a detached part of Ven's mind, the part not freaking out at Death's strange behavior, noticed his brother seemed to move and speak with a confidence he'd never possessed before. It seemed Ven wasn't the only one who'd undergone a change today. But what did it all mean? And was it for the good?

Death flicked Patrick a quick look, her forehead furrowing. "I need to test something. I think..." She turned back to Ven, regarding him with an expression he could only call guarded. "I need to take you both somewhere. Now."

"Where?" Patrick asked, and again, Ven was struck by the poise and self-assurance in his baby brother's voice and demeanor.

She looked at him, her teeth worrying her bottom lip. A tiny jolt of something that may have once been desire worked its way through Ven's chest at the sight, but he ignored it. Whatever he was, Death sensed it and was confused by it. Confused and apprehensive.

That wasn't good.

He stood up, brushing past her and his brother. "I'm not going anywhere until I've had a feed," he threw over his shoulder on his way to the front door. "I'm starving, I'm tired and I smell like fish piss. After I've had a bite, a sleep and a shower, probably in that order, then you can start drawing up travel plans. Until then..." He stopped at the door and turned around, tipping a sarcastic wave their way.

Death looked at him from across the room, eyes white. Glowing. "Sorry, Steven." Her voice rumbled through him like thunder. "But I'm not asking."

Apprehension flooded through Fred. She stared at Steven, even as she felt Patrick step up behind her and smooth his hands over her hips, as if he knew what she was about to do. That he may very well be able to do such a thing should have scared the metaphysical shit out of her and had her tailbone itching like an insane demon, but it didn't. Not anymore. Nothing about Patrick Watkins scared her anymore. His brother on the other hand...

She braced herself, knowing she was about to break one of the highest rules of the Realm, but unwilling to risk any other course of action. Not yet. Not until she had her answers. She needed those answers. The human race needed those answers.

Reaching out for the brothers with her mind, folding them into her existential vortex, she pictured her next location.

And transubstantiated them all to the Realm.

Patrick stared at Death, unable to take his eyes from her. They were somewhere dark, somewhere warm, but he'd yet to take in his surrounding. Where he was didn't matter at that very moment. At that very moment what mattered was how Fred was behaving.

Like she expected to be attacked.

She stood frozen, long, dark hair blacker than pitch, pale skin even paler in the soft, muted light. The infamous Grim Reaper's robe she'd worn in his living room was replaced by black denim jeans, black biker boots and black silk hoodie, but the casual items of clothing did nothing to hide the tension in her body, the sublime coiling of every muscle, ready to...what? Attack? Defend?

Moving his stare to her face, Patrick hissed in a quick breath. Her eyes smoldered with white, burning light, like the infinite fires of some eternal energy force. There was power in those eyes he'd never witnessed before. Power and pain and menace. For the first time since seeing her, he recognized her for what she was—an entity of sheer and absolute force. It sent a shiver through his body. It made his cock pulse.

Bloody hell, Patrick. Now is not the time.

He rolled his eyes and let out a harsh sigh, shaking his head in disgust.

"Well." The tension suddenly flowed from Fred's body and she smiled. "That clears up one thing."

"Clears up what?" Ven snapped, and it took a second for Patrick to realize his brother stood to his left. In full vamp mode. "Where the hell are we?"

"Not hell, Steven," Fred replied, turning to Ven. "Home."

Patrick watched her give his brother a wide, cheeky grin and a shard of something dark and wrong stabbed into his chest. Something a lot like jealousy. He ground his teeth, another surge of disgust roaring through him. Here he was, caught up in the middle of the coming Apocalypse brought about by some wanker with what, in Patrick's mind, could only be called "short-entity syndrome", and he was getting jealous? Jesus, he needed to get his act together.

"Gentlemen." Fred's voice jerked him from his self-contempt and he looked at her, noticing her eyes were once again their original glacier blue. "Welcome to the Realm."

"Great," Ven growled. "Bloody fantastic. Just where I wanted to be. Who does your decorating?"

The surly venom in his brother's snarl made Patrick blink. He turned, finding Ven had dropped into one of two leather armchairs positioned before an open fireplace, arms crossed, human once again.

Armchairs? Fireplace? He frowned and let his attention finally move to his surroundings.

The room was small, almost cosy, with polished wooden lamp tables on which sat squat, bronze lamps. Floor-to-ceiling shelves on three of the walls, stuffed full with books of all sizes and thickness, and a massive open fireplace made from what looked like black granite dominated the wall before him. A fire blazed in its guts, the flames licking the air in undisturbed tongues of heat, casting a warm yellow glow over the room and its comfortable pieces of furniture—and the silently snarling vampire hulking in one of said pieces.

"What's the point of bringing us here, Death?" Ven thumped his heels onto the low table sitting in front of the two armchairs, his expression grumpy. "Not satisfied with doing my brother in the real world anymore?"

"The real world?" Patrick turned his stare from his brother to Fred. "The Realm? Where are we?"

"The place between the void and the final destination," Ven answered, studying his feet—which Patrick realized, were bare.

"The home of the Order."

He frowned. "Of Actuality?"

Ven shook his head. "The Order of the Agents."

"How do you know that?"

Fred's demand swung both their heads in her direction. She was staring at Ven, the same intense light in her eyes he'd seen before she'd done whatever it was she did to bring them all here. An intense light that said she had discovered something terrible. Or incredible. "Tell me how long you've known about the Realm, Steven. And the Order of the Agents."

Patrick turned back to his brother.

Ven shrugged, but the firm set in his jaw and the stubborn look in his eye, a look Patrick had seen more than once, told him the shrug was a lie. "What's going on, Steven? The Agents of what?"

"Something has happened to your brother, Patrick. Something..." Fred stopped, and again that incredulous expression flashed across her face.

Ven snapped to his feet, fixing Fred with a hard stare. "What *has* happened to me, Death? Come on, you know all the answers. How come I *do* know all this shit about the Agents of the Order, and the Powers and the Realm and the Void now? One minute the sum total knowledge I have in my head is what I learnt growing up, the next, after my run in with the bloke in the black suit and his squid-faced friend, I'm a walking, talking encyclo-bloody-pedia on all things fucked-up and paranormal. How come I now know exactly what a seraph is? What a cherub is? Who Abaddon is and why it's best not to let him catch you unawares? Tell me that. Tell me what's going on and I'll—"

Fred cut him short. "I need to test my theory."

Ven's eyebrows knotted for a brief moment and then his jaw clenched. "And how do you do that, exactly?"

Fred's tongue darted out to wet her lips, a hesitant, almost nervous action that made Patrick's throat squeeze tight. Why did he get a bad feeling about this?

"Your blood. I need to taste your blood."

Ven vamped out. Instantly. Completely. He hissed, his fingers—longer than normal and tipped with thick claws—wrapped around Fred's throat and he jerked her from the floor.

"Steven!" Patrick shouted, lunging at his brother.

"No one is tasting my blood," Ven growled, his eyes burning with a wild yellow light.

"It won't—" Fred began, but Ven threw her across the small room before she could finish.

She arced through the space. And the space shifted.

The room shimmered and before Fred hit the wall, the wall wasn't there.

She twisted midair and landed feet first on the floor, her face set as she strode back toward him, the room reforming around her with each step she took. "The other choice is I kill your brother," she stated, matter-of-fact.

It felt like he'd been punched in the gut. Patrick gaped at her. Did she just say what he thought she said?

"You won't kill your lover, Death." Ven clenched his fist, glaring at her. "Pardon the cliché, but I've seen the way you look at him. What does it mean to the world that the Grim Reaper is in love?"

Fred's eyes hardened. "On imminent death, the soul releases everything into the Void. The person's life flashes before their eyes, as such. But to me, I see it all. Their life. Their past. Their entire connection to the mortal coil. If I kill Patrick…"

Ven shook his head. "No."

"Then let me taste your blood."

Ven shook his head again. "The last time one of your kind tasted my blood, I became a fucking monster."

His voice cracked, though from anger or something far more wrenching, Patrick could not tell.

Oh, Jesus, Ven.

Patrick's heart thumped and he closed his eyes, the

realization of what his brother had been through, what he'd suffered since they'd been attacked that night outside the pub all those years ago really sinking in for the first time—the torment and torture and sacrifice.

He'd died protecting Patrick. His neck had been torn open, his blood had gushed from his body, draining from his veins in thick, red rivers and yet he'd never been allowed the release death brought.

Gut churning, Patrick stepped between Fred and Ven, and gave Fred a level look. "No."

Her eyebrows shot up. "I need to know this, Patrick."

"Because it changes the balance of power in my upcoming confrontation with Pestilence? Or because you hate not knowing the answers? Because you hate being confused?"

The second the words passed his lips, Patrick knew they were the wrong ones. Fred's eyes turned white. Iridescent white. But it mattered not. He wouldn't let her do what she wanted to do to his brother. Even if it meant he, Patrick, went into battle against the First Horseman with nothing but a cricket bat and bad sarcasm.

"Patrick," Fred began, but he shook his head.

"No, Death."

She turned her white, glowing eyes to Ven. "I need to know, Steven. You should have died when I touched you eighteen years ago. I severed your life thread. No one survives that. You should never have transformed into a vampire. I need to know why. If you've become what I think you've become, I need to know how."

Patrick felt his brother shift behind his back. He turned, seeing confusion, fear and anger swimming in his eyes. And surrender? "No, Steven." He shook his head, giving him a dry smile. "Not this. I won't let her do this to you."

Ven looked at him, his every muscle coiled, his vampire's face tormented. "Pat..."

"It's not important, Ven," Patrick said. "Unless you say it

is."

A shudder passed through Ven's body and his human façade, so like Patrick's their parents complained often it was eerie, stood in the room again. His gaze slid to Fred, his throat moving up and down as he swallowed.

"She won't kill me, Ven." Patrick gave his brother a broad grin, ignoring the sound of Fred moving behind him. Talk about being caught in the middle. "She's all bluff."

"Hey!"

Fred's indignant shout made him grin wider.

Ven narrowed his eyes on Fred, the promise of lots of pain in their green depths, before he turned them back on Patrick. "I've had enough of this," he muttered. "I'm hungry. I'm going to Amy's. Call me when the Reaper's finished with the dramatics."

He flicked his stare to Fred again and disappeared.

"Holy *shit*!"

Fred's shout made Patrick jump. He spun about, finding her standing with her mouth open and her eyes—once more pale, pale blue—wide.

"Did you do that? Did you make him go away?"

She shook her head. "No, I didn't. But Ven shouldn't have been able to do it, either."

He frowned, wanting nothing more than to drag his hands through his hair and let out a roar of frustration. Just when he thought he had a handle on what was going on, his brother goes and stuns the hell out of his guide and tutor to all things otherworldly. "I guess that means you really *are* going to need to kill me now, aren't you? There's no way you can let something as inexplicable as *that* pass without needing to find out the answer. I can almost see you wanting to scratch your nonexistent tail."

She blinked, and for a split second Patrick saw her wavering with indecision. But then she let out a sharp sigh, shook her head and took the one step left between them to take his fingers in hers. "I'm not going to kill you, Patrick. I was never going to kill you. *Almost* kill you, maybe, but kill you? No."

He cocked an eyebrow. "Oh, *almost* kill me. Well, that makes all the difference."

Fred's low chuckle set his pulse into heated flight and he scowled. Once again, the woman was affecting him in ways she shouldn't. He should be worried about his big brother and his disappearing act. Instead he was getting turned on by a laugh. "Don't worry, lifeguard." She arched her own eyebrow back at him. "Something tells me even if I tried, it would be impossible to sever your life thread."

"And why's that?"

"Because Ven transubstantiating himself from the Realm shouldn't be possible. That he did so answers at least one question I had before bringing you here."

"And that is?"

"I'm one hundred percent certain your brother has become a second-order demon."

Patrick frowned. "How did Ven become a second-order demon? And why? Does this have anything to do with me?"

She pulled a face. "I don't know. But I think I have an idea."

Patrick pulled his own face. "So, we're back to square one."

A small smile, both nervous and hesitant, played with the corners of Fred's mouth. "Back to testing my theory? Yes."

"But you said you needed to taste Ven's blood." He looked around the room pointedly. "Bit tricky when he's not here."

There was a short pause as Fred studied him, and Patrick's gut twisted. "I said I needed to taste Ven's blood. I didn't say *only* Ven's blood. You're brothers. The answer lies in both your veins."

Patrick's heart smashed against his breastbone. He stared down at her, the twist in his gut turning into a full-blown knot.

"It won't hurt."

He let out a short, sharp grunt. "That's not the problem."

Fred studied him, puzzled uncertainty on her face. "Then what... Ahhh." She nodded, as if finally seeing the hidden 3-D shape in the image of nonsensical colors. "I'm not going to turn you into a vampire, Patrick," she said. "That ability is beyond my power. I'm Death, not a bloodsucker and only vampires can sire vampires."

Patrick narrowed his eyes, but before he could response—exactly how, he didn't know—she continued.

"What I said about the soul releasing its secrets to the Void on imminent death is true. I see it all. Their entire thread in the Weave. Where they came from, right back to their first ancestor. By the same token, I can taste it all, for want of a better way to explain it, in a living human's blood. In fact, the results are quicker. I would have suggested your blood first, but I was..." A soft blush tinged her cheeks and she looked away for a quick moment. "I was a bit concerned about how I would react."

"How you would react?"

The blush in her cheeks grew hotter. "I'm not a vampire, Patrick, but I am a demon. If you make me horny with just a look, imagine what the taste of your blood could do to me."

Patrick studied her, unsure what to say. Or think.

"But it's okay," she hurried on, her gaze holding his. "And all I need is one small taste. Honest."

Gut clenched, chest tight, he closed his eyes. Ah, Jesus, when had his life become so surreal?

"The moment you were born, Patrick Watkins," Fred murmured. "And I'm trying to find out why. Trust me."

Opening his eyes, he gazed down into her face. Releasing a sigh, feeling more than a little nervous, he nodded.

Fred's eyes shimmered to white. "Just one taste, Patrick. I promise. All I need to do is touch my tongue to your vein."

Her stare held him frozen. Mouth dry, pulse crazy, he watched her slowly lift his right hand level with her chest. She caressed his inner wrist with infinite care, her fingertips trailing over the sensitive flesh protecting his median antebrachial vein, the main source of oxygen-rich blood coming straight from his heart. Her warm breath feathered the delicate epidermal layer and he swallowed at the desert in his throat.

A ripple of tight heat rolled through him. He licked his parched lips with his dry tongue, unable to move.

She looked up at him, confident calm radiating from her. "This will be quick," she whispered.

God, does it have to be?

The dark, seductive thought floated through Patrick's hazy mind. He pulled in a swift breath, the sudden realization he was aroused, painfully, completely aroused slamming him in the chest. And still he couldn't move.

He stared at her, his blood roaring in his ears, his erection growing harder. He watched her lips curl into a small smile that revealed two short, pointed fangs. He watched her lower her head over his arm, the curtain of her midnight black hair cascading over her neck and shoulder to hide it from his view. He stared at the back of her head, his cock straining for release, his breath shallow.

The warm softness of her lips pressed to his wrist and a surge of liquid electricity shot straight through him. He tensed already taut muscles. His balls rose up closer to his body. His heartbeat tripled.

And then the tip of Fred's tongue touched his wrist, her teeth pierced his flesh and exquisite, elemental rapture exploded in his core.

He felt his blood flow from the wounds, felt her tongue bathe his wrist. He hissed in a breath through clenched teeth, every nerve ending in his body on fire. A surge of something carnal and primitive flooded into his groin and, unable to stop himself, he threw back his head and groaned, the sound as raw as the pleasure consuming him.

Fred's lips moved over his wrist, her tongue lapping at his weeping vein. Her fingers dug into his arm, gripped it with fierce strength so opposite to the gentle administrations of her mouth before, with a soft hitching gasp, she jerked her head up.

She stared at him, her pale skin aglow with an inner light, her lips glistening red with his blood. "By the Powers..." She trailed away, her fingers still holding his wrist and arm.

Patrick pulled in a deep breath, forcing his body back under control. He felt like a violin string wound too tight, thrumming with so much tension it was sure to snap with just one more touch. "What?"

She didn't answer him. Just stared at him with white-fire eyes.

"What?"

"You are of the Carpenter's line."

The simple declaration, uttered in a voice choked with shock and reverence, punched Patrick in the chest. He pulled his arm from Fred's fingers and took a step backward, the enormity of her statement filling him with...what? He dragged his hands through his hair, trembling, hot and cold at once, his throat tight, his chest heavy.

Oh, Jesus.

Fred's gaze held his. "Exactly."

Chapter Twelve

Amy looked at the man standing before her, her stomach more sick than it had ever been. She wanted to throw up—again—but the last time she had, the man in the black suit had touched his fingers to her temples and pain like a metal spike drilling into her skull had erupted in her head. She'd screamed and pissed herself, and now here she was, in some horrible room filled with candles and the stench of disease, held by Raz in a cruel embrace, blood oozing from the puncture wounds in her neck left by his teeth.

She wanted to go home.

The man in the black suit ran his palm over her bare shoulder and a wall of nausea crashed over her. She gagged, turning her head to the side, not wanting to contemplate the punishment he would deliver if she vomited on him.

"It was very nice of Raziel to transform you, was it not?" His fingers slid along the line of her collarbone, dipping into the cleft between her breasts. "So much easier to bring you to me than when you were human, and I did so want to meet you in person."

Amy rolled her eyes, her stomach lurching. She had no idea how she came to be here. One minute she'd been staring at herself in the bathroom mirror, tormented thoughts of Ven confusing her, the next, Raz had burst through the door, skin blistered, fangs extended, and smashed his fist into her jaw.

She'd regained consciousness exactly where she was now.

In this strange, putrid, stinking room, in her underwear, with the man in the black suit studying her closely, a leering smile pulling at his mouth and what felt like a thousand grasshoppers crawling over her feet and up her legs.

"How do you feel, my dear?"

Her stare jerked back to the man in the black suit before she could stop it and another lurching wave of nausea rolled through her. "Please..." She knew she was whimpering but she couldn't stop herself. "Please...where am I? What..."

"Is happening?" the man finished for her, each word he spoke like a finger of rotting filth shoved down her throat. "I needed to speak with you and my faithful servant brought you to me. Of course, you are no longer human. He had to initiate your transformation to a bloodsucker before you could travel to the Realm, but I understand that transformation has not yet been completed." His expression turned to one of concern and thick snot dribbled from her nose. "May I ask, my dear, are you hungry?"

Amy cowered backward, pressing herself harder to Raz's cold body. She wasn't hungry. She was sick. Real sick. She licked her lips, tasting snot and blood. "I want to go home."

Raz's claws sank deeper into her ribs and arm. "Pestilence will let you return when he is finished with you."

Amy stiffened. "Pestilence? As in the First Horseman of the Apocalypse?"

The man preened, smoothing one hand over his lank, unwashed hair. "You have heard of me? I am honored."

Swallowing the bile bubbling up from her stomach, she nodded. "My father was a minister."

Pestilence's smile spread wide. "A man of the cloth?" He turned his attention to Raz and Amy thanked the Lord for the small reprieve from his sickening gaze. "Raziel, you did not tell me she was a child of the church." A frown contorted his sallow forehead and the candles illuminating the room flickered, throwing wild shadows up the walls as if sharing his displeasure. "That was very remiss of you."

Behind her, Raz tensed, the claws puncturing her flesh digging in further. “I did not know, sire.”

Pestilence waved his hand, turning his smile back to Amy. “Tell me what you know of me, child. I am curious of how I am perceived in the world of man.”

Amy swallowed again, her stomach churning. Every pore of her body leaked perspiration, foul-smelling sweat that seemed to burn her skin. She licked her lips, horrified to discover they were not only cracked and bleeding, but crawling with tiny bugs. Oh Lord. What was happening to her?

“Well?” Pestilence snapped, and Amy’s bladder let go in a gush of hot, acrid piss.

She squirmed in Raz’s hold, desperate to be free. Her muscles held no strength however, and the vampire’s grip was impossible to escape.

“Just that Pestilence is the First Horseman of the Apocalypse,” she sobbed. “He comes before the others on a decaying horse and causes the destruction of the world’s crops and wildlife.”

Pale blue eyes narrowed. “That is all?”

Amy closed her eyes. She felt sick. Oh Lord, save her. She felt so sick. “Please, I want to go home.”

“So, I am just a pest? Like a grasshopper? A little munching on some wheat fields? Is that it?”

Feeling like she was about to pass out, she shook her head. She wanted to go home. “Revelations 6:2 ‘I looked, and there before me was a white horse! Its rider held a bow, and he was given a crown, and he rode out as a conqueror bent on conquest.’ My father always said the church view the other Horsemen more formidable. The Fourth Horseman is the most feared.”

She was babbling. She knew it. But she’d never felt so sick. Or scared.

“The other Horsemen are...” Pestilence’s growl faded away.

Maybe he’s gone? A tight spear of hope stabbed through

her nausea. *Maybe you can go home now?*

Cold, clammy fingers hooked under her chin and she cried out. Her stomach cramped, her head felt like it was about to explode. Every muscle and joint in her body erupted in agony and her bowels opened in a flood of stinging shit that dribbled down her legs onto the insects swarming there. Behind her, Raz let out a disgusted bark. He jerked backward, his claws tearing deep gashes into her flesh.

"*I* am the most powerful!" Pestilence's voice sliced into her like a blade and her eyes snapped open. "I am the *First.* The premier. I am the beginning of the end. Without me there is no Apocalypse!"

His fingers dug into her chin, forcing her jaw open. Wider. Wider. Her lips parted, the putrid air flowing onto her tongue. She gagged, vomit surging up her throat. Choking her.

The room swam. Turned grey. Black splotches blossom behind her eyes. But still she saw Pestilence, eyes wild, leaning towards her, lips stretched into a maniacal grin, his other hand reaching for her mouth.

"The lifeguard's brother will not be able to locate her if she is dead, sire."

Raz's statement seemed to be whispered from far away. Amy stared at Pestilence through the thick, grey haze. This was it. She was going to die.

The grip on her chin jerked away and she slumped, Raz's claws in her arm and torso the only thing keeping her on her feet.

"I am the First!" she heard Pestilence snarl. "The First."

Gasping for breath, blood and snot trickling from her nose, she lifted her head. "Why are you doing this? What do you think you'll achieve? I'm nobody."

Pestilence stared at her, his face contorted with fury. "You are the favored source of blood for the vampire, Steven Watkins." He curled his lip. "Well, you were. I'm not sure he will want you now you are a pathetic half-caste. No longer human, yet not demon either."

Amy's throat squeezed tight. She stared at Pestilence, unable to comprehend the words she heard. A half-caste monster? Ven? No longer human...

Tell me, dear. Are you hungry?

Bitter saliva flooded her mouth, coated her tongue. She *was* hungry. Starving. An insistent, powerful hunger gnawed at her stomach, almost devoured by the nausea consuming her. A hunger for blood. Human blood.

Repulsion and terror radiated through her. "What's going on? What's Raz done to me?"

Oh, Lord. What did they want to do to Ven?

Her fear filled her with strength. She lashed out, kicking at Pestilence, bucking in Raz's cruel hold. The vampire laughed and yanked her harder to his body, driving his claws so deep into her flesh their pointed tips scraped her bones.

"I *needed* to have you here, my dear." Pestilence threaded his fingers before his chest, giving her a patronizing smile. "You are the bait to reel in the lifeguard's brother. The only way you could travel to the Realm was to no longer be human." His smile grew wider. "Raziel sank his teeth into your neck and partially drained you, but he did not allow you to feed in return. You are in mid-coitus, as such. Not completely fucked, but very close to it." He smirked, flicking his gaze over her, and her heartbeat tripled, smashed against her aching breastbone in a frantic, painful rhythm. "But as I am sure you can see, you are just as pathetic as you always were. A victim, it seems, of your lust and addiction."

His smug words slipped into Amy's ear like an oily snake.

Lust.

Addiction.

She bit back a sob, guilt and scalding contempt crashing over her. Lord, she'd brought this on herself. Her craving for the burn of the feed, for the sexual high it created, had led her to seek out another vampire. And Raziel had delivered her to

Pestilence.

"Is that dawning realization I see on your face?" Pestilence asked. "I must admit, it is hard to see your face, what with the blood and snot and matted hair. Oh, and look, your skin is beginning to welter. Pus." He flashed a smile of such perverse delight that Amy's stomach clamped tight. "We have pus, Raziel. Your looks are improving with every moment in my company, my dear." He laughed, and Amy whimpered.

Oh, Lord. Ven. What had she done?

"Now that I have *you*," Pestilence continued, his euphoric smile evaporating, "you will give me the vampire. And once I have the vampire I will have the lifeguard." He closed the distance between them, hooking his nail under her chin to force her face up to his. "And with the lifeguard's only weakness in my power, with his brother's fate in my hands, the Cure shall surrender to me and the Apocalypse shall begin." He grinned, yellow teeth glistening in the flickering candlelight. "Sounds like fun, does it not?"

Ven appeared in the kitchen of Amy's apartment, every nerve and muscle on edge. Something was wrong.

How he'd got to Amy's home, he didn't know. He had a suspicion what he'd just done—leave the Realm without Death's aid—was not something he was meant to be able to do. But then again, changing into some freakish creature with wings and arms the size of tree trunks wasn't something he usually did either. Not to mention tearing apart an ugly-as-shit squid monster until it was just a pile of sushi on an isolated beach in the middle of the day.

All in all, he had to admit, things were not as one would expect.

What are *you, Steven?*

He ignored the unnerving, irritating question, along with

the roaring hunger gnawing at his gut, focusing instead on Amy's home. It was a tiny first-floor apartment that always smelled of tofu and incense, two narrow windows, one in the bedroom, one in the bathroom, and no secret nooks or crannies. A small living room, even smaller bedroom, a kitchen about the size of a shoebox and a bathroom with a shower cubicle so small you had to step out of it to change your mind. Amy loved it and had spent many, many hours searching flea markets and yard sales to decorate it in an eclectic mix of bohemian luxury and 1950s Australian retro. It was an unusual design choice, but it suited her so very well. Quirky and soft and welcoming at once.

A twist of cold apprehension knotted in Ven's gut and he narrowed his eyes. It wasn't just the silence of her apartment that put him on edge, it was a taint to the air. Like something malevolent had been there.

Something malevolent has *been here, Steven. You. Remember what you did to her last time you were here? Remember what you almost did to her?*

Ven's throat grew tight and he suppressed a growl, moving from the kitchen into the living room. He ran a slow gaze over the space, noting it was in the exact same state it had been that morning. "Amy?"

His call fell flat in the silent room.

A ripple of unease shot up his back and he felt his demon stir. No, it *wasn't* his demon, not like he knew it at least. It felt...different.

Crossing the living room, he pushed open the door to Amy's bedroom. Empty.

And why wouldn't it be. It's what, four o'clock in the afternoon. She's probably at work.

Ven curled his fists. He stepped into the room and crossed to its one small cupboard on the sidewall. The hollow ache of starvation he'd had in his gut for the last forty-eight hours was growing stronger. He needed to feed. Soon. The moment he found Amy he'd beg her forgiveness for his previous unforgivable behavior, on his knees if he had to, and hope to the Trilogy she would understand how desperate he was. How close he was to becoming weak. He would make it up to her, any way she wanted him to—shit, he'd even take her shopping—but if he didn't feed soon...

He yanked open the cupboard and another twist of cold apprehension knotted in his gut. Amy wasn't at work. Not unless she decided to leave all her equipment at home. He looked at her camera bag and laptop, throat getting tighter by the second. Unless she'd discovered a way to photograph children and babies without a camera, he was pretty certain she hadn't gone to work today.

Fuck.

He turned about, studying the room and its immaculately made bed and spotless side tables. Nothing out of place.

Again, the ripple of unease traveled up his spine. Again, the sense of something malicious on the air tainted his breath.

Fuck.

He strode from the room, the sound of the carpet pile crushed under his feet, the feel of the still air on his face almost making him scream. Damn it, what was the point of having hypersensitive senses if they couldn't tell him where one defenseless female was?

Scanning the living room one last time for anything he may have missed—not a thing—he shoved opened the bathroom door.

The stench of blood and piss smashed into him like a wave.

Amy's blood and piss.

He sucked in a sharp breath.

And tasted vampire. The same vampire he'd detected on Amy's neck that morning.

The entity inside him roared. Fierce and angry and purposeful.

Shutting out its rage, *and* his raging hunger, Ven studied the room. He needed to be calm, focused. Turning into bat boy wasn't going to save Amy. Not until he found her, at least.

The room seemed as spotless and pristine as the rest of the apartment. Except...a small smear of bright red blood on the white floor tiles beneath the vanity mirror caught his attention. A little further away, about the length of Amy's torso, was a puddle of urine. A few wavy strands of blonde hair lay scattered on the floor, the microscopic white nub of follicle root still attached to the ends of each one.

Ven ground his teeth, the image of those strands, along with about one hundred thousand others cascading down Amy's naked back flooding into his mind all too easily. His fingers had been buried in those strands a little less than ten hours ago.

He wiped at his mouth with his hand, his fangs digging into his top lip as he did so. "Shit."

Dropping into a crouch, he touched his fingers to the smear of blood and he lifted his hand to his nose.

The distinct scent of the other vampire threaded into his nostrils, played over his preternaturally developed olfactory bulb. It filtered through the hypersensitive cells; traveled over the olfactory nerves until, with barely a moment of time passing, he recognized the source.

Raziel. The lowlife scum vampire who frequented The Pleasure Pussy and fed from the hookers and tourists too stupid not to linger near dark alleys. The vampire who always seemed to turn up wherever Ven was, even once at the cliff beach.

Cold anger and guilt rolled through him. If he'd not been so freaked out this morning, if he'd not fled Amy like a rabid dog with its tail between its legs, he would have recognized the bastard's scent and done something about it. Like tear the lowlife dickhead a new arse-hole before ramming a piano leg through his chest. Or better still, a cricket bat.

He bit back a growl, silencing the enraged entity within his core.

Christ, what did he do? The bastard had Amy and it was all

his bloody fault.

Does he have her, or has he fed from her? Drained her of life and dumped her body somewhere? Worse still, has he turned her?

Ven ground his teeth. He didn't like the possible answers to *any* of those questions.

Okay, then how about this one? How did Raziel get here during daylight? How did he survive the sun?

Jesus, maybe he wasn't so unique after all? Frustration and worry fighting with his guilt and anger, he pulled in a long breath—and for the first time since entering the bathroom detected the faint taste of burnt flesh on the air.

He took another breath, a deeper breath, narrowing his senses onto the telltale odor. The taste and smell of barbequed white meat flowed into his nose and a cold grin pulled at his lips. The lowlife dickhead got singed pretty bad getting his skinny, pale arse over here. Pretty bad indeed.

Ven's lips curled away from his teeth. "Good."

Straightening to his feet, he ran his gaze over the small bathroom, searching for anything that would tell him something. Apart from the blood smear, urine, strands of hair and Raziel stench, there was nothing.

Letting out a harsh sigh, Ven dropped his head into his hands and raked his nails through his hair, scratching lines of hot pain in his scalp. Bloody hell. How was he going to find Amy? How was he going to save her?

If there is anything left to save.

He drove his nails into his scalp. "Shut up."

Closing his eyes, he forced the calmness to flow through his body again. He needed to get to Amy. Wherever she was, he needed to find her. If Raziel was with her, all the better.

Drawing the sweet, innocent scent of Amy's blood into his lungs, he formed an image of her in his mind. Concentrated.

And opened his eyes in hell.

Or something close to it.

"Aaah, Steven Owen Watkins."

He spun about, his stare locking immediately on the skinny man in the black suit he'd met at the beach. Pestilence grinned down at him from a throne made of bones, the hideous piece of furniture raised on a dais illuminated by what appeared to a thousand flickering candles.

"You've caused me quite a few problems over the years, Steven." Pestilence gave him a stern shake of the head, his grin stretching wider. "More than one attempt to end your brother's existence has been foiled by you."

Ven raised his eyebrows. "Foiled?" He snorted, folding his arms across his chest, keeping the rage boiling through him under tenuous control. The entity inside him, the force that had replaced his demon radiated furious purpose, but what that purpose was, Ven still could not fathom. "Foiled? You sure you want to go with foiled? Surely thwarted is a better word in this context. I mean, if I *have* prevented you from killing my kid brother all these years you'd have to be feeling pretty bloody frustrated by now. And really, the word foiled is just so melodramatic." He shook his head, scanning the room as he did so from the corners of his eyes, tasting the air for any sign of Amy.

Maybe...

He uncrossed his arms and shoved them into the pockets of his jeans, baring his fangs at Pestilence in a cold smile. "Sounds to me like you just weren't good enough."

The man's eyes bulged. He leapt from his throne, lunging at Ven in a blur of screaming rage. But Ven was faster. He met Pestilence halfway, sinking his claws into the demon's skinny neck and shoulders, driving him backward. Backward. Back into the depraved piece of furniture. Ramming him against the bone seat with driving force.

"You made a mistake trying to kill my brother," he growled into Pestilence's pain-contorted face, grinding his bony shoulders into the throne's backrest. "And now I'm going to—"

"Ven."

Amy's terrified scream punched through Ven's ice-cold fury. He froze, staring into Pestilence's suddenly smug face.

"Foiled again, Steven?" Pestilence laughed, the sound high and haughty. "Or should that be thwarted?" With barely a shift in his subjugated position, he planted his palms on Ven's chest and pushed.

Ven was flung backward, arching through the air before crashing to the floor on his shoulder. He slid across the granite floor at a wild, out-of-control speed, coming to rest at two pairs of feet. One pair booted, one pair bare.

"Ven," Amy cried again, the overpowering stench of her fear and blood pouring into his nose.

"If it isn't the surfboard-riding vampire." Raziel chuckled. "You smell hungry."

He raised his leg and smashed his booted heel down into Ven's chest.

Absolute agony erupted through Ven. He snatched out at Raziel's ankle, hooking his growing claws into the vampire's leg through course denim and tough leather. "I'm going to tear you apart," he ground out, struggling to escape Raziel's brutal stomp.

But with every ounce of energy he expelled, the monstrous hunger he'd denied for too long grew stronger. He writhed under Raziel's boot, drawing on the entity within to come to the surface, to consume him and destroy the vampire who'd brought Amy to this hellish place. The only thing that consumed him however, was his hunger. Sucking him of his strength, of the entity's strength. Draining him. Draining them both.

A wave of sick giddiness rolled over him and he let out an enraged roar, the sound weak even to his own ears. Forcing his starving body to obey—*come on, damn it*—he sank his claws harder into Raziel's ankle, fighting another crushing wave of lightheadedness. "Let…Amy…"

The vampire laughed, his clawed fingers closing tighter around Amy's throat. Her blood oozed between his fingers, and as Ven looked up at him through a smoky curtain of grey starvation, he dropped his head to her neck, extended his long tongue from between his thin lips and licked the bright red liquid from his knuckles. "It seems we have something in common, doesn't it." His eyes flared violent yellow. "Thanks for neglecting her, by the way. If you hadn't missed a feed or two, she never would have gone looking for another vamp to sate her appetites." He flashed a smile at Ven, Amy's blood painting his lips and gums bright red.

Ven stared at him from the floor, his hunger devouring him from the inside. He struggled with Raziel's pining hold one more time, trying to escape the booted foot grinding into his breastbone, but to no avail. His stare rolled to Amy and he moaned, the sight of her fear sucking what little strength there was left in him. *Oh, Jesus, baby, I'm sorry, I'm so sorry...*

"You see, Steven," Pestilence said, arising from his throne. "You are correct. I *did* make the mistake of trying to kill your brother all these years." He crossed the distance between them and lowered himself into a crouch beside Ven, studying him with glowing eyes. "What I *should* have done is exactly what I did today." He grabbed Ven's chin, increasing the pressure of his grip until Ven's jaws began to separate. "Bring the older brother to me so the younger brother will follow." He smiled, tracing Ven's parted lips with cold fingertips. "Simple really. Use the Cure's weakness against him."

His smile grew wider and, eyes glowing a sick yellow light, he plunged his fingers into Ven's mouth.

Chapter Thirteen

Patrick sat in the armchair, his face stunned. He kept opening his mouth, as if knowing he should say something, but not having a clue what that something should be.

He stared at Fred, hands hanging between his knees, eyes wide, and shook his head. "No."

She frowned at him. "What do you mean, no?"

He shook his head again. "I can't be...Ven can't be..." He held out his hands to her, as if the claim she'd just made rested on his palms and she could just take it away. "Our parents were not... Shit, I don't even think we were baptized. I went *surfing* most Sundays." He dropped his hands and shook his head one more time. "No."

"Blood doesn't lie, Patrick."

He opened his mouth to say something and then closed it again.

Fred bit back a sigh. His unspoken response had floated through her mind like so many other times, but this time she'd not only heard the words of his thought—*But you might*—she'd felt the confused torment behind them. He still didn't trust her. Not enough to believe her without hesitation, at least. She didn't blame him for being angry. What she'd laid on his shoulders was huge, bigger than huge, gigantic, gargantuan, but she needed him to deal with it and move on. Quickly. Her spine was itching so badly she was beginning to feel like a flea-ridden mutt.

They were running out of time.

Whatever Pestilence was up to, he was about to do it.

She looked down at the Australian lifeguard. *Come on, Patrick.*

He sat motionless, head bowed, shoulders slumped.

Fred suppressed the urge to fidget. She would help him deal with the enormity of his bloodline later, after the upcoming confrontation with Pestilence, when they had all the time in the world, but she needed him to be with her now. To be the sarcastic, determined, stubborn bastard she'd fallen in love with.

Finally admitting it, Fred?

She scrunched up her face and balled her fists. Yes, she was. She'd fallen in love with the guy, damn it, but just as Patrick needed to come to terms with who he was later, she would deal with her feelings for him after this whole shit fight was done. Until then, all that mattered was getting him ready. Really ready.

She fixed the back of his head with a hard stare. *Come on, Patrick. Please.*

For an eternity, he didn't move, and then Fred heard a ragged sigh.

"Fuck it," Patrick said, pressing his hands to his knees and pushing himself from the chair. He looked at her with unreadable green eyes, a wry lopsided grin playing with his lips. "If I'm going to die, it may as well be saving mankind."

Relief swept through her. She laughed before she could stop herself, closing the minute space between them with one step and smoothing her hands up his back. "So, does this mean we can recommence your training now?"

He rolled his eyes and slid his own hands down her back to grip her arse, tugging her hips harder to his. "What? You didn't get enough the last time?"

She gave him a grin, touching the tip of her tongue to her top front teeth, letting him see her fangs. "We were interrupted last time."

Patrick cocked his head to the side, his eyes shining with a light Fred could only describe as merriment. "Wait, we are talking about my 'training' aren't we?"

She chuckled and pressed her sex to his groin. "I tell you what. *When* you finish kicking Pestilence's butt from here to the lowest level of hell, I'll let you tie me up and do whatever you like to my body. Is that a deal?"

The sudden spasm of his cock and his quick intake of breath told Fred it was very much a deal. He didn't need to seal it with a kiss. But that didn't stop her from stopping him when he captured her lips with his and did just that.

She slid her hands up his shoulders and tangled her fists in his hair, the cool strands like spun silk in her gasp. They didn't have time for this. Not at all, but she sensed in Patrick the need to take this moment. He was the most amazing human she'd ever met, a human with more internal strength than all the entities she'd ever known. A being of immense power still untapped and unrealized. A being more at home on the water than in the Realm where he belonged.

A man faced with something no mere mortal should.

She would no more deny him this last moment of pleasure than she would deny him water to slake his thirst.

Parting her lips, she plunged her tongue into his mouth, tracing the edge of his lips, his teeth.

He groaned, gripping her arse harder, yanking her closer to his body. A fire roared through him. Fred could feel it heating her own blood and existence. She returned his groan with a soft whimper, the sound turning into a moan when he removed one hand from her butt to place it on her breast.

His fingers teased her nipple, pinching its puckered tip. She moaned again, ribbons of exquisite tension unfurling through her body. Her breasts grew heavy, swollen with pleasure. Her pussy grew wet and thick with anticipation. She deepened their kiss, arching her back to grant Patrick greater access to her breasts even as she ground the curve of her sex against the rigid length of his erection.

Oh, God, yes. This feels so good...so good...this woman...she is... Oh, God...I love...

The frenzied thought threaded through Fred's own pleasure-clouded mind, feeding the inferno rapidly building in her core. She dragged her mouth from his, letting his lips burn over her neck, her jaw, up to her ear and back down. His tongue touched the curve of her shoulder and she realized she was naked. Wonderfully naked.

Patrick raised his head, staring down into her face with smoldering eyes, the hand on her ass squeezing tight, the one cupping her breast massaging with infinite care. "Jesus, you are gorgeous."

She smiled, rolling her hips so her exposed mons stroked the impressive length of his boxer-short-covered erection. "I'm not sure you can say that anymore."

His eyebrows rose, even as he captured her nipple again with his fingertips. "What? You *are* gorgeous."

She chuckled, her sex flooding with liquid joy at his words, and carnal heat at his touch. "You know what I mean."

A mischievous light flared in his eyes and he lowered his head to her neck. "The beauty of family," he murmured, his voice caressing her flesh in soft little whispers of warm air, "is that you don't have to change who you are."

As if to prove his point, he pinched her nipple between his fingers and bit her neck with ungentle force.

Explosive pleasure rolled through her. She cried out, thrusting her hips forward. He chuckled into her neck, twisting her nipple, flicking it, pinching it until she cried out again, all the while charting a wicked path along the line of her shoulder with his teeth and lips.

Fred's sex constricted, pulses of wet need gripping the memory of Patrick's cock. By the Powers, she wanted him inside her. They were almost out of time, but she wanted him inside her. Thrusting. Pumping. Stretching her to the limit. Claiming her completely. Possessing her utterly.

She raked her hands down his back, letting her nails become claws as she did so, scoring lines into his flesh until she reached the waistline of his boxers.

His cock twitched, jabbing into her belly as she slipped her hands past the elastic band and gripped his arse.

Oh, yes...on fire...I'm on fire. This feels like...

She squeezed his ass cheeks, rolling her head to the side and leaning slightly away from him. He knew what she wanted. His lips traveled over her collarbone, his back bending as he moved his mouth, in tiny nibbles, down her chest to the fullness of her other breast.

Oh, Jesus...she tastes so good. I never want this to end.

She closed her eyes, Patrick's thoughts heating her pleasure as much as his mouth and teeth and tongue and fingers. She agreed with him. She never wanted this to end. She never wanted to be apart from him. He was her future, her past, her eternity.

Unless Pestilence—

Patrick's lips closed over her nipple, destroying the terrifying, unwanted thought.

She cried out. "Yes!"

He sucked on the puckered tip. Hard. Pain exploded in her breast. Blissful pain that flooded her sex with cream and stole her breath. She gasped, sinking her claws into his ass cheeks.

Patrick's teeth sank into her nipple in reply and she bucked, her body shuddering as a sharp, abrupt orgasm rocked her.

She whimpered, feeling her juices wet her thighs.

"You taste so good," he growled against her breast, the utterance sending gentle vibrations through its swollen weight.

Her still-throbbing sex constricted and she pressed her thighs together, the tiny nub of her clit a button of sheer, agonizing rapture.

He moved his mouth from her nipple, back up her neck,

along her ear to her jaw. "I want to taste you everywhere."

He didn't give her time to respond. The hand on her breast moved down her body, over her ribcage, down the curve of her hip. Her pulse quickened and she shifted, breaking the contact between their hips just enough to slide her hand from Patrick's ass to his cock. Its long, thick heat filled her grip, just as his fingers delved between her thighs and parted the folds of her pussy.

"Oh, yes." Fred bucked, ramming her hips forward. He stroked the pad of his fingertip over her clit, once, twice. She shivered, waves of concentrated pleasure rippling through her. "Yes."

"My sentiment exactly," he said, the words leaving his lips in a ragged breath. His cock jerked in her fist, its steel length seeming to grow even as she held it.

Her pulse tripled and she pressed her sex to his hand, knowing her desire coated his fingers. Damn, she wanted him inside her. The teasing strokes on her clit were like torture, driving her closer and closer to another climax she could barely believe was possible, robbing her of breath and control and focus. She squeezed his cock, gazing into his eyes. "Please..."

With languid torment, his nostrils flaring, his stare locked on hers, he slipped one finger past her folds, sliding it deeper into her sex. "Is that what you want?"

She nodded, grinding her clit on his knuckle. A hoarse whimper vibrated in her throat and she closed her eyes, feeling the building tension of her orgasm approaching.

Patrick withdrew his finger. All the way out.

Fred cried out in protest, snapping her eyes open to glare at him, squeezing his cock in punishment.

He chuckled. "Maybe you'd like more?"

Before she could nod, he slid his finger back into her sodden pussy, this time letting two others join its delicious journey.

Fred's sex contracted. She thrust into his hand, liquid

electricity stabbing into her core as she came again with a raw scream.

Again.

The violent climax claimed her. She trembled, Patrick's hand between her legs the only thing keeping her on her feet. By the Powers, how did he do it?

Her legs grew wet with her cum, her breath shallow and quick with exertion. She was Death and as such, should never feel weakened or drained by physical activity. Yet making love to Patrick Watkins seemed to defy those metaphysical laws and she reveled in the mortal state.

Fred rode his fingers, her grip on his erection pumping up and down in perfect sync with her orgasm. He moaned, his body stiffened.

My love, my Death...oh, for the love of God, I'm going to... And, as his balls rose up and his cock strained tight, she released her fingers around its length, dropped to her knees and took him in her mouth.

Tasting his desire for her.

Loving him with every molecule of her existence.

Ven looked at Amy through the tangled mess of his hair, blood and sweat trickling down his face, his eyes fierce and dead at once.

Behind him, knuckles red, grin insane, stood Raziel, his stare fixed on Ven's back, his foot pressed to the bowed curve of Ven's spine. He snapped his leg straight, slamming Ven to the floor, grin stretching wider.

"Ven!"

The scream tore at Amy's throat. She tried to move, to crawl over to him, but she couldn't. Pestilence had not been kind to her while he'd waited for Ven to arrive and her body barely functioned anymore.

A shudder convulsed through her—a reaction to the swarm of locusts Pestilence had poured into her mouth or the result of the sickness he'd filled her with, she didn't know. If she were human, she'd be dead already. Now, she survived it all, in more pain than she believed possible to endure, too weak to escape, too demonic to die.

Tears and snot stung the gashes on her cheeks but she refused to cry. If Ven saw her cry he might give up and if he did that, they were both lost.

"This is all rather entertaining, is it not, my dear?"

Amy cringed, shying away from Pestilence as he hunkered down beside her. He smiled, yellow teeth dripping saliva. The foul stench of his breath—decay and rot—fanned her face and before she could stop herself, she threw up, blood and bile spewing from her mouth in a violent spurt.

"Leave her alone."

Pestilence laughed, swinging his attention to Ven. "Why, the vampire finally speaks!" He reached out for Amy, stroking the back of her head as if she were a cat. No, change that. She'd seen him playing with a kitten earlier, a tiny little ball of white fluff. He'd touched the kitten with more care than he favored her now.

"After all this time trying to pull the words from your mouth and all I needed to do was smile at the female?"

Raz chuckled. "Not as much fun for me though."

Pestilence nodded. "True. I have not seen one demon inflict such pain on another since the Fallen Star punished those who tried to change sides in the failed uprising."

"Really?" Ven's laugh sounded more like a choked cough. "I didn't think my face was hurting Raziel's knuckles that much?"

Raziel hissed. "Why you—" He stamped his heel into the small of Ven's back.

The sound of snapping bones filled the air.

"Ven!"

Ven roared, and for a split second Amy swore she saw his

face shift before he slumped to the floor.

Pestilence laughed again. “I like your spirit, Steven. It is commendable, given the situation.” He stood and walked over to where Ven lay motionless. “It is a pity, all things considered, that you and your brother were not on my side.”

“I...disagree.” Ven’s voice was almost inaudible, chocked by pain and muffled by the floor. He lifted his head and Amy’s heart stopped. Fresh blood trickled from his mouth and nose, staining his lips and chin. “Even if...” he coughed, and bright red blood bubbled from his mouth. “...even if I was a sad, pathetic fuck...like you, I don’t think...I could...handle the stink.” He pressed his palms to the floor and pushed, lifting his upper body partly from the cold black marble. “Seriously...” He spat out a wad of blood. “When *was* the last time you cleaned...your teeth?”

Amy’s throat squeezed tight. “Oh, Lord, Ven, don’t,” she sobbed, shaking her head, reaching out a trembling hand to him. “Don’t...”

Pestilence’s face contorted. His eyes flashed white, the veins in the side of his neck popped and suddenly Ven went flying through the air, flipping over and over in a blurring arc before slamming face down to the floor again.

“Ven!” Amy scrambled on her hands and knees towards him, tears stinging the cuts on her cheeks. She shuddered, the disease and insects in her body fighting with her terror. Oh Lord, she needed to get to him...*to feed.*

She froze, cold horror flooding her veins. No. Oh, no no no no no. “Ven?” *Oh, Lord, please save me, please save us. Forgive me my sins and save us. Please...*

Pestilence swung to her. “I doubt the Trilogy is interested in a sinner such as yourself, my dear.” He flicked a look at Ven, prostrate on the floor. “And I think the bloodsucker will not be of any use to you, either.” He turned back to her. “You see, this is what happens when you don’t eat.” He cocked an eyebrow. “A perfect example of why breakfast is the most important meal of the day.” His expression turned dark, psychotic. “Steven should have known better. Instead, he chose to put his brother ahead of his hunger. The sign of a sad, pathetic fuck if you ask me."

Mouth dry, stomach clenching, Amy stared at Ven, willing him to move. *Get up, Ven. Please...get up. Move...*

He didn't.

Raziel laughed, strutting over to jab Ven's ribs with the toe of his boot. "I guess that's what you'd call a wipeout."

"Someone...should tell you..." The raspy, stilted whisper destroyed the smile on the vampire's face. Ven shifted, fingers curling into a fist. "You suck...at comedy."

Raziel hissed.

Just as Ven snatched his ankle and yanked his foot from underneath him.

Raziel tumbled backward and Ven leapt, crashing him to the floor with a growl that made Amy's mouth turn to dust.

What was that?

The thing inside her, the *thing* Raziel had turned her into, gibbered and cowered, Ven's growl petrifying it beyond measure.

She stared at the two vampires, watched Ven rise up over Raziel and sink his fingers into the other vamp's neck, his face—the face she loved unconditionally—still completely human, his green eyes the same green eyes she dreamed about every time she fell asleep.

Yet something *in* him scared something *in* her.

She swallowed, her throat tight.

"Get off me!" Raziel screeched, bucking under Ven, arms and legs lashing out. The blows bounced off Ven. He barely blinked in response.

Another one of those growls rumbled low in his throat and Amy shivered, her stomach churning.

His muscles seemed to grow. Shift. His pale skin darkened, his eyes glowed. The thing Amy had become squealed and tried to flee, but she was frozen, rooted to the spot in fear. Lord, what was Ven doing?

Pinned underneath Ven, Raziel thrashed and clawed at

Ven's arms, his eyes bulging. "Let...me..."

Ven's lips curled and Amy gasped at the row of needle-sharp teeth filling his mouth. He sank fingers that looked more like claws into Raziel's chin. Forced the now wailing vamp's head to the side. "Look at her. Look at what you've done to her."

Raziel stared at her, bug-eyed. "I'm sorry," he blubbered. "I'm sorry, I'm so—"

Ven dropped his head down to Raziel's cheek, his darkening skin contrasting sharply with Raziel's pasty white complexion, his burning pupiless eyes casting the vamp's terror-contorted face in a pale fire. "Sorry doesn't cut it, dickhead."

His shoulders bunched. He pulled back his right arm, his hand hooked, as if ready to tear out Raziel's heart, when a shudder wracked his body.

And another. Another.

His skin, almost a shimmering shade of charcoal, bleached to white, the fire in his eyes extinguished and he slumped forward, collapsing to the floor beside Raziel.

Amy's heart stopped. "*Ven?*"

Her scream was lost in a laugh. She tore her stare from Ven's still form, swinging about to watch Pestilence clap his hands. Lord, she forgotten he was even there.

"What a truly amazing display." He continued to clap, walking over to Ven even as Raziel, bloody and bruised, scurried to his feet. "You really have impressed me, Steven Watkins." He bent at the waist, snagged a fistful of Ven's sweat-tangled hair and jerked his head off the floor. "When did you become a Principatus?" He lowered his head, gazing with obvious surprise into Ven's slack face. "That is a nasty little secret you have been keeping from me. I have never seen one of the Trilogy's demon hunters in the flesh before, I have to admit." He released his grip, letting Ven's head drop to the floor with a hollow smack before straightening to his feet and sighing with melodramatic disappointment. "What a pity you have been starving yourself. I would have enjoyed the challenge."

He flicked the still-cowering Raziel a disgusted look. "Steven is exhausted, Raziel. He has depleted his energy reserves and is no longer a threat to you." Turning to Amy, he gave her a sorrowful smile. "Or you, my dear. The Principatus are not known to show mercy to our kind...no matter how many times they fucked you in the past."

"What...what have you..." Amy couldn't finish. Pestilence's gaze made her joints scream in agony and her stomach roll with nausea. She struggled to raise her hand to her lips, wiping at the foaming blood trickling from her mouth. *Dear Lord, please help us...*

Pestilence's eyes turned hard. Contemptuous. "What have I already said about that, Amy Elizabeth Mathieson?"

Her body cramped. Just like that. Every muscle contracting at once. She cried out, unable to move, unable to do anything but squeal and sob and stare in horror at the First Horseman of the Apocalypse as he bent down to Ven again, jerked his head from the floor and shouted into his face:

"Now call your brother to me."

Pestilence's breath, as foul as a rotting corpse, blasted over Ven's face. He looked at the First Horseman through the blood-matted tangle of his hair, his broken body growing weaker with every second passing. "Clean your teeth," he snarled with a cold smirk.

Pestilence hissed and what felt like a million tiny lice lashed Ven's face. Swarming over him, into his eyes, his nose, his ears. He threw back his head, incapable of escaping them, the sound of Raziel's laughter and Amy's screams almost drowned out by the screech of minute insects' invasion.

The entity within him roared, furious, but his body, starved of food and drained of energy, could not draw on the power to transform. He was dying, and as such, it was too.

With a million bites of his flesh, the lice disappeared, replaced instead with the sickening caress of Pestilence's stare. "Call your brother to me."

Ven spat, the wad of phlegm and blood writhing with live insects. "Go take a shower. You stink."

Amy's sobs in the background squeezed Ven's chest, but he could not look her way. If he did the dying entity inside him, the Principatus, would roar in deep-seated rage, and the human he once was would crack at the sight of her suffering and he would surrender to Pestilence.

With a *tsk tsk*, Pestilence blew a fine stream of air onto Ven's feverish face. Fire rained down on him. He felt his skin blister, boil after pus-weeping boil erupting over his cheeks and forehead and lips.

"Call your brother to me."

Ven laughed, the sound more rasping hiccup than anything else. "Go fuck your hat."

Raziel laughed again. Pestilence hissed, his teeth flashing in a snarl. He touched Ven's bottom lip with his fingertip and Ven's gut erupted in acid. "Call. Your. Brother."

Ven coughed, blood spurting from his mouth to splatter Pestilence's black shoes and trousers. "Fuck. Your. Hat."

With another hiss, Pestilence hooked his nails into Ven's jaw, gouging deep wounds into his weeping skin. "Are you always this stubborn, Steven?"

Ven managed a faltering smile, feeling the bruised flesh of his lips tear open and ooze fresh pus. "Only with you, love."

Snapping upright, Pestilence let out a screech and drove his foot into Ven's ribcage.

Piercing agony ripped through him. He ground his teeth, biting back the scream tearing up his throat. Fucked if he was going to scream for the bastard.

"I have tried to be nice to you, Steven." Pestilence stormed around him, stopping to give him a wild glare, eyes glowing cat-piss yellow. "But you leave me no alternative." He dropped into a crouch, grabbed a fistful of Ven's hair and yanked his head off the floor. "I cannot kill you, as much as I would like and I so wanted to keep the female alive to use as a bargaining chip against the Cure in case your survival was not enough to sway him, but your stubborn refusal to call your brother leaves me with no other option." He nodded to Raziel.

There was the sound of a scuffle, Amy screamed and Raziel laughed.

"No," Ven cried out, the word nothing more than a choked wheeze. He struggled onto his knees, fighting to get to his feet. Instead, he stumbled back to the ground, Pestilence's grip on his hair ripping out tufts as he collapsed.

He watched, sick with horror and rage, as Raziel dragged Amy closer, claws puncturing the column of her neck just above the jugular. A surreal memory flashed through Ven's head—kissing Amy on that very spot, her sweet, soft body moving under his, her wet sex gripping his length in rapid pulses the very moment he pierced her neck with his fangs and fed on her life force.

Oh, Amy...I'm sorry.

His stare found hers and guilt smashed through him. She was petrified and he could do nothing to save her.

He squeezed his eyes shut. No matter what Pestilence did, no matter what the First Horseman thought, Ven would not give up his brother. He would die, Amy would die, before that happened.

"Open your eyes, Steven." Pestilence's whispered order stabbed into his ear. "Let us see what happens when I fill her battered, diseased body with ants, shall we. Bull ants should do it. An Australian ant for an Australian monster. Quite apt really, particularly when you take into consideration the bull ant's bite can induce anaphylactic shock in those allergic to insect stings." He paused, and Ven opened his eyes, staring at Amy struggling in Raziel's grip. "Did you know Amy was allergic to insect stings, Steve-O? I wonder how the...*thing*...she has become, thanks to Raziel, will react to a bull ant's bite?" He chuckled, returning to his feet. "This should be fun."

"Leave her alone," Ven rasped. He tried to shift, to move. The entity inside him screamed. His overpowering hunger roared.

Pestilence cocked his head to the side. "You have a better option, Principatus. I am more than happy to accommodate."

Ven slid his stare to Amy imprisoned in Raziel's insidious hold.

Amy...Patrick...Jesus, I can't...

Amy's eyes widened and she shook her head. *Don't.*

"Hey! Pestilence!" she suddenly shouted, struggling against Raziel's arms. Anger flashed across her ravaged face. "Do you know there's a church in the USA that has declared the First Horseman less annoying than a hurricane? And another in Italy that's stated of all the players in the Apocalypse, Pestilence is the least worrisome."

Pestilence's nostrils flared and he swung his head in Amy's direction. "Excuse me?"

She grinned back at him, the expression cold and predatory. "In Sweden, the First Horseman is seen as a false agent of the Apocalypse, an imposter riding on the coattails of the other three, more effective and fearsome Riders."

Pestilence's expression grew black. He narrowed his eyes, the knuckles of his fists stretched to a taut white.

Ven shook his head. "Amy, don't." He knew what she was doing and his lifeless heart twisted in agony.

But she didn't stop. Her grin grew wider, her eyes fixed firmly on Pestilence.

"There's a second-rate rock band called The Four Horsemen," she shouted, "and only the Second, Third and Fourth 'Horsemen' have fan clubs dedicated to them."

Pestilence hissed, a ripple shuddering through his form. "How do you speak of such things?"

Amy shrugged, the action contemptuous and bored at once. "My dad stopped being a preacher when I was sixteen. He found the whole notion of the Apocalypse rather humorous."

Another shudder rippled through Pestilence's body. "Humorous?"

"Amy, no!" Ven shouted, pushing himself but an inch from the floor.

Amy's grin turned cold, the expression triumphant even as her eyes—eyes he'd gladly have drowned in for the rest of his existence—grew lost. Sad. "And in most versions of the Bible," she went on, "The First Horseman is referred to as Strife. You, Pestilence, don't exist at all."

Two things happened at once. Pestilence's human façade shattered, replaced by a skeletal demon of terrifying proportions, and Amy threw off Raziel's hold and launched herself forward.

Straight into the enraged First Horseman's shrieking charge. Head back. Arms wide. Her grin as wide and free as the burgeoning brown fire in her eyes.

Patrick closed his eyes, breathing in Fred's subtle scent. He'd never forget it, no matter how long he—

An invisible wrecking ball smashed into his chest, sending him flying backward.

He manipulated the space around him and twisted mid-flight, landing on his feet to glare at the woman across the room from him. "Not fair."

Fred cocked an eyebrow, studying him from the other side of the "training area" she'd created in her part of the Realm. "Do you think the First Horseman will play fair?"

Patrick rubbed at the white-hot pain throbbing through his body. When it came to Death, the pain always seemed to be white hot. "I don't think Pestilence is going to attack me with the scent of your sex. At least, I hope he's not. That would be just wrong."

Fred folded her arms, her face serious. "No, Pestilence will use much nastier tricks to distract you."

A sudden shimmer on the air beside her became Patrick's

mother.

Patrick's stomach dropped. His throat slammed shut. He stared at the tall, slim woman with the laughing green eyes and dark red hair. "Mum?"

The woman smiled—the same smile she'd given him every night of his childhood before kissing his forehead and tucking him into bed. "Heads up, Pat."

The wrecking ball hit him again, this time harder. He smacked against the far wall, a kaleidoscope of agonizing colors detonating behind his eyes on impact. But before he could drop to the floor, the ball crashed into him again and again and again, his mother watching the brutal assault, her smiling green eyes crinkling with mirth and joy. "I always said you were the weaker of the two."

Patrick screamed, the ball mashing him into the wall with blow after blow, his mother's words crushing him far deeper. "Oh, God, Mum!"

Focus.

The single word whispered in his head, barely penetrating the white agony engulfing him.

Focus.

"And to think I had the choice of aborting you," his mother went on, her smile growing wider. "What was I thinking, letting a pathetic joke such as you live?"

"No!" Hot tears stung Patrick's eyes. "That's not true."

He reached out for his mother, numb with grief, on fire with pain. The ball smashed into him, again, again, again, pummeling him with such force he could no longer draw breath.

"Mum," he croaked, staring at her through a black fog. "Mum."

Focus, Patrick.

"It is for the best that you will die." His mother nodded, her green eyes calm, her face soft with maternal love. "You really are just a disappointment to me and your father."

"Noooo!"

Fury poured through Patrick. He lashed out with his mind.

But the ball kept hitting him.

Again. Again. Again.

He was going to die.

He was going to—

Focus.

A ripple of control ran through him. He pulled in a long breath. His heartbeat slowed. *Thump thump, thump thump...thump...thump...thump...thump...*

The ball struck him, smashing him harder to the wall.

His heart slowed further still. *Thump...thump...thump...thump...thump...thump...*

He pulled a deep breath, stare locked on his smiling mother.

Thump...thump...thump

She shimmered. The ball smashed into him.

He absorbed the blow, stare fixed on the smiling woman before him. "You are not my mother."

Patrick's core erupted with golden fire, existence shuddered. He struck out. A tsunami of composed force aimed straight for the apparition.

And then it was just Fred standing before him, her eyes glowing white, tears streaming down her face. "I'm sorry, Patrick. I'm sorry, but I had to."

He stared at her, his heart rate returning to normal, his heart squeezing in misery. "*That* was not fair."

She studied him, eyes unreadable, tears unchecked. "I know."

He turned his head, unable to look at her. What she'd done was unforgivable. What Death had done was—

Prepare you.

The voice reverberated through Patrick's anger. He blinked, feeling as if someone had punched him in the gut. Dragging his hands through his hair, he let out a sharp sigh and turned back to Fred.

She watched him, expression pinched and on guard.

He crossed the room to stand before her. "I get your point." His body *and* soul felt like he'd been put through a shredder, and he was surprised he was still on his feet. "It's not going to be pretty and I'm completely unprepared. I just wish I had more time."

Fred shook her head, the training room around them shimmering back into the small, intimate library in which he'd first arrived. "I don't think you need it, Patrick. I threw everything at you then and you beat me."

He studied her for a moment, the thought both terrifying and...and...what?

Fred smiled. "Amazing?"

Patrick chuckled, the lighthearted sound surprising him. "Well, yeah, that's one word for it."

"I think it's a very good word." Standing up on tiptoe, she pressed her lips gently to his. "You *are* amazing, Patrick Watkins."

A soft blanket of warmth folded around him. Sliding his arms around Fred's waist, he smiled down into her face. "So, I guess I've just destroyed the notion held dear by hundreds of philosophers for thousands of years."

Fred raised her eyebrows. "And what's that?"

He let his smile turn into a grin. "You can't beat Death."

She burst out laughing, and raked her hands down his back to grab his ass. "*You* can beat Death. But that's only because she's in love with you."

The second the words past Fred's lips she gasped, her face growing a bright red. She gaped at him open mouthed, her body tense against his, her eyes wide. "By the Powers," she groaned, "I did not mean to say that aloud."

Patrick gazed down at her, every memory of pain and despair evaporating in an instant. He pulled her closer to his body, reveling in the infinite energy of her existence, loving the entirely human reaction to her confession. "Does it help if I tell you the feeling's entirely mutual?"

Pale blue eyes studied him for a long moment. "You know," she finally said on a smile, "I think it does." She placed her lips on his again, the tip of her tongue tracing the edge of his teeth with delicate care.

He chuckled into her mouth and threaded his fingers into her hair, holding her to him as he deepened the kiss. Regardless of what Fred said, by his reckoning, he would survive probably a grand sum total of about two minutes facing the First Horseman—*if* he was lucky. More than anything he wanted to experience the last moments of his life truly enjoying them with the woman he loved.

Fred's hands smoothed up his back, across his shoulders and back down to his arse, tugging his hips closer to hers as her tongue delved into his mouth, exploring it thoroughly. Wet licks of passion and desire flowed all the way into his core. He dragged his hands from her hair and grabbed her butt, lifting her from the floor without breaking their kiss.

Their time was running out. He could feel it. The itch in his gut had returned, his skin prickled, as if the air was electrically charged. The end raced toward him without remorse or pity.

Let me have this moment. Whoever is pulling the strings, please let me have this moment. Just this one and I will gladly forfeit my life. Just this one moment...

Fred's heart thumped against his, a soft moan vibrating in her chest.

One moment will never be enough. Let us have an eternity. Please...

Her unspoken plea slipped through his mind and soul like silken mist and his heart squeezed tight. An eternity. Oh, yes. An eternity of—

Death. You are summoned.

The call roared through Patrick's head and he reeled

backward, dropping Fred from his hold and slapping his hands to his ears. Bloody hell. What the fuck was that?

Staggering backward, he looked at her.

"Damn it." Her eyebrows knotted and she shook her head, worry flittering across her face. "I've gotta go. Stay right here. I won't be—"

She vanished.

Patrick stared at the spot she'd just occupied, the blood roaring in his ears. *"Fuck!"* he shouted, the curse echoing around the empty space.

Like the deafening rumble of thunder.

Chapter Fourteen

Fred glared at the whiteness, fury turning her blood to mercury. She hated this place. Its ambivalence drove her crazy. “What do you mean, interfering?”

The path of the First Horseman cannot be deviated. The First Horseman must continue his course without interference.

Her eyebrows shot up. “The path? The fuckwit has been messing with the Order of Actuality. I think what *I've* been doing is a little less significant, don't you?”

Silence followed her outburst and Fred got the sense a collective scowl of disapproval was leveled her way at her choice of words.

“Fuck it,” she muttered, tilting her chin and ramming her fists on her hips. “I'm pissed off. Let's see the Powers deal with that little piece of interference.”

The First Horseman must be left to choose his path.

Fred ground her teeth. “Are you not listening? Ol' sick and weedy is messing around with the Order. With the Weave. Shit, he's trying to bring about the Apocalypse. As far as I know that event has been declared null and void!”

Another pause followed, this one less disapproving and more weighted.

The Fabric of the Order has been rethread.

Fred's heart stilled. “Rethread? What does that mean?”

Again, a pause.

“This is not good, Fred,” she whispered, shaking her head.

"Not good at all."

The pause continued.

"What does rethread mean?" she shouted, staring into the whiteness. "What's going to happen? Is Patrick Watkins going to survive?"

Had she thought the previous pause heavy? This one almost crushed her.

"Well?"

The Fabric's new pattern is indeterminate.

"Fuck, are you kidding me?" She threw up her arms. "You lot are meant to track these things. The pattern is by your design. For crying out loud, the big guy's omnipotent! How do you *not* know? Indeterminate? What in the name of all the levels of hell is going on?"

Silence.

"Tell me."

Silence.

"Tell me!"

Death, you are forbidden to continue your interaction with the lifeguard. You are hereby ordered to resume the ultimate purpose for which you were created. Now.

Fred's mouth fell open. "I'm forbidden?" She blinked, unable to believe what she was hearing. She was Death. Not a child. No one forbade her anything. "Ordered?"

If you refuse to resume your purpose you shall be confined.

"Confined?"

The matter is finished. Return the lifeguard to the world of man and resume your purpose.

Fred clenched her jaw. "No."

Silence again.

"This is not right. What Pestilence is doing is not right. If you lot want to sit on your collective thumbs and see what happens then so be it, but I'm not going to."

The silence stretched.

She glared into the whiteness one last time, shook her head and transubstantiated.

To nowhere.

Fred throat slammed shut. Why wasn't she back with Patrick?

As forewarned and foretold, The Fourth Horseman has refused a divine command and is hereby confined.

Ice-cold disbelief rolled through her. "What do you mean, forewarned? When? By who?" There was no answer coming, and something told Fred she was alone. She gaped into the whiteness, heart hammering, blood roaring. Muscles frozen.

She swallowed, unable to do anything else. *Oh, Shit. Patrick.*

For the umpteenth time, Patrick walked about the room. Or was it one hundred and ten minutes? Time didn't seem to exist here. After the initial stunned shock following her abrupt disappearance, and an uncomfortable few seconds still waiting for her to return, he'd explored the library. Discovering there was no exit, he moved about the small space just to keep his mind from his upcoming confrontation with the Disease.

Perusing through a random selection of books pulled from the surrounding shelves had achieved nothing. None of the tomes made much sense, most referencing periods of time long before, as far as he could tell, dinosaurs walked the planet. Those that were dedicated to man were violent diatribes that left an unsavory taste in his mouth and made him long to meet the writers in person.

With each passing minute, his mind tried harder and harder to contemplate his future.

He refused to let it do so, and in an act of sheer desperation, he'd finally dropped into the more comfortable looking of the two armchairs and pondered his past. Or more to the point, his family's past.

Had his parents known? Had they suspected? On what side did the bloodline come from? His mum's? His dad's? His father had run his own landscaping business and his mother had been a high school English teacher and, as a consequence, he and Steven had grown up with a love of the outdoors and a passion for reading. Both brothers had prayed regularly of course, at the altar of the surf gods, and paid regular homage to those deities' bikini-clad priestesses as often as they could, especially Patrick during his late teen years. But as for church, nadda. They were just two typical Australian boys growing up on the coastline of the world's largest island.

Nothing in his life had pointed to an ancestry of such...*divine*...significant heritage.

Except for predicting the future on more than one occasion? Or resuscitating drowning victims seemingly beyond saving?

"Bloody hell," he muttered, pushing himself to his feet. He shook his head in disgust at the conceited train of thought. "Next you'll be throwing a barbeque for all the swimmers on Bondi with just one fish, a loaf of bread and a bottle of water."

Moving around the small room again—damn, what he'd give for a door—he wondered what Ven was doing.

A sudden realization struck him and he bit back a curse. He'd yet to ask Fred what she thought his brother had become. What exactly did a second-order demon mean? Ven was obviously more than he once was and if it wasn't for the fact they *both* were now targets for the First Horseman, Patrick would have a wonderful time giving his brother all sorts of hell. He grinned. If he survived this, he was going to pay back thirty-six years of nagging and lecturing.

If you survive this? What if Ven *doesn't survive this?*

The black thought sent a shard of numb unease into Patrick's chest and he ground his teeth. Ven was a target now. The attack from the *q'thulu* wasn't just a random incident. Shit.

A desperate sense of helplessness began to build in his chest. Trying like hell to ignore it, he searched the room again, looking for an exit.

What? The one you know isn't there?

Shit.

He needed to get to Ven. He wasn't safe. He was—

Stop it.

Pulling in a deep breath, Patrick force himself to calm down. Ven was fine. He was no doubt at this very moment with Amy, sating his long-denied hunger and, knowing his brother, probably sating his other more carnal appetites as well.

Patrick chuckled, dropping back into the armchair and crossing his ankles on the low table before him. "Good onya, brother," he murmured, settling himself in to wait for Fred's return. "Enjoy your self."

"Amy!" Ven roared. Just as bleached-white talons sank into her pale, bowed neck. The demon shrieked again and a swarm of black locusts spewed from its maw, engulfing Amy in a second.

"*This* is the power of the First Horseman," Pestilence screeched, gaunt face a white mask of insane fury and rapture. "*This* is the might of the Disease, of Pestilence."

The swarm of locusts turned into a frenzied black cloud, whipping around and around Amy, their wings slicing the air like razors. They raged over her, Pestilence's arms disappearing into their writhing mass, his hold on Amy hidden by their massive number. "*This* is the fate of the Cure." His skeletal shoulders bunched, his arms snapped wide and the wet sound of tearing flesh filled Ven's ears. Amy's scream pitched higher, and then died on a thick gurgle. Pestilence grinned, eyes burning with vile yellow flames. "And the world of man will suffer in my wake."

He turned to Ven. The locusts rose above him, swirling above his head before streaming back into his body through his laughing mouth, his flaring nostrils. Revealing the decimated corpse they'd left behind.

Amy dropped to the floor with a hollow thud, her neck torn open, her face, the face Ven had kissed a hundred times, lacerated and shredded to nothing but a bloody mask of flesh and bone.

Pestilence smiled at him, once again wearing his deceptive human shape. "And so ends the first act of the First Horseman. Now, call...your...brother."

"No."

Ven's cry rent the very air, a tortured wail of absolute grief. His mind cracked, his soul shrieked. The human he'd once been and the Principatus he'd only so recently become screamed with agonized horror...and then, fell silent.

Destroyed completely by the engulfing blackness of absolute sorrow and guilt.

Patrick stood frozen, Fred, the Realm, the upcoming battle and his bloodline forgotten.

An overwhelming, total knowledge his brother was dying flooded through him. No words. No images. No sounds. Just a terrible knowledge Steven was dying.

"Ven?"

His brother's anguish smashed through him, a force of unending grief and hate and guilt.

Oh, Jesus, Ven.

He looked about himself, frantic. Fred's study offered him no answers and no exit. He had no way of leaving, no way of calling her and no way of knowing when she'd return. Damn it, he was useless.

Another wall of concentrated anguish hit him, claimed him like a devouring shroud. A snarl burst from his lips. Fuck this, his brother was in trouble. He had to leave.

Where is he?

Without knowing exactly what he was doing, Patrick drew the memory of Ven's essence into his mind and core.

Nothingness.

Emptiness.

A cold fist reached into his chest. He had to find Ven. He had to find his brother and save him. Like Ven had saved him, protected him all these years. He had to return...

"Home."

The word formed on Patrick's lips, a second before his body became molecules of existential dust, moving through space and time, from one dimension to another. From the Realm to the...beach.

Patrick stared at the empty expanse of Bondi Beach, the late dusk sky the deep, wounded purple of a fresh bruise, stretching on forever, the shifting grains of sand swirling about his feet in the hot, gustless wind.

His throat grew thick. Tight.

The beach from his nightmares.

The beach of the beginning and the end.

Deserted, save for the Disease standing at the high-tide line. Waiting for him, his shadow stretching across the sand, a dark stain on the ever-moving grains.

"Hello, lifeguard." Pestilence smiled. "Shall we begin?"

Chapter Fifteen

Patrick attacked, hurling a wall of concentrated air particles, twisted and folded upon each other until they formed a force as solid as a steel sheet at the First Horseman.

He didn't move. He didn't think. He attacked.

And Pestilence reeled backward.

One step.

Two.

The Disease's arms flailed. He stumbled backward, the sand puffing at his heels in little balls of displaced grains and then, with a wide grin, regained his footing. "Well, we have been training, haven't we?"

Patrick glared at him across the distance, the air charged. The deserted beach seemed to shimmer, and for a split second he swore he saw the undefined ghosts of people hurrying over the sand. People there and yet, not there. People dressed in swimming cozzies, enjoying the dying light of the summer day even as their eyes shone with unease, as if their souls knew something they did not. And then the second passed, the ghosts vanished and it was just Pestilence and Patrick. Facing each other on an empty stretch of sand.

"Where's my brother?"

Pestilence smiled again, adjusting the cuffs of his suit. "This is an interesting development, lifeguard. I did not expect it, I must say. I figured you would choose this location—you seem to be emotionally handcuffed to this pitiful place—but not the dimensional plane. A simple temporal shift and we are here and yet not. Effective. Still, it makes sense when you consider your incessant desire to maintain human life." He shrugged, a totally indifferent action and Patrick had to bite back the urge to leap forward and ram his fist into his smug face. "It will make no never mind though," he went on. "When I destroy you, the world of man will fall."

Patrick balled his fists. "I didn't choose anything, Pestilence. Now, tell me where my brother is before I tear you a new arse and shove your head into it."

Pestilence pulled a contemplative face. "You did not? Now is that not interesting? Hmmm."

A hot ball of anger rose up in Patrick's chest. He looked at the Disease, drawing on the inert power lying dormant in the air around him. "There's nothing remotely interesting about this, Pestilence. Sad, yes. Pathetic, definitely, but interesting?" He shook his head.

Pestilence chuckled and took a few steps forward. "Are you not intrigued by this all, Patrick Watkins?" He lowered his attention to his feet, studying the disturbed sand sliding from the black leather toes of his shoes. "How do you have the strength to determine the location of our...altercation...yet not know it? How can you transubstantiate to your brother and still not control your destination? How do you have the ability to propel me backward and yet still be so naïve to leave your guard down?"

A black wave appeared from nowhere. It dwarfed Patrick, blocking out the low sun, casting him in a light-devouring shadow. It crashed down, knocking him to his knees and it was only then Patrick realized what the wave was—a million gnats, their tiny bodies sticking to his face, blocking his nose, his ears.

He thrust out with his mind, slicing into the wave of gnats, carving them apart, sending them tumbling over each other. Crushing them. Molding them. Reforming them.

Into a thick, writhing spear he flung straight back at Pestilence.

They struck the demon in the chest. Hard. Direct.

Pestilence squealed, eyes igniting in baleful yellow hate. His arms flailed, his mouth gaped open.

With a flick of his mind, Patrick sent the gnats down the demon's throat, a pouring, writhing punch that choked Pestilence's squeal.

The demon slapped at his own neck, claws tearing at his pasty flesh. His eyes rolled and—as Patrick watched, sweat trickling down his temple—Pestilence stumbled, the wind-lashed sand collapsing beneath his heels until he fell backwards, lost in a thick mass of gnats.

Patrick staggered to his feet, exhaustion making his lungs burn. Gasping for breath, sweat stinging his eyes, he released his "hold" on the insects. If he didn't, he would pass out. He had no idea how he'd just done what he had—taken Pestilence's weapon and used it against him—but his body and mind felt scorched. Drained.

He watched the swirling cloud of stray insects blow away in the wind, his patience tested as he waited for Pestilence to move. Waited for him to attack again.

It can't be this easy. It won't be this—

Pestilence rose to his feet, eyes on fire, gnat corpses stuck to his chin. "Impressive." He brushed at his sleeves with one hand and then the other. "You have improved since we last met."

Patrick glared at him. "Where is my brother?"

Pestilence curled his lip. "Is there nothing more in that pathetic human brain of yours?"

Rage smashed through Patrick. He struck out, hurling a wall of sand at the First Horseman. "Where is my brother?"

Pestilence cried out, arms raised, hands shielding his face from the blasting grains. He stumbled backward, cowering from the onslaught of sand and force.

Pulling more sand from the beach, Patrick flung it at the faltering demon. More. More. Fury fueled him. Fury and fear.

Where was Ven? Was he alive? Dead?

"Where is my brother?" he roared, pummeling Pestilence with grain after grain after grain of raw glass. Slicing at his skin. Stripping it from his bones. "Where. Is. *My. Brother*?"

"Hey, fuckwit."

Patrick swung to his left, his stare locking instantly on the strange vampire standing beside the wind-frenzied dangerous-surf flag.

The vamp grinned. "He's here."

He shoved something forward, a large something covered in blood that fell to the ground with a boneless thud, looking like it belonged in an abattoir from a horror movie and not on a beach in Australia.

Oh, Jesus...Patrick's own blood ran to ice and his heart stilled. *Ven*.

"And now," Pestilence smirked, rising to his feet. Blood trickled from a thousand tiny wounds in his flesh and a foam of black vomit dripped from his mouth and nose. Swiping sand from his shoulders, he crossed the beach to Ven's motionless form and shoved his foot between Ven's shoulder blades. "So are you."

A heavy knot of fury twisted in Patrick's chest. "Let Steven go."

Pestilence laughed, his smirk triumphant and smug. "Why would I do that, Patrick Watkins?" He held out his arm and Ven snapped upright, eyes dazed, face bloody and bruised. "While I have Steven, I have you."

With a wild laugh, the vampire spun about, smashing Ven in the jaw with his heel. Patrick screamed, leaping forward. Intent on tearing the vampire to pieces.

But before Patrick could destroy the distance between them, Pestilence grabbed Ven's neck, holding his limp form as if it were a shield. "Not a good idea, lifeguard. Not unless you want me to rip your brother's throat out. I think even a Principatus would fail to survive such an attack from an entity of my stature."

"You mean short-arsed and stinky?"

The barely audible mumble came from Ven and Pestilence hissed, a shudder wracking his frame. He flung Ven against the vampire, who snatched his neck in blood-tipped claws, driving him to his knees in the space of a heartbeat.

"He will be dead before you can draw breath, lifeguard," Pestilence shouted, blazing stare locked on Patrick. "Move and he dies."

Patrick froze, every fiber of his being feeling his brother's pain. He stared at Ven's slumped frame, the sight of his once-pale-but-healthy flesh now sallow and covered in weeping sores, filling him with agony. The sight of his brother's once-unassailable strength beaten beyond death filling him with misery.

His throat slammed shut. He couldn't do this. He couldn't let his brother suffer. Not the one soul who'd spent his life, his *death*, doing everything in his power to protect him. The one person who always knew when he was sad, angry, scared. The one person who sacrificed it all to make sure Patrick lived.

Patrick choked back a sob. He couldn't do this. Not to his brother. Not to Steven.

He turned from Ven's shuddering, broken body and fixed Pestilence with a flat stare. "My brother's life for mine."

The wind picked up his words. Whipped them from his lips.

Pestilence smiled. Gleeful. Smug. "Of course."

Driving his fingers into the soft center of his palms, Patrick drew a deep breath. What was to come would hurt, but for his brother he would face it all.

I'm sorry, Fred, but I can't let Steven suffer for me anymore.

He began to drop to his knees, Pestilence's stretching grin burning into his brain.

"Yes," Pestilence whispered, his voice ringing with supreme elation. "Yes. *The Cure shall surrender to the Disease and the Disease shall destroy the Cure.*"

"Don't you bloody dare!" Ven's growl shattered the silence of the beach. A ripple distorted the very air around them and he surged to his feet, arms flinging wide, body transforming into a creature of immense size and might.

"The Principatus!" Pestilence screeched.

Ven spun, massive black wings unfolding from his impossibly wide back, long, muscled arms reaching out to snare the vampire around the neck. His skin, blacker than midnight pitch, shimmered in the dusk, his eyes twin balls of burning white light. "For Amy," he said, lifting the gibbering, squealing vampire up to his unrecognizable face. "For the heinous creature you are, for the heinous acts you performed." His voice rumbled, thunder in a storm. "By the decree of the Order of the Agents, by the power of the Principatus, I hereby declare you punished."

He sank talons the size of daggers into the vampire's ribcage, just below his armpit and, with barely a shift in muscle, tore the squealing demon in two.

The two parts spurted blood, bright red arching showers that drenched Ven's black flesh crimson. And then, as the Principatus threw back his head and roared, arms wide, wings spread, both parts fell to dust and were scattered to nothing by the gusting wind.

Patrick stared at his brother, his pulse pounding in his ears. *Jesus, is that Ven?*

The Principatus turned to look at him, eyes white fire, lips curled away from needle-tipped teeth in a sardonic, cheeky grin. A grin Patrick had seen many, many times before. "Was that too melodramatic?"

Patrick's laugh took him by surprise. "Well, you always were one for the—"

A shudder wracked Ven's giant frame, once, twice and he pitched forward, collapsing face first into the sand, changing back into human form before his body came to rest.

"Ven!" Patrick screamed. He sprinted forward, stare locked on Ven's motionless form, on the blood pouring from his slack

mouth and nose and ears, staining the sand around him a dull red. Like a shadow of blood on the beach.

He ran, desperate to reach his brother. To save him.

And was picked up and flung backward by a savage blow of invisible force.

Fred fumed. She stormed around the tiny "space" the Powers had afforded her, an area in the whiteness no bigger than the average public toilet cubicle. What the fuck did she do now? She couldn't leave, she couldn't return to Patrick, she couldn't even track down Pestilence and beat the crap out of him. Shit, with the Powers' ridiculous confinement she could barely scratch herself.

She stomped her foot. "Aarrggh!"

Well, that was entirely childish, wasn't it, Fred.

Huffing into her fringe, she glared at the ubiquitous white. Yes, it was childish, but it was better than just standing around accepting her fate.

She narrowed her eyes. Fate? Was that who had blabbed about what she was doing with Patrick? The last Fate? Before she'd mysteriously up and vanished from the Realm, had the last Fate gone all soothsayerish and revealed what role Death was planning to play in the confrontation between Pestilence and the Cure?

And what role was that exactly, Fred? Coach? Umpire? Cheerleader for the Cure? You know you cannot directly wage war on your own brethren, even if Pestilence is *a megalomaniacal piece of shit that needs to have his skinny ass kicked from one side of the Realm to the other. The Horsemen cannot attack each other, no matter how much you wished you could. To do so would rend the Weave asunder. So, what role* were *you planning to play? Wingman?*

A numb coldness unfurled in her belly. She hadn't allowed

herself to think that far ahead. Once she'd discovered Pestilence's plan, once she'd discovered all the players involved, she'd been so focused on preparing Patrick, she hadn't stopped to question what she was going to do once the "battle" had began.

Preparing Patrick? Is that what you've been so focused on? Really? Are you sure?

The cold numbness growing in her gut grew icy. Shit. Preparing him had *not* been her sole focus, even though it *should* have been. Making love to him had been her primary focus, feeling his body move over hers, feeling his body move *in* hers... Shit. Instead of trying to equip him for what he had to face, she'd been thinking only of the way he made her feel—alive, wonderful, gloriously amazing. Her own selfish greed may have delivered to Patrick the very thing she was created to do. Death.

Standing motionless, she closed her eyes. By the Powers, what if she never saw him again?

No. She wouldn't let that happen. Time was irrelevant to her. If need be she'd go back to Patrick in a moment of history...

The rebellious thought trailed away and she let out a sigh. The Powers would prevent her doing so. Of that she had little doubt, and if imprisoning her in the whiteness was their reaction to her falling in love with Patrick, what would they do to her if she broke the first law?

"Fuck," she muttered. "Fuck fuck fuck."

"You really need to do something about your language, Death."

She froze, gaze flicking around the whiteness. Her heart smashed against her breastbone. Was that who she thought it was?

"Yes. It is. Now, tell me, Death. Why do you want to return to Patrick Watkins?"

Fred's mouth went dry. Should she really answer that question?

"Yes. You should."

"I love him."

It was the simple truth.

"Is that the only reason?"

She frowned. The thought of all mankind—children, babies, the innocent, the guilty—destroyed by Pestilence's ego, by his hunger for power and glory rolled through her. She thought of them all. She thought of Patrick...and shook her head.

"Does there have to be any other?"

Silence answered her.

"Does there?"

Silence. And the sense of a low, wise chuckle.

"Well?"

No reply.

Fred frowned. "Well?"

Again. Nothing.

She threw up her hands, shaking her head as she stormed around in...circles.

Circles. Large circles. Circles bigger than a toilet cubicle.

Holy shit, she could move!

"Just you and me now, lifeguard." Pestilence's voice rose above the wailing wind, his eyes ablaze. "Your pitiful brother has finally exerted all his energy. Not even the power of a Principatus can defeat starvation. Especially when their own blood flows so freely from their body." He laughed, the sound cold. Inhuman. "As the last Fate foretold, it has come to pass. The Cure and the Disease."

He laughed again, and as Patrick scrambled to his feet, tiny grains of sand lashing at his face, slicing into his eyes, he saw the First Horseman walk toward him.

No, Patrick. Limp toward you. He's limping.

Cold hope surged through him and he bared his teeth in a dead smile. Good.

He straightened, glaring at Pestilence. Ven's lifeless body cut into the corner of his vision but he refused to look at him. He had to end this. Now. "As the last Fate foretold," he growled, *"The Cure shall face the Disease on the shifting dunes and the end shall begin and the beginning shall end."*

The words of the prophesy boomed across the empty stretch of beach, their volume impossibly loud. Pestilence reeled backward, eyes wide. "How do you know those words?"

Patrick gave him a dark grin. "Someone much more powerful than you told me." Without thought, he threw the beach at the demon. Sand, rocks, metal trash cans, the needles cast aside by junkies. Everything he could reach with his mind, he hurled at the First Horseman.

Pestilence stumbled, arms pinwheeling. His eyes erupted in yellow hate, and suddenly Patrick's gut cramped.

Every pore in his body seemed to piss acid, every joint screamed as though crushed in a vice. He staggered, stomach surging up through his throat, hot bile and vomit flooding his mouth.

"The Disease!" Pestilence screamed, and another wrecking ball of illness smashed into him. "The Disease!"

Patrick spat, swiped at his mouth and sent a red and yellow safe-to-swim flag straight for Pestilence's head.

The sand-crusted steel point pierced the First Horseman's forehead, sank into his head and burst through the other side.

Pestilence screeched. And his human form vanished in a shimmer.

Long, skeletal arms reached up, claw-tipped fingers wrapping around the metal spike. "You think that will stop me, lifeguard?" The sound of metal on bone sliced the air as he pulled the flagpole from his skull. A soft, liquidy pop filled the air and blood, thick and black and stinking of decay, gushed from the hole in his forehead—followed by an equally thick, equally black fog.

It shot across the beach, engulfing Patrick before he could move, turning the dusk to midnight and the air to a suffocating shroud.

He lashed out, but to no effect. The blackness invaded his nose, his mouth. It seeped into his eyes, pooling at the corners, ice cold and scalding at once.

"Did you really think a pathetic human such as yourself could stop me?"

The black fog trickled into Patrick's ears.

"Did you really think a lowly mortal could stop the First Horseman?"

It threaded down his throat.

"I am the Disease."

Into his lungs.

"Pestilence."

Choking him. Suffocating him.

"He who destroys life in the world of man."

An image of his lifeless brother's body flashed through Patrick's air-starved mind.

"He who brings the end with the beginning."

Damn, I'm really getting sick of his voice.

The thought wasn't Patrick's, but he grabbed a hold of its familiar sardonic wit. Ven. Forever alive in his heart. A golden heat radiated through him and swelled into a tangible, potent force, almost an entity in itself. He threw back his arms and head, drawing the blackness into his being, devouring it, letting it permeate his core.

A heatless world of illness and pain and abject misery consumed him. Tried to possess him. It turned his bones to chalk and his blood to water. It squeezed his heart still and turned his stomach inside out. But before it could render him empty, before it could undo him completely, he purged it from his being.

In a blinding wall of light and warmth.

The dark beach bleached white.

Pestilence squealed. His arms whipped up to protect his face, his feet scurried backward. The flesh on his bones began to flay, as if scoured away by the golden heat pouring from Patrick's being. His demonic form convulsed, twitched. He fell backward, thrashing in the pure light on the wind-whipped sand, eyes bulging, tongue bloating.

That'll teach the skinny bastard to mess with my brother.

Again, the thought didn't belong to Patrick. He jerked his stare from the convulsing First Horseman to Ven, expecting to see him sitting up, grinning at him with that same old sarcasm he'd counted on his entire life.

His brother still lay prone on the sand. Lifeless. As still as a corpse.

Aching hollowness exploded in Patrick's core. The light flooding from his existence guttered and he collapsed to his knees. Drained. Exhausted. Sapped of all energy.

Get up.

He stared at Ven.

Get up.

"As...I suspected." Pestilence's hoarse snarl sliced into his desperate sorrow. He jerked his stare from his brother's body, cold horror twisting around his heart as the First Horseman slowly rose to his feet. "The...Cure's weakness...will be...his...end."

With a shudder, the Disease shook the grains of sand from his bleeding, flayed limbs and, as Patrick watched, the wounds in his flesh disappeared.

Struggling for breath, Patrick drew on all he had within and threw it out.

Pestilence laughed. "Is that it?" Healed and grinning with smug satisfaction, he strode across the beach, closing the distance between them. "Is that all? I am disappointed."

Patrick pushed himself to his knees, every muscle in his

body trembling with fatigue. Every molecule of his existence drained. Empty. Breath ragged and shallow.

The First Horseman lowered himself into a crouch before him and Patrick's gut rolled as the demon's stench assaulted him.

"I have known of this moment for over a millennium," Pestilence murmured. "True, I tried to prevent its occurrence, but I must admit I am glad I failed." He tilted his head to the side, smiling. "Although killing your parents was quite enjoyable."

Patrick screamed. Hate and fury ripped through his body, charging him with new life. He lunged for Pestilence.

But it wasn't enough.

He collapsed face first into the sand.

"Oh, how glad I am I failed." Pestilence laughed again. "This is so much more fun."

"You..." Patrick struggled onto his hands, pushing his body from the beach, so weak he could barely draw breath. He lifted his head, just, and glared up at the grinning First Horseman, "fucking...bastard."

Get up, Patrick. Get up.

Pestilence lowered his head closer, his yellow eyes glowing. "That may be, but I am not the one on all fours, am I?" His grin stretched wider and he raised his hand, fingers hovering near Patrick's mouth. "The one about to be filled with all the disease of the world."

And then suddenly he blinked, surprise flashing across his face. "Is that..." He drew his head closer, eyes narrowing, tongue flicking at the air. "By the Powers, it is!" A chuckle bubbled up his throat, the sound cold and furious and ripe with mirth at once. "The Fourth Horseman."

An invisible fist slammed into Patrick's gut. He cried out, recoiling from the brutal blow, his stomach boiling with agony and burning vomit.

Pestilence rose to his feet. "You have been fucking the

Fourth Horseman!" He shook his head, eyes yellow fire. "And they accuse *me* of reaching above my station."

Another invisible fist smashed into Patrick, snapping him backward in a violent somersault. The world spun, a blur of darkening sky, emerging stars, dying sun and never-ending sand.

Pestilence followed him across the beach, fury turning his eyes to yellow pits of hate. Thick fingers of sickness wrapped around Patrick's throat, pushed at his lips, into his mouth. He gagged, struggling against the assault. He needed to get up, get up. Goddamn it, get up!

"You have been sticking your tiny, pathetic *human* dick into the Fourth Horseman's cunt!"

An image of Fred filled Patrick's head. Fred in jeans and a Bob Marley t-shirt. Fred in a flowing black hooded robe. Fred in nothing but her sublime, pale skin.

For fuck's sake, Patrick, get up!

With a roar, he forced himself to his feet, sucking in breath after breath, body screaming in agony, core screaming in rage. He glared at Pestilence, letting the rage and agony fuel him.

It's not enough, Patrick. It's not what you need. You need—

The First Horseman stumbled backward, eyes widening a fraction, fear shimmering in their depths for a split second before his lips curled into a sly, smug smile. "You know what, lifeguard?" he said, recovering the ground he'd lost with one defiant step. "So have I. Often. I too have sunk my cock into her cunt. I fucked her regularly, pumping her cunt so full of my diseased seed it looked like she was drowning in come. And as soon as I am finished here, as soon as I destroy you and rend the world of man asunder, I will return to the Realm, flip the Fourth Horseman onto her stomach on my bed and do it again. And again. And again."

Sound disappeared.

So did the sense of touch. Taste.

All that Patrick could see was Pestilence standing before

him on the empty beach, speaking vile words he didn't hear.

All that Patrick could smell was Fred. The secretive scent of her body, the soft musk of her pleasure.

Her pleasure for him. Her love for him. Pure and real and untainted.

Golden heat consumed him.

He reached out for Pestilence and enclosed him in an invisible grip so fast and tight the demon could not move. Sickness seeped into his mind from the contact and he accepted it, drew it from the First Horseman's existence, letting it fill him. The only way to beat a disease was to know it.

Pestilence screamed, eyes wide, thrashing in the invisible hold. "No! No! Let me go!"

Swarms of insects surged through Patrick's mind, filled his core. He took them all, their furious energy like black electricity. Fogs of darkness folded over him, and he pulled them into his being.

He took it all from the Disease, milked him of his existence and understood what he was.

A pest. Just a pest. And what was the cure for pests?

Eradication.

He smiled at the First Horseman. Lifted him high from the sand and tore open the ground beneath him.

"No!" Pestilence squealed, bucking in Patrick's hold. His eyes bulged, his pale face drained of color. *"No, I beseech you! Not there! Not there!"*

Patrick raised his eyebrows. "Nobody fucks with Death but me, Horseman. Remember that."

The chasm in the sand roared. Black light poured from its mouth.

Pestilence screamed.

And Patrick released him. Watching him fall, screaming, into abyss.

The chasm roared again, a silent sound vibrating though Patrick's body, and then it was gone. Bondi Beach was again perfect and empty and bathing in the young moon's growing light.

Patrick stood still, looking at it all, looking at the smooth, unmarked sand. Completely calm. Completely composed.

"That was probably the most romantic thing I've ever heard."

He spun about, the surreal calm evaporating with the first note of Fred's voice.

She stood behind him, dressed in black jeans, black biker boots and a black Midnight Oil t-shirt, her black hair tumbling about her face, her brilliant blue eyes shining in the pale moonlight.

He was scooping her up in his arms before he knew he'd even moved, his mouth crushing hers, kissing her even as he laughed and cried.

Her fingers tangled into his hair and she kissed him back, the cool warmth of her body like a salve, healing him, nourishing him. He plunged his tongue into her mouth, needing to taste her. He pulled her glorious scent into his being, letting her fill him.

She was his five senses—she was his life, his existence. She'd saved him. Just the mere thought of her had saved him. Saved the world, in fact.

A chuckle rumbled in his chest and he dragged his mouth away from hers, grinning at her.

"What?" She grinned back, her hold on him not relaxing a bit.

"If it wasn't for you, Pestilence would probably be knee-deep in bodies by now." He nudged her forehead with his. "You do realize, my sexy-arsed Horseman, that Death just kept every creature in this world alive?"

She looked at him, eyes twinkling. "Shhhh. You'll ruin my reputation."

He laughed, kissing her again and spinning her around. Everything was right in the world. Everything was as it was meant to—

"Can you pair...get a room?"

The whispered grumble, barely audible, shattered Patrick's joy. Shit. Ven.

He dropped Fred, a cold knot twisting in his gut. He sprinted to his brother, falling to his knees beside him in the sand. Guilt squeezed his chest. Jesus, how could he forget his brother?

"Ah, shit, Ven."

Ven looked up at him with sunken cloudy eyes, his grey, lacerated skin weeping pus and blood. A shudder wracked his body and he coughed, bubbles of bright red blood splattering his lips. "I take by the expression on your face..." he wheezed, fresh blood trickling from his nose. "...I'm not...looking my best."

Patrick shook his head, not knowing what to do. He'd never seen someone so badly brutalized. "I can't lie, brother," he laughed, the raw sound desperate and harsh. "I've seen you better."

Ven coughed again, the tip of his tongue—ashen grey and covered in sores—scrapping over his cracked, bleeding lips. "Could still...pull the girls...better...than... ...you." A weak chuckle fell from his throat and his body went limp, his eyes fluttering closed as his head rolled to the side.

"Ven?" Numb terror seized Patrick. He grabbed his brother's shoulders and shook him hard, grief destroying rational thought and years of first-aid training. "Ven?"

Nothing.

"Steven!"

"Bloody...hell...mate," Ven slurred, head lulling on his shoulders, eyes barely opening. Blood continued to ooze from his nose and ears. His body twitched, as if something tried to escape it. "Can't...a...bloke...get some peace...around here?"

He is going, Patrick.

Fred's voice slipped through Patrick's head. He turned,

glaring at her. No. He wasn't going to go through all this shit to lose his brother. He wasn't.

Turning back to Ven, he shook his head. "I've spent thirty six years putting up with your shit, Ven." He took his brother's hand in his, holding it as firmly as he dared, dismay taking huge bites from his hope at how fragile Ven's bones felt in his grip. "I think it's time you put up with some of mine."

A small, wavering grin pulled at Ven's lips and his head lolled to the side again. "Annoying...little pain...in the...arse, aren't...you?"

The words faded away to barely a whisper and Patrick choked back a sob. *No. No.*

"Stop being a lazy bastard, Steven, and get up. Who the hell is going to do my ironing if you die? Again."

His brother chuckled, a soft, liquidy hiccup of a sound that made Patrick's heart ache. "Fuck...off."

Fred's cool palm touched Patrick's shoulder and he dragged his stare from Ven's ashen face.

"Tell me how to fix this," he ground out. "Tell me."

"I don't know, Patrick." She shook her head, eyes unreadable. "I don't know the cure."

Patrick's throat squeezed and he sucked in a swift breath. The cure. *He* was the cure. Did that mean...?

The same surreal calm that possessed him during Pestilence's last moments flowed through Patrick again. He extended his arm from his body, hand open and fingers spread, and then closed them around the shaft of the Fourth Horseman's scythe as it materialized in the air beside him.

Fred gasped but he ignored her. A prickling wave of heat rolled through him and he turned back to Ven, lowering his lips to his brother's ear. "I think it's time you had a feed, brother."

Ven didn't respond.

Patrick straightened a little, brought the tip of the scythe to his neck, pressed it directly above his pulse and sliced open his flesh.

White pain ripped through his neck and down into his shoulder. He hissed through his teeth, biting back a sharp shout. Warm fluid oozed from the clean wound and trickled down his neck. He opened his hand, releasing the scythe back to the Realm and moved, repositioning himself over Ven's lifeless form, an inferno of hope burning in his chest.

Please. This has to work.

Blood flowing from his torn vein, he lowered himself closer to his brother and pressed his wet neck to Ven's cracked, parted lips.

Nothing happened.

And then, it did.

Ven's mouth opened. A gentle pressure nuzzled Patrick's neck, like the innocent kiss from a young child. There was a soft moan, and then Ven's tongue touched the bleeding wound and his fangs punctured Patrick's flesh.

Sizzling heat shot through Patrick. Exquisite agony and terrifying joy. His lips parted, a cry catching in his throat. Ven sucked gently at his neck, and Patrick could feel his blood drawing through his veins, flooding his brother's mouth. With every swallow Ven took, Patrick's heart smashed against his breastbone. With every explosive beat, his blood pumped faster into Ven's mouth.

He closed his eyes, feeling his life force drain from his body, feeling his soul erupt in golden existence.

Ven's hands gripped his arms. His nails sank into his biceps. A growl sounded in Ven's throat, low and wild and suddenly—after an eternity—he yanked his mouth free of Patrick's neck. "Bloody hell, brother." Flopping backward, he wiped at his mouth with his hand—his large, strong, healthy hand. He gave Patrick a look of comical distaste. "That was the most disgusting thing I've ever done." He looked up at him, his face once again belonging to a perpetually twenty-seven-year-old surfer, his eyes glinting with green mischief, his skin smooth and pale and almost luminescent. "Don't ever, *ever* do that again."

"That's the thanks I get?" Patrick grinned and, before Ven could move, gave him a damn good punch to the arm.

"Ow!" Ven curled himself up into a ball, tucking his head under his arms. "This is no way to treat your brother! After everything I've just been through. Help! Help!"

Rolling his eyes, Patrick climbed to his feet, shaking his head at Ven's dramatics. "Fair dinkum, Ven. Remind me again why I just saved your life?"

Stretching onto his back, hands behind his head, Ven gave him a grin the Cheshire cat would have envied. "Because you love me and your life would be boring without me."

"Yeah, right, that's it. Now I remember." Patrick snorted, shaking his head again as he reached out for Fred and slid his arm around her back, pulling her into the side of his body to hold her close.

Ven chuckled, turning his attention to Fred. "Guess you missed me again, Death. That's twice I've denied you."

Fred pulled herself closer into Patrick's embrace and smiled. "I'm getting the feeling it will be impossible to miss you, fang face. You're now the third constant in the universe." She arched an eyebrow. "Me, taxes and Steven Watkins."

With a wide smirk, Ven leapt to his feet and brushed the sand from his arse. "Well, you know what they say? You can't keep a good vamp down. Or should that be a good Principatus?" He gave them both a puzzled look. "What the bloody hell is a Principatus anyway? Pestilence kept carrying on about it. Figured it must be something important."

Fred laughed. "As you have pointed out before, Steven, a Principatus is an Agent of the Order. A hunter—of sorts—controlled by the Powers, who gets to kick the shit out of...how should I put this...otherworldly scum who step out of line. I'm afraid your bad-boy days are behind you."

A dark light ignited in Ven's eyes and an expression of furious grief etched his face. "If it means I get to kick the shit out of arse-holes like Pestilence and Raziel, consider me signed up for life."

Patrick studied his brother. There was more to Ven's uncharacteristic response than physical pain and he would ask him about it, as well as fill him in on their family connections, a little fact his brother would probably find highly amusing, or irritating. Just not now. Not while his obvious anguish simmered so close to the surface.

Later.

He turned to Fred, smoothing his hands up her back. All he wanted to do was bury his head into her neck and breathe her in until he was giddy on her scent, but something still troubled him. "Tell me," he said, fixing her with a steady look. "Where did I send Pestilence? Cause frankly, I haven't got a bloody clue."

Fred laughed. "The only place befitting an egomaniac asshole with delusions of grandeur. The lowest pit of hell. Kinda like being sent to detention for demons and entities."

"Can he come back?"

A distant expression crossed her face for a moment, her eyes glowing a brilliant white before they returned to their normal blue and she shook her head. "No. The First Horseman is where he is meant to be. The punishment is sound and the Weave has been rethread. The Order of Actuality is restored."

Patrick suppressed a sigh and tugged her closer. "Is that it? Is it over? Can I go back to being just a lifeguard now?"

She gave him a long look, gnawing on her bottom lip. "Well..."

He cocked an eyebrow. "If you say no, you're going to miss out on the best sex of your existence."

"Oh, in that case." She grinned. "It's over. The beginning has ended."

Patrick touched his lips to hers. "About bloody time."

Epilogue

Death looked at herself in the mirror and sighed, a smile curling her lips. She looked good naked. Damn good. Maybe that's why the lifeguard couldn't keep his hands off her, a situation completely acceptable in her opinion. For the last five human days they'd done nothing but make love and when it came down to it, she could definitely go the rest of eternity with Patrick Watkins unable to keep his hands off her. Definitely.

"Are you done yet? Or do I have to come over there and help you check out how goddamn gorgeous you are?"

Fred threw him a grin over her shoulder. "Promises, promises. And you should probably rethink the blasphemy. You're going to piss off the family."

He cocked an eyebrow at her and straightened from the bed. "The thing with family," he murmured, walking towards her, his lean, surfer's body as naked as hers. "They've all got that embarrassing cousin that just can't seem to keep his mouth shut."

The pit of Fred's belly twisted. Her nipples pinched tight. She watched him approach her, her sex growing heavy. Thick. Wet.

Yes. An eternity of Patrick Watkins she could really go for.

An eternity she didn't have.

She sighed and turned back to the mirror. Despite the fact Patrick had no date of death she was aware of, one day he would die. She couldn't see it any other way. He was mortal. All mortals died eventually. The Order of Actuality demanded it so. One day, Patrick's number would be up and no matter how much she hated it, she would—

She cut that line of thought dead and sighed again. By the Powers, she didn't want to think about this. She really didn't.

"That's a lot of sighing for a woman just paid a blasphemous compliment." Patrick slid his hands over her hips and tugged her back against his body. "Is there something you want to tell me?"

Fred closed her eyes and leant into his delicious embrace. He felt so damn good. So damn *right.* How did she tell him they didn't have an eternity? That she would continue long after she'd brought his life to an end? How did she tell him one day he would—

"Die?" he murmured in her ear, pressing her closer to his body. "By your very hand?"

She stiffened, closing her eyes. "I thought we agreed to not peek inside each others thoughts."

Patrick lowered his head, nibbling on her neck. "Didn't need to be in your head to know what you were thinking, babe." He smoothed his hands up over her ribcage, skimmed his knuckles along the bottom curve of her breasts. "I seem to be able to read your face better than I do the waves."

She laughed, shifting her weight until her ass nuzzled his very impressive erection. "That well?"

"Hmmm." He trailed his fingertips up the under swell of her breasts, circled her nipples once. "Scary isn't it." His lips moved over her neck, explored the little dip below her ear. "Just out of interest, why do you think you *are* going to claim my soul one day?"

The damp heat blooming between Fred's thighs cooled and she frowned. She didn't want to have this conversation. Not while they were both naked. Not ever. She tried to pull away from him, but he wouldn't let her go, his lips charting a slow path down to her shoulder, as if he wasn't asking her about his removal from the mortal coil. She swallowed, the churning in her stomach overwhelming. So this was fear? By the Powers, how did humans live with it? Handle it?

"Fred?" The tip of Patrick's tongue drew a line along her shoulder, and she shivered.

"Because you are mortal. One day your time will come."

She expected his hands to stop their slow torment of her body. Instead, he scooped each breast into a gentle grip and rolled the pad of his thumb over her taut nipples.

"Hmmm," he murmured against her neck again. "If I told you we had the rest of forever, would you be upset?"

Fred twisted in his embrace, studying him from the corner of her eye. "Why would you say that?"

Patrick's lips twitched. "Let's just say I've been talking with the family."

She frowned at him, her heartbeat growing quicker. Louder. Thumping in her chest, her throat, her ears. "With the family? What are you—"

Patrick chuckled, sliding his hands from her breasts, down to her hips to rotate her slowly in his hold. "Turns out that embarrassing cousin is very good at weaving."

Fred's heart thumped harder. Her lips tingled. "Weaving?" She paused a moment, gazing into Patrick's laughing green eyes, not wanting to believe the squirming hope unfurling in the pit of her belly. "As in rethreading? As in rethreading the Order of Actuality? As in..."

"Not now, Fred." He pressed her body to his, hip to hip, sex to sex, heart to heart. "Ask me again in a millennium."

About the Author

Lexxie's not a deviant. She just has a deviant's imagination and a desire to entertain readers with her words. Add the two together and you get darkly erotic romances with a twist of horror, sci-fi and the paranormal.

When she's not submerged in the worlds she creates, Lexxie's life revolves around her family, a husband who thinks she's insane, a pony-sized mutt who thinks he's a lapdog, two yabbies hell-bent on destroying their tank and her daughters, who both utterly captured her heart and changed her life forever.

Contact Lexxie at lexxie@lexxiecouper.com, follow her on Twitter http://twitter.com/lexxie_couper or visit her at www.lexxiecouper.com where she occasionally makes a fool of herself on her blog.

My Bookstore & More
www.mybookstoreandmore.com
Green for the planet.
Great for your wallet.

LaVergne, TN USA
30 May 2010
184489LV00006B/2/P